A LOVE OF THEIR OWN

Amara was having the most wonderful dream. The man she loved also loved her and had told her so several times throughout the night. He'd stroked her hair, kissed her, held her hand, and told her that from now on, he was going to be the man she'd always dreamed of. Then the light of day pierced her eyes as she opened them. She struggled to breathe. Her chest hurt as if an elephant had been sitting on it. And she was so tired, she felt queasy. Somehow she managed to turn her head. Ross Hayward sat beside her, smiling gently, holding her hand.

At least *part* of her dream was real.

BOOK YOUR PLACE ON OUR WEBSITE AND MAKE THE ARABESQUE ROMANCE CONNECTION!

eated a customized website just for our very special readers, where you can get the inside scoop on everything that's going on with Arabesque romance novels.

When you come online, you'll have the exciting opportunity to:

- View covers of upcoming books

- Learn about our future publishing schedule (listed by publication month and author)

- Find out when your favorite authors will be visiting a city near you

- Search for and order backlist books

- Check out author bios and background information

- Send e-mail to your favorite authors

- Join us in weekly chats with authors, readers and other guests

- Get writing guidelines

- AND MUCH MORE!

Visit our website at
http://www.arabesquebooks.com

A Love of Their Own

KIM LOUISE

ARABESQUE
★BET
BOOKS™

BET Publications, LLC
http://www.bet.com
http://www.arabesquebooks.com

ARABESQUE BOOKS are published by

BET Publications, LLC
c/o BET BOOKS
One BET Plaza
1900 W Place NE
Washington, DC 20018-1211

All Kensington Titles, Imprints, and Distributed Lines are available at special quantity discounts for bulk purchases for sales promotions, premiums, fund-raising, and educational or institutional use. Special book excerpts or customized printings can also be created to fit special needs. For details, write or phone the office of the Kensington special sales manager: Kensington Publishing Corp., 850 Third Avenue, New York, NY 10022, attn: Special Sales Department, Phone: 1-800-221-2647.

First Printing: February 2004
10 9 8 7 6 5 4 3 2 1

Printed in the United States of America

*This book is dedicated to Julie Woodard,
Brenda Woodard, Angie Trask, and Linda Miller.
We miss you.*

ACKNOWLEDGMENTS

I had so much help with this book, there isn't room to thank everyone. Here's my attempt anyway.

Thank you to Alicia Rasley for planting the seed. Thank you to Pam Crooks and Marie Huggins for plotting with me. Thank you to Kathy Shriver for sharing stories of her daughters, and to her husband, Dr. Mark Shriver, for walking me through the healing process. Thanks to Dee Dee Fales for letting me hang out at her house and watch her children be themselves. Thank you to Sharon Edmonds and Sue Neff-Richards for explaining what they do with business resumption. Thank you to Karen Thomas for believing in my work. Thank you to my book club, Sista Girl, for being the force in my life that "keeps it real!" Thank you to ReTonya Lasley for her unique insight and always, always being there for me.

Thanks without end to the almighty Creator—for thine is the kingdom.

Allgood Family Tree

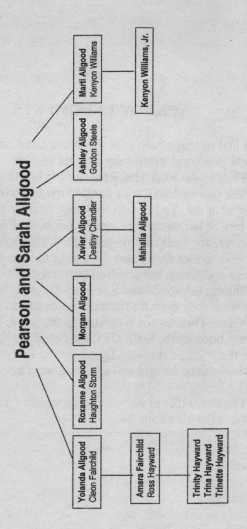

Chapter 1

"Are you sure about this?" Amara Fairchild's mother asked for the fifth time. Her face reflected all the confusion that her daughter felt but was determined not to show.

"I'm sure, Mom."

"There's still time. You just say the word, and I'll go out there and tell them it's off."

"I'm not going to let her down," Amara said, rising. The small church dressing room was just large enough for her, her mother, and one or two attendants—if she'd had any. But today, only her parents and a few others would witness the most important event in her life—her wedding.

She stood before the oval-shaped mirror thinking her aunt had worked a miracle. Her wedding dress was spectacular. Full of angel-white satin, French lace, and pearls. Within three weeks, Morgan Allgood had created an elegant gown. Even in her apprehensive state, Amara swelled with a sense of euphoria seeing herself in the gown.

Her face held the perfect reflection of calm. Her breathing was regular and deep. Even her hands, which usually twitched with nervous tremors, had not betrayed her. They looked as steady as a surgeon's.

Amara turned from side to side. At last, a weak smile penetrated her unease and she turned to her mother.

Tears threatened the corners of Yolanda Fairchild's eyes. She returned her daughter's smile and then fumbled with the latch on her purse. Walking up to her daughter, she held out four objects. Amara's eyes grew wide with recognition.

"Something old," her mother said, pinning on a brooch that had been in their family for five generations. "Something new," she continued, placing a cluster of fresh baby's breath in her daughter's hair.

"Something borrowed," Amara interjected tearfully, recognizing one of her uncle's monogrammed handkerchiefs.

"The something blue is really your father. But you can't take him with you after the ceremony, so I got you this."

The cobalt garter belt looked foreign in her mother's hand. Its delicate lace was a marked contrast to the ivory, satin gloves she wore.

"Mom, I don't think—"

"I know, dear. But take it anyway. Every bride should have a garter belt."

Amara did as she was told, then enveloped her mother in her arms. "I love you," she said.

"I love you, too, sweetheart."

The two women were still holding on to each other when the door to the dressing room creaked open. "All right, break that stuff up. It's time."

Amara stole one long look at her mother, then took her uncle's hand and walked out of the dressing room. Her father was waiting in the vestibule. Her uncle's hand was replaced by her father's and she stood nervously before him. He was a tall, strapping man who looked just over half of his forty-five years.

The butterflies in her stomach had morphed into hummingbirds, and Amara fought desperately to calm the fluttering.

"You look beautiful, Princess," Cleon Fairchild said to his daughter. "Are you ready?"

"Yes," she replied, squaring her shoulders.

He gently reached down and pulled the veil over her face. Then he executed a perfect ninety-degree turn and stuck out his arm. She took it and together they walked to the church entrance.

For years, Amara had done what most young girls do—she had imagined what her wedding day would be like.

"Purple and gold," she could remember telling her best friend, Debbie. "When I get married, the church will be decorated in purple and gold, and I'll have ten bridesmaids. There will be lilacs and yellow roses everywhere and the church will be so full of people that there won't be any more seats!"

She had wanted a thick carpet of lilacs to lead her way down the aisle, and there at the altar would be the man of her dreams. He would be the one who loved her unconditionally and doted on her every whim.

Once she had imagined that during the ceremony, when it came time for her to say, "I do," she would hesitate for the briefest moment and watch as her beloved dropped to one knee—proposing again, pleading once more for her hand.

Alas, those were the fantasies of a child. And right now, before her, was the reality of adulthood.

The colors worn by those in her small wedding party were white and black. The only flowers to speak of were in the bouquet of lilies she held in her hand. And there were fewer than twenty people in attendance.

As for her fiancé, he stood before the altar like a large, immovable monolith. His black tuxedo hung crisply against his body, tailor-made.

Amara remembered the first time she had seen Ross Hayward. It was six years ago. She had accompanied her mentor, Brenda Hayward, home for dinner. She had been sixteen then.

"Amara, I'd like you to meet my husband, Ross."

Amara had never seen a more handsome man in her life. None of her boyfriends came close. Even Denzel didn't compare. Ross was everything she and her high school friends giggled about between classes and while walking home from school.

Like a living breathing pheromone, Ross Hayward exuded sensuality in a way that Amara's sixteen-year-old hormones had only begun to experience. His naturally curly hair was cut close to his head. His thick brows centered wildly over deep expressive eyes. His sensuously symmetrical nose and mouth sat perfectly on his angular face. And as if that wasn't enough, he had smooth, unblemished skin the color of Hershey's dark chocolate.

"Welcome to our home, Amara," he had said in a cavernous baritone. Then he took her hand in his and she thought the world had stopped turning. It was only the fire and excitement in his eyes that helped her to keep her balance that day. It was something she saw as soon as Brenda had entered the room—a kind of life-affirming resonance that lit up his whole face.

As she and her father made their slow approach to the altar, she wondered what it was she saw in Ross's face now. Scorn, disdain, contempt? His glare was venomous and a shudder moved through her.

Well, Ross Hayward would not ruin the most important event of her life. Her days of crying and tears were over. She recalled the memory of her reflection in the mirror and walked toward her intended like the beautiful bride that she was. A slight smile curved her lips and she was beside her husband to be. A stern look from her father tempered Ross's disposition somewhat, and his expression was now blank and sort of hollow.

The moment she took Ross's hand and they turned to the minister, she thought about Brenda, the woman whose memory she would love and cherish forever. *I won't let you down, Brenda,* she thought. *I will make you proud.*

Chapter 2

There was no reception. After the short ceremony, the small contingent of spectators dispersed, and Ross drove himself and his new bride to his home in Buckhead.

His cousin Suzette had actually suggested that he allow her to put a *Just Married* sign on his Lexus LS. For the first time in his life, he entertained the brief thought of choking a woman.

There was nothing celebratory about this marriage. Nothing he wanted to proclaim or write in gold letters. How could he? His precious Brenda was gone only thirty days from him, and already . . .

"Argh," he growled, gripping the steering wheel tighter. The pain of his betrayal piercing him.

"We should talk."

"No," he responded. "We will not talk about this now."

The newlyweds rode in strained silence until they pulled up to the house.

"Ross, we probably should discuss how we're going to—"

"Look, Amara. This isn't going to be easy . . . for either of us. Now I've thought about this and the best way to handle this arrangement is for you to stay home with the girls. It will save money and give you something constructive to do. I'll stay out of your way. You stay out of mine. We'll be civil of course, especially around the girls. Heck, we may even deepen our friendship. But whatever happens, we'll give it our best shot, right?"

A twinge of unease flickered through her. He sounded as if they were taking aim at a basketball hoop. She wasn't sure what to make of his little speech. Either he didn't take their relationship seriously or he felt so strongly about doing the right thing that he was trying to come up with a plan.

She decided to take the situation one day at a time. And her first priority was to the girls, not the man standing in front of her.

"That sounds okay for now. But things may change. I may want to go to school or work or . . . something."

"I'm going to get the girls," he said.

He had left his four-year-old triplets with his cousin, persuading her to baby-sit instead of making a sign.

He let Amara off at the curb, then without a look, handed her a key and drove away.

She stepped into the living room and a ribbon of sorrow twisted through her. It was the first time she'd been inside the house since Brenda died.

Among the rows of lilies and more leafy plants than she dared to count, her mind registered the same furniture, the same paintings, the same fixtures she'd seen a hundred times. But now, even with all the greenery, everything seemed darker and smaller somehow.

A finger across an end table told Amara what she expected. In Brenda's last days, Ross had devoted all his time to her care while neglecting everything else. She wondered if there were also dishes to clean, clothes to wash, floors to scrub.

She made her way into the area of the house that would be hers. Her father and uncle had moved her things in the day before. If she had told them that the den where they'd put her things was also where she would be sleeping, they would have dragged her out of the house kicking and screaming.

She didn't have much. What twenty-two-year-old did? Just her clothes, shoes, books, a few CDs, and a hope chest of items she'd accumulated for the past five years. They were all still in boxes stacked in the small room where she would sleep—far away from the master bedroom where her new husband would be at night. Amara sighed.

She'd stepped over the threshold alone.

In less than ten minutes, she was out of her wedding dress and into jeans and a T-shirt. She found a bucket and some cleaning supplies in a pantry. She grabbed them and went to work.

The Haywards had purchased an old house. The nearly eighty-year-old structure still had the original interior doors and oak moldings lining the ceiling and floor. Amara spent time learning the intricacies of her new home by washing, waxing, polishing, and dusting nearly every inch of it.

She gathered clothes and washed them. She washed a small load of dishes and dusted. And after hours of Ross being gone, she refused to let herself dwell on his whereabouts. Instead, she kept busy in the kids' room. Picking up the seemingly endless supply of toys and making up their beds. She would have thought that if she were going to cry, it would have been in the girls' room. There the essence of her friend and mentor was alive and vibrant. It was where Brenda's unique thumbprint was evident on everything from the drapes on the window to the plaques on the wall, and where the aura of her soul would always resonate warmly in the smiles of her daughters. She was wrong.

The tears didn't come until she was watering one of the many plants sent by Brenda's myriad of family and friends. She'd almost missed it—a small life fading amidst all the vibrant growth around it. It was a chrysanthemum—tiny and unattended. She pulled it forward and examined it. Its vines faded pale green and its leaves yellow. Many were brown and shriveled. When she touched a flower to remove it, it disintegrated in her fingers.

That's when it hit her just how fragile life is and how at any moment, someone she loved and cared for deeply could be taken from her. It struck her just how much she would miss her friend.

The realization dropped her to the ground. A tidal wave of despair overtook her and she sobbed uncontrollably.

"What am I doing here, Brenda? Why me?" But there was no answer. Only rooms that were too quiet, the lingering smell of sickness and dust, and hardwood cold and unyielding beneath her.

Oh, God, she thought as a pain greater than she ever imagined gripped her. *If this is grief, I'll not survive it.*

"What are you doing on the floor?"

Ross's dark voice broke through her anguish, but just barely.

"Mara!"

The girls' happy voices jolted her at the core of her pain. She couldn't allow herself to sink any deeper or to let the girls see her writhing with grief. If she couldn't be strong for them, what good would she be? Her promise to Brenda would be for nothing.

She pulled herself up to her knees just as two small bodies piled on and hugged tight.

"Daddy said you were here!" Trina said.

"Will you make us some cookie faces?" Trinity asked.

Discreetly, Amara wiped her face clean of her sorrow and hugged the two girls who had nearly toppled her with exuberance.

"Of course, we'll make cookie faces!" she said.

"Yeay!" the girls squealed with four-year-old enthusiasm.

"It's too late for sweets."

Amara looked up from the two little girls who yipped around her like puppies. The vision she saw brought the pain back with full force.

Ross's handsome features had gone hard and bitter. His entire body stood in the doorway stiff and rigid. He was not going to make fulfilling their promise easy.

Beside him stood Trinette. She could tell because of all the triplets, Trinette had the darkest, most penetrating eyes. And right now those eyes had grown cold. Unlike her sisters Trina and Trinity, Trinette had not moved an inch from her father's side.

A twinge of unease turned in Amara's stomach. Of the three sisters, Trinette had taken her mother's death the worst. She'd grown quiet and her delicate facial features were drawn into a constant frown. Trina had cried and once her crying was through, carried on like business as usual. Trinity still had bouts of sadness or days when all of her skies seemed black. But for the most part, she was moving through her grief.

Trinette, on the other hand, had all but taken herself out of the world. Amara had suggested that Ross take his daughters to see a psychologist to help them cope with their loss. She even volunteered to go along. But he would have nothing to do with that idea. He'd told her that all his girls needed was time to heal. So she hadn't raised the issue again.

However, seeing the two standing in the doorway and staring at her as if she were the enemy made her think that maybe both father *and* daughter needed counseling.

"Trinette, would you like to help me and your sisters make cookie faces?"

The angry little girl growled and turned her face into her father's pant leg.

I guess that means no, Amara thought.

Ross dropped his hand to his daughter's shoulder. His gaze remained on Amara. "Didn't I just say it's too late for snacks?"

Amara smiled down the anger she felt building and rubbed her new daughters' shoulders. "You said we weren't going to talk about this," and her eyes narrowed, "but we're going to talk about it."

A nerve at the base of Ross's jaw throbbed angrily. "Girls, go play in your room."

"Aw!" came Trina and Trinity's pained replay. "What about the cookies?"

Ross kept his eyes on Amara. "I'm not going to tell you a second time."

Three little girls, all dressed in the same yellow and white dresses, trudged off toward the stairs. Two were sulking, one more robotic in her march.

The second they were out of earshot, Amara stood up and laid in. "What's the matter with you?"

His eyes hardened with anger. "I just buried my wife and married a new one in less than thirty days, and you have the audacity to ask what's wrong?"

"Do you think this is easy for me?" Remembering her breakdown before the girls came in, she added,

"Brenda was like a second mother to me. She was my *best* friend."

Ross turned away, his face riddled with pain. "Look, we made an agreement. Let's just stick to it and—"

"And what? It's not like this thing will end . . . unless we get a divorce."

Ross stiffened. The thought of betraying his wife cut him like a sword. He had granted her last wish. He could still see her lying on the settee. The cancer that originally started in her breasts had spread throughout her limbic system and had reduced his beautiful wife of fifteen years to skin, bone, and grit.

They had been through a double mastectomy, chemotherapy, and every other treatment the doctor had recommended. They even tried homeopathy and several types of natural remedies. Nothing stopped the progress.

For two years, Ross had been her only caretaker. As his wife's condition worsened, he soon quit his job as a recovery consultant, and attended to Brenda full-time. To help ease the burden, Amara, who had become like a member of their family by then, had helped take care of his three daughters.

One day, when he was so exhausted he couldn't see straight, Brenda took a turn for the worse and he knew it was time for hospice care. He was determined to make the last days of her life as comfortable and painless as he could for the woman who had been the love of his life and brought him such incredible joy.

It had become too difficult for her to talk. Sometimes she would moan or mumble her requests. Miraculously, Ross was able to understand much of what his wife had wanted. It was only when she actually spoke to him on that day that he couldn't figure out what she could possibly mean.

"You . . . must . . . married."

"What?" he asked, staring into eyes that had long lost their brilliant color, yet somehow held a cold fire now.

"Get married," she said, her voice as thin as thread.

He dropped to one knee beside her. He'd gotten used to the way her body smelled of the soap he used to wash her, and of ripe decay. But this time there was something different. He could smell death.

He shook with fatigue and fear. "I'm already married." He tried to smile, but couldn't. "Brenda, I love you and—"

"If you love me . . . get married."

He took her thin hand in his. It was so light, he could barely tell it was there. "Brenda—"

"I'm dying, Ross. Right . . . now. I'm so tired, I want . . . to go."

Ross's shaking made his teeth chatter.

"God is waiting for me. But, I won't go until you promise."

She's talking out of her head, he thought. Several of their many, many doctors had mentioned delirium as a possibility. *My poor Brenda.* And then she smiled for the first time in months.

"I know what I'm saying, Ross. I can't go . . . unless I know the girls . . . have a mother."

She was breathing awkwardly now. Straining.

"Brenda." He stroked the stubble on her head. "I can't promise that, I can't." He lowered his head and sobbed as the realization of life without her overtook him.

"Ross Hayward," she said.

He looked up at her through the tears glistening in his eyes. She looked like an angel.

"I want to see my daughters and Amara."

Ross peeled himself away from his wife's side and

went down to the basement. He stopped at the bottom of the stairs, where Amara was braiding Trina's hair. They were watching the movie *Snow White*. He looked on as the prince bent down to kiss Snow White and she awakened from her slumber. He knew that when his wife closed her eyes to sleep tonight, no kiss, not even his own, would awaken her.

Amara turned to him then. He wiped a stray tear.

"Girls," she said, her voice quivering. "Let's go upstairs."

When they returned to the sunroom, Brenda Hayward was breathing heavily and staring straight ahead. Her daughters approached tentatively and her eyes flickered brighter.

"Come give your mother a hug."

They did as they were told and streams of tears covered their mother's face. "I love you," she said. "I'm going to miss . . . Go downstairs now. I have to talk to Daddy."

"Come on," Amara said.

"No," came Brenda's faint reply. "Stay with me, Amara."

Amara turned to the girls. "I'll be down in a minute."

When the girls were gone, Brenda took a hard and deep breath.

"You must marry Ross."

"What?" Amara said, eyes widening.

Ross sank into a chair and stared at the ceiling.

"Promise when I'm gone you will take care of my girls."

"I promise."

"And you will marry my husband."

"Brenda, I can't do that."

Brenda shook and coughed, then gasped for air. Ross

and Amara knelt at her side. Her tears had slowed to steady trickles.

"My babies," she said, shaking. "I love them so much." She coughed again. "I cannot rest in peace until I know they will be safe and loved. Please . . ."

Brenda's words dissolved into hacks and coughs. Then she stopped breathing.

"Brenda!" Ross bellowed. "Brenda!"

"Oh, God," Amara said, tears flowing.

Then Brenda pulled one last long breath from her lungs. "Promise," she said, looking beseechingly into both their eyes.

Amara spoke first. "I promise," she said.

Ross knew Brenda was holding on to her last breath. He had never disappointed his wife. Ever. "I promise," he said, with a pain so great he thought he might die with her.

Brenda Hayward had let go then, of her last breath and everything she'd ever been afraid of, and quietly passed on.

Even now, one month later, Ross could still feel her fragile hand in his, could still smell her, could still hear her last words. A hot tear rolled down his cheek.

Amara clasped his arm. "Ross?"

He yanked away, toppling her in the process. "I said we weren't going to talk about this now."

He turned and marched away, making Amara almost regret the promise she had made. But the anguish she'd seen in Trinette's eyes gave her even more conviction to fulfill it.

Chapter 3

A child's cry startled Amara from sleep. She jumped out of bed and hurried down the hall. Yesterday, when she'd carried her life in suitcases and bags down the corridor, it had seemed endlessly long. Now, it seemed stretched beyond her memory of it. The screams grew louder. Amara ran faster, her long cotton gown flowing in white billows around her ankles.

She bounded into the girls' room, worry streaking through her mind. Trinette squirmed and kicked in her father's arms. Her face doused with tears. Ross's gruff and groggy voice croaked out admonitions.

"Trinette, calm down and tell me what's wrong. Are you hurt?"

Amara moved to Ross's side and knelt beside the little girl. Her *daughter* thrashed frantically. Her eyes large and round with fear shot bolts of pain into Amara's soul. "What happened?"

Ross worked diligently to keep his daughter from squirming out of his arms. "I don't know. Bad dream maybe. I heard screaming. When I came in, she was rolling on the floor."

Amara reached out. "Trinette?" she cooed. "What's the matter?"

Trinity sat up in her bed, eyes bright with concern.

Trina huddled in the corner, tears threatening to spill from her eyes.

Ross slid Amara a hard glance. "Go back to bed. I can handle this."

His word's sliced into her.

"We're married now. You have to let me help."

"Then that makes me your husband, and I *said* go back to bed."

His words stung. *One day you're going to regret shutting me out,* she thought. Amara trudged back to her room on what was supposed to be her honeymoon, her wedding night, feeling that it was everything but. She paced in front of her bed. Three minutes. Eight minutes. After ten minutes, Trinette's cries subsided, and Amara's began. She'd married a man who didn't love her and she was the new mother of children living in the aftermath of their real mother's death. What had she gotten herself into?

For the next hour and a half, Amara tossed from one side of the twin bed to the other, but did not sleep. Her mind replayed the scene in the girls' bedroom and couldn't let go. She winced at the image of Trinette thrashing in Ross's arms. And despite her better judgment, she warmed at the sight of Ross's brown muscular frame shirtless in pajama bottoms.

He was her husband, and she dared not touch him.

At five-thirty, she got up, showered, and went out into the kitchen to make coffee. As soon as a steaming cup was in her hand, she allowed her mind to contemplate the day. In the month since Brenda's death, Amara's thoughts had been consumed by fulfilling her friend's wishes with no thought as to how. Now, in the early morning silence of her new home, she wondered what her routine with the girls would be and how she would fulfill the duties of a wife. She'd approached Ross about the subject of the girls three times in the past few weeks. Each time his answer was the same. "I don't have time to talk about that right now."

Well, he would have to talk about it today.

Her heart sank as she stood in the kitchen where she'd had many meals and lively conversation. It was a chef's arrangement with only the finest cookware and utensils. Brenda had loved to cook. It seemed to Amara that Brenda had loved everything about being a wife and mother and had performed each role to perfection. Amara knew she would never measure up, but somehow she had to try. She had to make everything perfect, as if Brenda had never passed away, or else she would face a lifetime of scenes like the one she'd experienced a few short hours ago.

A small body wiping sleep from her eyes wandered into the kitchen. Although the little girl wore the same Pooh pajamas as her sisters, Amara could tell Trinity from a mile away. She was like an old woman in a child's body. Amara remembered seeing her in the hospital nursery hours after she was born and knowing right away that there was something different about her—something in her eyes wise and haunting.

"I knew you were up," Trinity said, in her little girl voice. "I came to see if you need something."

Ross awakened teetering at the edge of his bed. His tiny daughter had managed to hog all of the bed and left him with only a sliver of mattress on which to sleep. He swung his legs to the floor and glanced behind him. Trinette lay sprawled behind him breathing soundly.

Ross shook his head in amazement. "Just like your mother," he said.

While he still had a few moments before the girls woke up, he headed off to the bathroom for a quick shower. The last thirty days of Ross's life were as foggy as the mist rising from the hot water. It was as if he'd been sleepwalking. As soon as he'd opened his eyes, he'd wondered if it was all true. Did Brenda really die? Did he really marry Amara? He had only to inhale to get his answer. He could smell the new woman in his house as vividly as he could smell the soap in his hand. She smelled young, and vibrant, and colorful like a fist full of flowers.

"Ahgh!" The last thing he needed was something that reminded him of sunshine when all he wanted to do was slump into a dark corner and grieve for his departed wife. But there had never been time. There had been funeral arrangements to make. Followed by wedding arrangements. He moaned and pounded a soapy fist against the wet shower wall. His life had gone to shit.

Ross stepped from the steam-filled room and the aroma of buttery maple overcame him. Since he knew Brenda's mother had flown back to Detroit days ago, there could only be one explanation. He pulled on his clothes, stepped from his closet, kissed his sleeping daughter on the cheek, and headed down to the kitchen.

The sound of voices surprised him. Walking through the swinging doors, he entered the kitchen where Amara stood over a griddle ladling pancake batter onto the hot surface. Trinity stood barefoot in a chair at the kitchen table. She was powdered with flour. She busily stirred another batch of batter and didn't even notice her father when he came into the room.

The shock of seeing another woman cooking in his kitchen jolted him. "Do you know what time it is?" Ross asked.

Amara looked up. "It's breakfast time. We thought you and Trinette were going to sleep the whole morning away."

"I found it!" a small voice called from the pantry. Trina ran in with a box of cookie cutters. She too looked as if she'd just taken a lazy roll in a vat of flour.

"Are you crazy?" he asked Amara, appalled at the bedraggled state of his daughters. "They look like they've been—"

"We've been cooking breakfast for you, Daddy," Trinity said.

Trina handed the cookie cutters to her sister. "Yep. Mara is our susistant."

"Uh-sistant," Trinity corrected.

Ross's anger flared. "You two go upstairs right now."

"But we haven't finished breakfast," Trina said, pouting.

Amara sighed. "Ross—"

"Upstairs!" he bellowed in his "I mean business" voice. To make sure Trinity didn't fall, he lifted her from the chair onto the floor. He watched as they slow-footed it to the stairs. Heads bowed and faces sad. Ross couldn't believe that Amara was corrupting his daughters already.

The young woman turned off the griddle and placed her batter-covered hands on her narrow hips. "What was that about?"

"That was about order and expectations. I expect both from my daughters. You haven't been here twenty-four hours and already you are trying to turn them into ragamuffins. What's the idea of four-year-old girls cooking? They can't even spell *cook*. They're not interested in cooking. They want to play in the kitchen and make a mess."

Amara's eyebrow rose. "I've got news for you . . . that's what four-year-old girls do."

"Not in this house. Brenda never—" He stopped himself. He would not compare this young woman to his deceased wife. There *was* no comparison. And he'd known that. He'd also known that this marriage was doomed from the start. He promised himself that at the first sign that their union was hurting his girls, he would get an annulment. As a matter of fact, he was planning on it.

Just one false move, he thought. He almost said it too, but the expression on Amara's face sent a cold wave of sorrow traveling through his body. She looked as though someone had stolen all her happiness.

Why was she so gung-ho about this arrangement? he wondered. "Look, I'm . . . I'm sorry. We just live by a set of rules in this house. You've been around us long enough to know that. Those things don't change just because . . ." *Brenda's dead. Go on, say it.*

He tried to ignore the discomfort he saw in her eyes. It was hard. She looked so vulnerable standing by the stove, salvaging pancakes. Her delicate form looked breakable, broken even. He had an overwhelming urge to wrap her innocence in his arms until the expression on her face relaxed. But that urge changed to revulsion. Brenda was only thirty days cold in her grave. He would not betray her memory by embracing another woman in their kitchen.

"I don't have three roughhousing boys, Amara. I have girls whom I will raise to be ladylike, just as their mother was." He turned and exited the kitchen, leaving her to clean up the mess she'd made.

* * *

If Trinette poked her lip out any more, Amara believed, it would be permanently deformed. "Trinette, honey. Aren't you hungry?"

When Ross left for work, Amara and the girls had sat down to breakfast. Amara had tried some of the fun food ideas her mother had used with her like putting faces on the pancakes or cutting the pancakes into fun shapes with cookie cutters. Trina and Trinity dove in with zest. Trinette just held on to her seat and poked her lip out.

She'd noticed the child's odd behavior and mentioned it to Ross before he left. He'd passed it off as nothing more than drowsiness from a bad night. Amara hoped that was all that was wrong.

When the doorbell rang, Amara thought for a moment that Ross had forgotten his key. Then she remembered that the man she married functioned like a well-oiled machine. He would never do something as careless as that. Squinting out of the peephole, Amara saw a short, pudgy woman with a pie dish in her hand. Amara smiled, and swung the door open.

"Hi," she said.

The short woman smiled from the inside out. Her cinnamon-cream-hued face radiated with joy. "Welcome to the neighborhood, Amara!" she said, holding out the pie.

Amara took it and stepped aside. "Come in, Shasta."

Shasta Martinez was a newcomer to the neighborhood herself. Having moved in about six months ago, she and Amara had exchanged greetings one day when Amara had come over to take the girls shopping.

Shasta lived next door and had decorated her yard

with the most unusual fixtures—a unicorn lamppost, Snoopy mailbox, Victorian wind chimes, to name a few. When Amara asked about the unique items, Shasta quickly explained that she was a professional contest winner. Her job, as she loosely described it, was to enter fifty to seventy-five contests per day. Some on paper. Most on-line. In no time, she'd told Amara the story of how she entered contests with cash prizes, but she also entered contests that offered prizes of things she could use, like a year's supply of toilet paper or free hamburgers each week, every week, for her entire lifetime.

"I only enter the legitimate ones. Not the scams. And I've been doing this long enough to know which is which," she'd said.

According to Shasta, she won an average of 5 percent of the time. So nearly every day, she received large packages, small boxes, and envelopes containing amounts from a few dollars to several hundred. When she threw in coupons, rebates, and Tupperware parties, Shasta's "job" took care of her every need without her having to "get out into the real world and work."

"Did you make this?" Amara asked, opening the dish and revealing a Dutch apple pie that made her mouth water just to look at it.

"Who has time to bake?" Shasta responded. "I won that in a raffle at a bake sale yesterday." The woman's bright smile dimmed. "How's . . . everything?"

From the sound of the girls in the next room, things were all right there, but after last night and this morning with Ross, Amara was starting to wonder if she'd made a good decision getting married and becoming an instant mother. She cut two slices of pie and placed them on plates. The women sat down at the kitchen table.

Amara kept the girls in her sight. "I just have to get used to everything."

"Well, just so you know, I'm on your side. I didn't know Brenda. I only got to see her a few times when Ross wheeled her outside for some fresh air. But even in as bad a shape as she was in, she seemed like a very smart woman. And it was painfully obvious that she loved her children. So if she picked you . . . then you're the one that is supposed to be here—for her girls *and* her husband."

Amara lifted a forkful of pie to her lips. In her heart, she knew Shasta was correct. She was grateful for the reminder that she was doing the right thing. And no matter how hard Ross was determined to make it for her, she was determined to ride out his dispassion until it mellowed into an amiable relationship they could both live with.

The pie melted in her mouth. The tastes of cinnamon, nutmeg, and creamery butter competed for attention on her tongue, but nothing overpowered the flavor of fresh sweet apples dissolving between her teeth. She moaned and licked her lips.

"Hey now!" she said. "I wish you had baked this. I'd ask you for the recipe or another pie." Amara smacked her lips. "I hope you didn't want another piece."

The women shared a laugh and two of the triplets entered the kitchen. "Can I have some pie, Mara?"

"*May* I have some pie?"

"*May* I?"

"Yes, you may," Amara said, rising for another plate. "Would you like a slice too, Trinette?"

Trinette stood next to her sister, not really looking at anything. She wore the same bleak expression she'd had all morning. A wave of sadness moved through Amara.

She was afraid for Trinette. The child hadn't smiled in a month's time. Ross seemed to think it was okay to allow her to grieve in her own way. He was confident it would pass. Amara wasn't so sure.

She placed two small pieces on two plastic plates and offered them to the girls. Trina took hers eagerly. Trinette only stared.

"May I have Trinette's piece?" Trinity asked.

"Yes," Amara replied.

The three little look-alikes sat down at their Fisher-Price table in the corner of the kitchen. It's where they went for snacks and coloring. Amara slid back into the seat across from Shasta.

"She's not doing so well, is she?"

"No, Shasta. She's not."

"Have you thought about therapy?"

"Thought about it. Suggested it. Ross rejected it."

"Hmm," Shasta said, finishing the last of her pie. "Well, if you need it, I've got six free consultations with United Methodist Treatment Centers."

Amara couldn't hide the shock on her face.

Shasta shrugged, licked her index finger, and proceeded to polish off the remaining crumbs on her plate. "You never know when stuff like that will come in handy."

Chapter 4

Three of everything! Dresses. Dolls. Toothbrushes. Pajamas. Books. Pairs of shoes. Jackets. Socks. The girls had the largest bedroom in the house, and rightly so. They had enough stuff to fill two rooms. Amara found the sheer number of things the girls had accumulated overwhelming.

Now she understood why Brenda and Ross had sometimes protested at her frequent gifts. There was only so much space in the house.

And the triplets didn't seem satisfied until every toy they owned was out of their numerous toy boxes and on the floor.

Amara had to work like a madwoman to keep the girls clean, their room organized, and the house in livable condition. She dared not think about any shopping, cooking, and errands she may have needed to run during the week.

One day, and she felt as though she'd stepped on a treadmill with no off switch. When the girls took a nap, she did too, and dreamed that she'd fallen asleep and forgotten something—Ross's lunch, a load of laundry in the washer, or worse, something burning on the stove.

Even her nightmares came in threes.

After only a few hours of running herself ragged,

Amara made up her mind that she was not going to keep up the superhuman pace. She couldn't. Her plan was to let one thing go per week and pick it up next week. This week, it would be the girls' hair. If they wanted their hair combed, they would have to do it themselves. Besides, there was no rule that said their hair had to be combed every day. And she was sure she wouldn't be jailed for it.

It was also one of the most taxing things on her to-do list. Not only did the girls not like their hair combed, they'd been tender-headed since birth. So instead of enduring the tears and the wailing, Amara decided she could spend that time vacuuming.

She pulled the Kirby out of the utility closet knowing full well what to expect. It had happened every time she'd taken out the vacuum cleaner in the past.

"Can I turn it on?"

"I want to turn it on!"

"Can I put the tachments on?"

"I wanna do it! You did it last time!"

While Trinity and Trina argued over whose turn it was to turn on the vacuum, Amara counted to ten.

"Trina, since you started the vacuum the last time, let's give Trinity a turn."

What a reaction! She didn't know Trina could scream that loudly. Her high-decibel voice frayed the last of Amara's nerves.

"All right then, Trina, why don't you go in the kitchen and color?"

Trinity smiled and pressed her small brown thumb against the on switch. The vacuum whirred to life. Trina marched off sniffing.

"And you two, keep your sister company," she said to the girls standing by her side. Grudgingly, they stomped away. Grateful they were doing as they were told, Amara let out a steadying sigh and went to work.

By the time she had cleaned her way to the end of the upstairs hall, something made her hesitate.

Ross's bedroom.

It always felt like a *forbidden zone*. In fact, she'd only been in his room a few times. Once to take out a plate of half-eaten dessert and another time to empty the trash can.

For the most part, Ross was a neat man. Everything in his bedroom had its place. Tie tree for ties. Shoe racks for shoes. Special drawer for cuff links, watches, tiepins, and sunglasses.

Although she appreciated his neatness, the fact that he organized his clothing and socks by color always made her chuckle.

She placed a new plastic liner in the small basket where he discarded his trash and thought, *You should have been in the military, Ross*. She knew if she opened his closet and picked up one of his black leather shoes, she'd be able to see her reflection in it.

Before she left the room, something she didn't understand drew her toward the bed. She stood there for a few moments. Staring.

The place where Ross slept. The place where he'd slept with his former wife.

A place she would never know.

She wondered if she and Ross would ever come to any kind of understanding, ever be more than civil to each other. They would have to if this arrangement was to work. She didn't dare call it a marriage or think of it as a union. Ross had made clear what it was. A deal. An agreement. To take care of the children. To provide good lives for the girls.

And as soon as those girls grow up, that will be the end. She knew it as sure as she knew the scent of Paradigm cologne in the room. Ross's scent. Ross's terms.

Maybe, she thought, walking toward the door, they would find their way back to the feelings they had once had for each other. Feelings of family and appreciation, and respect.

She would pray for that, Amara thought, and closed the door behind her.

She would pray hard.

By the time Ross got home, Amara was tired. She realized that in the four years the girls had been alive, she'd never been alone with them for more than a couple of hours at a time. Having them all day was more than a notion. Between periodic screaming matches and tugs of war with toys, they had kept her hopping. If she was going to get some things done around the house, she might have to put them in day care part-time until she could get used to having them on an all-day basis.

She'd been so busy picking up after the girls and preparing meals and snacks that she hadn't had time to eat. She was hoping to remedy that situation soon.

Her stomach grumbled while she added the finishing touches to dinner. Swiss steak with onions, carrots, mashed potatoes and gravy, steamed broccoli, and strawberry fluff. Just in case the girls were fickle, she'd warmed some hot dogs.

Hearing his weighty footsteps, Amara cut a slice of apple pie and popped it in the microwave on a low setting.

"Hey! Where are the women in my life!" he said, coming into the kitchen.

Trina and Trinity jumped up from the coloring books at their table and ran. "Daddy!"

He scooped them both into his thick muscular arms

and lifted them easily. They covered him with kisses. Amara smiled. The sight warmed her heart as it always did. Ross loved his girls more than anything. His affection was obvious.

Trinette stayed behind at the table.

"Trinette, come give Daddy a kiss."

The little girl rose slowly from the table and walked trancelike to his side. He placed the other two on the floor and knelt down beside Trinette. She did as she had been told and kissed her father on the cheek.

"That's better," he said, rising. He tousled her unkempt braids and patted her on the behind.

Immediately Trina and Trinity launched into a chatter-fest about all the things they had done that day with Amara. Trina took great pride in telling all the bad things that her sisters had done. Trinity seemed focused on reporting all of Amara's good deeds.

"Okay, okay!" Ross said, smiling. "It sounds like you had a good day."

"Can we stay home again tomorrow, Daddy? I don't want to go back to day care."

"Sure, sweetheart," he said, patting Trina's head. "You can stay home tomorrow, too."

"Yeay!" the girls shouted. All except Trinette, who hadn't moved or smiled since she'd walked over to her father.

"Hello, Ross," Amara said.

"Amara."

"Dinner's ready."

Trina tugged on her father's jacket. "Mara made Swiss steak, Daddy! Swiss steak is your favornet."

"Fav-or-ite," Trinity corrected.

Ross's face held a combination of surprise and suspicion. "You didn't have to—"

"I wanted to."

"Amara, I have some unusual dining habits. I prefer to eat—"

"In the kitchen. I know."

Annoyance twisted his facial features into a frown. "I always have a—"

"Warm dessert first."

There wasn't anything Amara didn't know about Ross. She knew he only wore one kind of cologne. She knew he brushed his teeth in the shower. She knew that he put his socks on before anything else. And yes, she knew his eating quirks. Most of what she knew was things she'd observed over the years. Other things she'd been told by Brenda during their numerous woman-to-woman talks.

He swept a glance in the kitchen. The table was set just as Brenda used to set it for dinner. His favorite foods simmered on the stove. At the ding of the microwave, Amara thought she'd probably overcome all of Ross's objections.

She moved to the unit, took out the piece of pie that was now piping on the plate, and placed it before Ross's seat at the table.

Ross's look of incredulity pleased her. "Hungry?" she asked.

"I just need to change my clothes," he said, and headed upstairs.

While he was gone, Amara propped each one of the girls up in a chair. She fixed their plates and ones for Ross and herself. When it came to arranging them at the table, she wasn't as sure. For years, she'd been the guest. Whenever she had dinner, she'd always taken a seat in what obviously was a guest seat. Ross and Brenda typically sat at the ends of the table.

For a few flabbergasted moments, she vacillated on where to place her plate.

"Wait for Daddy! Mara! Trinity ate a broccoli!"

"I just wanted to taste it!"

"Okay, you two," she said, placing her plate next to Trinette's, "no arguing at the table."

Trina folded her arms in a huff. "I'm not arguing!"

"Trina!" Ross's deep voice bellowed throughout the kitchen. All the girls' heads snapped in his direction—including Amara's.

"Don't ever let me catch you raising your voice to an adult again. Do you understand me?"

Trina's body deflated as if it were a popped balloon. "Yes, Daddy."

"And since you have such a smart mouth this evening, why don't you say grace?"

Trinity smiled. Trinette just stared down at her food. Amara took a seat beside the solemn child and Ross took his position at the head of the table.

"Trina . . ." Ross said, authority flattening his voice into a potent order.

She huffed, glanced quickly at her sisters, and began to pray. "God is great. God is good. Let us thank Him for our food. Amen."

"Amen," they all said in response.

For the first few minutes of their meal, there was silence. Blissful, blessed silence. And then the first argument ensued.

"You know, that's something we might need to talk about in the future," Amara said, trying to take as much of the disappointment out of her voice as possible.

"What?" Ross asked, looking at her as though she had no business speaking at the table.

"Day care. There will probably be times when the

girls may have to go to day care. It occurred to me today that it might be better for all of us if the girls went to day care on a regular basis. Like maybe two times a week."

"You're kidding," Ross said, letting his raised glass of water clink to the table.

"No!" Trina whined. Trinette's eyes widened. "I like it here with you, Mara."

"No one's going to day care," Ross said to the girls, but stared at Amara. "You've taken care of the girls all of twelve hours and already you want them in a facility?"

"I'm ready to do what's necessary to take care of this family. If that means that sometimes the girls can't be around while I clean the house or wash clothes, then so be it."

Suddenly the food in Amara's mouth tasted rank and she thought that was awfully strange, because she knew she could cook.

"Why don't we discuss this later?" Ross asked, a dismissive tone lacing his words.

"I don't see anything wrong with letting the girls know we're human and that sometimes humans disagree with each other."

"We will not have this discussion now," he said, and returned his attention to the remaining food on his plate. There wasn't much left. So without saying it, he let her know she'd won the first battle. But this new tension between them troubled her. Would it be like this every day? No matter what she did, he would find fault with her actions.

No, she thought. She would not let him rule her that way.

The triplets had stopped their little girl chattering, and stared back and forth between Amara and Ross as if they'd been watching Venus and Serena in a championship match.

"Ross . . ." Amara began carefully measuring her frustration. "How many times have you been alone with the girls? I mean completely alone with them?"

"Plenty," he responded, never taking his eyes off of his plate.

"For how long? An hour? Two?" Amara gulped down a healthy portion of her water to cool her heating feelings. "I love these three little munchkins, but oh my gosh! If you haven't had an entire day alone with them, you have no idea how much energy it takes."

Amara braced herself. She knew what was coming. She could see it on his face. *Brenda never had any problems*.

But he remained silent. Then the hint of a smile tugged at the corner of his mouth. "If you can't handle it, just say so."

At that moment, all of the grand feelings she'd ever had for Ross Hayward soured. It took all of her strength and resolve as a respectable black woman not to slap the handsome off of his face.

Instead, she finished the smile he started, took a bite of her steak and chewed it slowly. When she finished, she forced his gaze with her own. "Now, you ought to know me better than that."

Ross's eyes widened. She couldn't tell if it was in surprise or conciliation. Either way, she knew. She'd won victory number two.

She finished the rest of her dinner, helped the girls get ready for bed, and wondered with a concerned heart if tomorrow would bring yet another battle.

Chapter 5

Back at the corporate grindstone, and Ross was uneasy. For years, this was the life he loved—project planning, attending meetings, making presentations. His job as director of risk management gave him the opportunity to work in a business setting making the kind of money he liked, yet it was flexible enough that he could be mobile and not just stuck behind a computer in a cubicle.

During Brenda's illness, he'd quit his day job to take care of her. To make ends meet, he'd used his skills as a risk analyst to do consulting work out of his home. He hadn't realized what a comfort it was to be home with the girls until he was forced to be away from them. This was his second week back. The Facilities Planning Department had been kind enough to reinstate his position. As he reviewed the script for his PowerPoint presentation, the off-white walls of his cubicle seemed to close in on him. Even though his work area was large, more like an office than a cubicle, it was suddenly too small. Ross stood abruptly and grabbed his coffee cup. He could use an excuse to get up and stretch his legs.

He worked on the twenty-eighth floor of a thirty-story building. The corporate headquarters of Braum Technologies was home to all of the executive vice presidents, directors of the company, and their first level staff. Everyone here was in charge of something. Ross's floor, Facilities and Building Management was in charge of the disaster recovery and contingency planning of the organization. It was Ross's job to make sure that if there were a disaster—flood, tornado, major power-outage, sick building syndrome, crippling computer virus, or terrorist attack—the company would still be able to function fully at an off-site location. Since 9/11, his job duties had tripled. But he was grateful to be part of the solution.

Ross made his way to the coffee machine, passing row after row of off-white cubicles. If seen from above, the room probably resembled a maze, like the kind popular in his daughters' puzzle and game books. Suddenly, there were too many straight lines and corners, too many conversations muffled by cloth-covered walls, too much sterility, too much order. He filled his cup with the steaming black liquid, thinking that he missed his girls terribly and wondered what they were doing at this very moment.

When he sat down at his desk, he picked up the phone. He'd made it through the entire morning without calling. Before he went to lunch, he had to check on his daughters. He knew their voices could make him feel better and remind him of why he had to be away from them in the first place.

He didn't even hear the phone ring. All he heard was "Let me answer it!" "No, me!" "Mara! You said it was my day!"

"Hey, hey!" he said. "What's going on over there?"

"Daddy, Trinity won't let me answer the phone, and it's my day."

"Your day for what, sweetheart?"

"To be the helper."

In the background he heard voices. "Let me talk!" "I want to talk to Daddy."

Helper? He wondered what Amara had them doing now.

"Well, Ms. Helper, you practice your letters today, okay?"

"Okay, Daddy."

"Good. Let me speak to Nettie."

He heard the familiar rustling sound as the phone changed hands. "Hi, Daddy."

"Hi, baby girl. You miss me?"

"Yes."

"Well, Daddy will be home in a few hours, okay?"

" 'Kay."

"You be good. Let me talk to Trinity."

"Bye, Daddy."

"Bye, Nettie."

"Daddy, tell Trina to let me answer the phone!"

Ross laughed. He might have to start calling the eldest of the triplets Ms. Drill Sergeant. She was always giving orders. "Why?" he asked.

" 'Cause I said I wanted to."

Apparently Trinity's comment made Trina angry. Her voice became loud and accusatory. Ross did not like the tone of it. "Sweetheart, let me talk to Trina again."

"Ooh, you're in trouble, you're—"

Ross pulled the phone away from his ear as a high-pitched shriek shot across the line.

"Ross?"

It wasn't the voice he was expecting. "Amara, what's going on over there? Why is Trina answering the phone?"

"I asked Trina to be my helper for the day. I told her she could answer the phone."

Ross blew out a hot breath. "That just causes commotion. If you let one answer, you have to let them all
answer. And *you* may not keep track of how many times
they each get to answer the phone, but *they* will. Pretty
soon—and from the sound of things, it may be sooner
than later—there will be no pleasing any of them."

"That's why I have helpers. They each get a day. That
way, there's no misunderstanding on who gets to do
what, when."

"Really? So, that's not a misunderstanding I'm hearing?"

"This is the first day," she said, sounding like she was
straining to keep two girls from tearing into each other.
"They just have to get used to it. Now, I don't mean to
be rude, but were you calling for something special?"

"I just needed to hear their voices."

"Oh. Okay. Anything else?"

"Are you rushing me off the phone?" Ross asked,
irritated.

"Yes. I've got lunch to make. So if there's nothing
else . . ."

"No, nothing else."

"Okay. We'll see you when you get home."

Before the click, he heard a chorus of wee voices saying, "Bye, Daddy."

He hung up thinking Amara had a lot to learn about
taking care of children. And as long as it didn't hurt
the girls, he was prepared to let her learn the hard way.

That evening, when Ross came home expecting
World War III, he was surprised by the silence that
greeted him and the aroma that welcomed him. His
three little monsters were quiet. So quiet, he wondered

if they were even home. Curious, he left his briefcase by the couch and walked straight toward the kitchen.

"Daddy!" *How can children so small make noises so big?* he wondered, knowing he really didn't care. Their enthusiasm at his return was all the incentive he needed to hit the job in earnest every morning. He picked up Nettie, who'd been Little Miss Quiet for far too long.

"Well, you all sound happy," he said, thinking of how they were all seated at their play area coloring when he'd walked in.

"We did our numbers and everything, Daddy!"

"Yep, and we made cookie faces."

"And I was Mara's helper."

"We all were Mara's helper."

"Yep, and then a man came over and we got to color."

Ross stiffened. He turned toward Amara, who was stirring something on the stove. "What man?"

The thought of a strange man around his children drew Ross's concern.

"My uncle Zay. He came by to see me."

"Really?" Ross asked, letting Nettie down. "Do you often get visits from your uncle?"

"With my family, there's no telling who'll pop by. We're very close. Remember?"

Remember? He'd never forget the time he'd given Amara a ride home after she'd come over for dinner. It was several years ago, before the girls were born. Amara and Brenda had just started the mentoring program and were getting to know each other. When Ross had volunteered to give Amara a ride home afterward, he had no idea what he was getting into.

When he pulled up to her house, several women had come strutting out and asked him a boatload of questions.

He remembered all right.

He remembered feeling like the patsy in a shake-down. How long had he been married? What did he do? How did he feel about his wife being Amara's mentor? What did he see his role as in their relationship? Where did he live?

These were questions he was sure Brenda had already answered, but he could tell they weren't as concerned with the answers as they were getting some insight into the older man who'd driven home their niece. He'd finally cut to the chase by assuring them that he would never harm or allow any harm to come to Amara. The expression on their faces told him that they would hold him to that promise.

The idea of someone having a family that loved them that much stuck with him. "Yeah," he replied, finally. "I remember."

A cold dizziness gripped him. It was as if he were walking without moving. Suddenly the house was too small; it was swallowing him. The girls were swallowing him. Amara was swallowing him.

Brenda's memory was swallowing him.

He couldn't breathe. "I have to get out," he said, heading for the door.

His collar was too tight. He tugged at it. Tore at it. Popped a button.

"What?" Amara called behind him. "Ross!"

"I'm going out!" he said, almost running now.

He fumbled with the keys, and then seconds later he was in his Lexus, driving away.

By the time he pulled into the club parking lot, he'd been driving for hours. The whole thing was a blur, as if he'd been only partly conscious the whole time. He had no clear idea of how he ended up where he was.

He stepped out, eyes on the verge of tears he hadn't allowed himself to shed. He was standing in front of Ventana's, a bar and grill. The place where he and Brenda had first met.

He checked his wallet to make sure he'd brought enough money to tie on a good one. At the sight of several twenties, he almost smiled, then headed inside.

Just like his life, Ventana's had changed—drastically. The wood floors had been replaced by something gray, metallic, and shiny. The cream-colored walls were now a stark bright white. The old-fashioned square wood tables with black leather and metal chairs were gone. In their place were round glass tables and skinny white art deco chairs.

He closed his mouth, which had obviously been hanging open, and approached the bar. When he sat down, the pristine masonite counter looked like a place where one would order a shot of wheat grass instead of a Courvoisier.

But that's what he intended to order, and if they didn't have it, he would grab the bartender by the neck and squeeze until someone brought him what he wanted.

"How can I help you?" the young woman asked.

Damn, he thought. *Young women everywhere. I can't get away from them!*

"Shot of Courvoisier. Make it a double."

She smiled. "You got it."

Ross settled back into the chair, but couldn't relax. Ventana's had been *their* place. But now, it was barely recognizable. Glancing into the bar mirror, he realized that so was he.

As the bartender returned with his drink, he wondered why he'd agreed to marry Amara. Was it really to honor Brenda's last wishes? Was it because he didn't want his girls to have to go without a mother? Or was it because he valued the comfort of a woman and knew how lonely he'd be without one?

The cognac burned like a warm memory inside him. Their first hello. And contrary to popular love stories, she came to him first. Pursued him. Romanced him.

And he had fallen head over heels.

"How ya doin'?" the young woman asked. She was African-American, slender, perky. The kind of woman that probably smiled in her sleep.

"Come back in a few minutes," he said, trying to sound as civil as possible. What he wanted to say was, *Just bring me a bottle and leave me the hell alone.*

He rotated the snifter in his hand. Images of the past floated in the golden brown liquid. Ross took a deep breath and gulped it down.

"Ahh," he said, gasping for air.

He wiped his mouth with the back of his hand. "We said our first hello here, my love. It's only fitting that we say our good-byes here, too."

In the background, Muzak pumped a steady stream of happy-feeling instrumentals. It set Ross's teeth on edge. "Bartender! Another double!"

There was a train in Ross's head. A big freight train, rolling hard with a loud and unforgiving whistle. He pressed his palms to his temples and prayed for the iron horse to stop its charge through his skull. But to no avail. It kept rolling and rolling and . . .

"Ross? Are you all right?"

After the third double shot, he and the bartender had addressed each other on a first-name basis.

"Bring me notherrr double, Ruby." Another round of Courvoisier would stop that runaway train on its tracks.

"Ross, I think you've had enough. As a matter of fact, I'll call you a cab."

"I don't need a cab! I can dr—dr— I can steer!"

The train in his head was picking up speed, making him dizzy. He held on to the bar counter to steady himself.

"Ruby, this darn thing is gonna jump the tracks!"

"Hold on, big guy. Your ride's coming."

When the headlights flashed through the bay windows, Amara jumped up from where she was sitting. She didn't want him to know she'd been waiting up.

But she had.

And she was worried out of her mind. Ross had been so distraught before he left. She thought he'd take an hour, two at the most, to cool off. But it hadn't been a couple of hours. It had been seven.

Even when he was working late hours or out with his friends, he was always home in time to put the girls to bed. Tonight, they'd gone to sleep without a kiss on the forehead from their father.

Amara headed down the hallway, grateful that her worst fears hadn't been true. Ross hadn't been hurt or in an accident. And he was finally home.

Waves of relief calmed her until the knock came at the door.

She tied her satin robe around her and headed back to the entryway wondering who was at the door at this time of night.

Rather than turn on a light, she took a glance through the peephole. Her heart fluttered when she saw the condition of the man swaying on the porch.

She yanked the front door open. "Ross! What happened to you?"

"He threw back about five too many, ma'am," a man standing next to Ross said.

The cab in the driveway and the rocking man on her porch told her all she needed to know.

"I said I can drive! Now give me back my nose or I'll punch you in the keys!"

The cabdriver helped Amara get a good grip on Ross. She leaned Ross toward the house and looked back.

"Thanks so much for bringing him home. What do I owe you?"

"Nothin'. The bartender at Ventana's already paid me. And he's got his keys. He's just too drunk to get 'em outa his pocket."

"Okay," Amara said, staggering a little with her husband's weight. "Thanks again."

The cabdriver shut the door behind her and she headed toward the couch. She couldn't believe this was the same handsome man she saw every night. His bright piercing eyes were bloodshot, his crisp fitted clothes hanging askew. And his cowboy swagger now reduced to a lopsided stagger.

"Where are we going?" Ross asked.

Amara winced and turned her head. Ross's breath was foul, rotten. As if he'd never brushed his teeth in his entire life. The cabdriver was wrong. Five too many was definitely an understatement.

"I said where are we going?"

"As heavy as you are, we're barely going anywhere right now. But the plan is to get you to the couch so you can sleep this off."

"No couch!"

"What?" Amara said, stumbling. By sheer dumb luck

she was able to keep them both from falling on their faces.

"No couch. Take me upstairs."

"I can barely get you into the next room, Ross. You're deadweight."

He stared at her through his stupor. His gaze made her shiver. There was pain there. An acute pain shining in his eyes so brightly she felt blinded by it.

"Please," he said.

Amara relented and hobbled with him to the staircase. She'd climbed these stairs every day without care since her marriage. Now the steps looked more like obstacles than a means to the upper floor.

Amara tightened her grip. "Okay," she said. "On one . . . *One.*"

Amara stepped up, but Ross did not. She pulled, tugged, and hoisted until his right foot lifted a little. With a groan he stepped up.

"Two," she said, again using her strength. After her exertion, Ross followed suit in lifting his left leg. At this rate, they would only make it three stairs before all her strength would be gone.

"Ross," she said, agitation sharpening her voice.

"I want to go upstairs," he insisted.

"Then you're going to have to help me here."

He groaned in protest.

"Ross, I can't do this by myself! Now if we don't work together, we're never going to make it!"

A sickening wave of awareness washed over Amara as she realized that it was not just the mounting of the stairs she was referring to.

The feelings she had for Ross surfaced in a way that surprised her. She held on to him tightly. "Stop working against me," she said, catching his gaze.

Their eyes held for a moment. Then Ross nodded, his head lobbing as if weighed down by a great burden.

After that, their ascent went much more smoothly. Though still a challenge, Amara managed to get Ross up the stairs and into his bedroom. The closer they got to the bed, the more the man in her arms groaned.

"Ross? Are you all right?"

"No," he said, collapsing on the mattress. "I'm drunk."

And sweaty, she wanted to add. "Don't I know it? You're not going to be sick, are you?"

"No," he said, closing his eyes.

Just to be on the safe side, Amara retrieved the wastebasket from the corner and placed it on the floor near the head of the bed. When she looked up, Ross was sprawled on the bed, passed out, clothes bunched in a weird and uncomfortable-looking way.

The sight saddened her. She'd never known him to be so out of sorts before. The great and terrible Ross Hayward. Reduced to a heap by a night of drinking. She sighed and went to work.

"Oh, God, Ross," she said to the unconscious man. "How much do you weigh?" She used every bit of her remaining energy to take off his shirt, shoes, and pants. Without reservation, she allowed herself a few silent moments to admire his body. Everything she'd imagined about his manly frame was true in the flesh in front of her. On impulse she stroked the length of his arm, hard and firm even in his sleep.

Angry, happy, and any emotion in between. It didn't matter. Wearing a frown, a smile, or a drunken stupor, Ross Hayward was still the most handsome man Amara had ever seen. Everything about him was deep, thick, and imposing. The deep parts were his eyes and the way they were set into his face, his voice, dimples that only appeared when he smiled, and the cut of his gaze. His eye lashes, eyebrows, moustache, and physique were the thick parts. His hair begged for stroking, his muscles too sometimes, if Amara admitted the truth to herself. And his presence—his stride and surefooted determination, the confidence with which he did everything, and the way a room got smaller every time he stepped into it—was what made Amara think he was imposing. Everything about him commanded attention. And Amara knew it. She just wished she could be a little better at fighting off the effect it had on her.

The last test of her strength came as she rocked Ross from side to side, inching the bedsheets down. After pulling them at an angle, she'd rescued enough fabric from beneath his drunken torso to cover him with. He breathed hard and heavy and smelled like a tangy mixture of booze, cologne, and sweat.

"You beautiful and tormented man," she said, amazed by her compassion. "I hope you sleep your demons away."

Another impulse and her hand touched his cheek, stroking, caressing, savoring. Even though she was Mrs. Ross Hayward, Amara never dreamed that she would ever touch him in this way. It felt good. Then it felt guilty. But before she could take her hand away, Ross grabbed it. His grip on her wrist was incredibly tight considering his condition.

Her heart lurched up into her throat. She'd been caught.

His eyes opened and he looked at her dreamily.

"Thank you," he whispered, "for putting . . . me . . . to . . ."

The grip on her arm disappeared and his hand dropped to the mattress. He was out. Before anything else could happen, Amara hurried out of Ross's bed-room and down the stairs to her own bedroom——her hand still throbbing and warm from where it had touched Ross's face.

Chapter 6

Ballet lessons! What a disaster! Not only did the girls hate it, but their instructor was a crotchety old woman with a penchant for barking orders.

Drill sergeant would be a better descriptor. Along with "Rule Queen." Mrs. Casey had rules for everything. The girls' hair had to be pinned into buns. They had to wear their dance-wear to the lesson—they were not allowed to change when they got there. There were to be no smudges, rips, tears, or unsightly wrinkles of any kind in their suits. And their shoes had to be sparkling clean at all times.

The girls were ready to go after fifteen minutes of the first lesson.

But still, she'd tried to make it work for a month—taking the girls three times a week to Mrs. Casey's Ballet School. But neither she nor the girls were happy and the girls were so unhappy that Amara felt bad about just dropping them off, and so Ross's wonderful idea about how she could get some much needed free time was shot to shinola.

"That's the last time I listen to you!" she declared, scrubbing the sink.

In rebellion of Mrs. Casey and Ross, she and the girls had left for ballet lessons, but instead of going to the dance studio, they'd gone to her aunt Marti's house where the girls had the run of a magnificent house and played happily with Kenyon Jr., their cousin by marriage.

When she'd called Ross to tell him where they were, his voice had grumbled his disapproval. But Amara held fast to her decision and was determined not to allow Ross's rigidity to get in the way of what she believed was the best interest of the girls.

Her decision felt good. It would hold her contented until the next day.

The aroma of freshly baked sugar cookies filled the kitchen. Amara and her three helpers were busy doing what had become a ritual for them, making cookie faces.

Amara used to make them for the girls when their mother was ill. At first, she baked the cookies at home and brought them over. Then once, when she had wanted something to do that would take her mind off of her ailing friend, she had baked the cookies right there in the Hayward kitchen.

Now that she'd moved in, not only did she make cookies on a regular basis, but she let the girls help her. Even Nettie seemed to be getting a kick out of it.

But Amara was still worried about her. Nettie was going through the motions. They were just slow motions, as if she'd been caught in a terrible instant replay and no matter what she tried, she couldn't get out.

The cookies were cooling atop racks on the kitchen counter. This was the girls' favorite time, making the icing.

They did it the old-fashioned way with powdered sugar, water, and food coloring. Each girl was responsible for a color. Trinity blue. Trina red. And Trinette yellow.

When they finished making the icing, Amara loaded decorators with each color. The girls took turns using the colors to create smiley faces on the cookies.

When it was Nettie's turn to make a face, she just shook her head instead.

"What's wrong, Nettie? Don't you want to make a cookie face?"

Again, she shook her head.

The scent of vanilla, sugar, and butter hung heavily in the air. The smell and excitement worked its magic on everyone except Trinette. No matter what Amara did, she couldn't make the good times last. She couldn't keep a smile on her face, couldn't keep her laughing or engaged. No matter what, Nettie always retreated to her shell, cheerless and alone. Even with a roomful of people.

Suddenly it wasn't the Hayward kitchen Amara was in but the Fairchild kitchen. Her mother was making cookies and humming. Yolanda Fairchild had a wonderful voice and Amara had loved to hear it growing up. Then something had happened. She began to feel miserable and left out of things. She felt liked but not really loved. And her connection to her mother grew more distant by the day.

Except one day that was exceptional. It had been as if her mother was making a special effort to be a mother. To talk to her. Spend time with her. Laugh with her.

Listen to her.

The highlight of the day was when they were in the kitchen baking cookies. As Amara reflected on how gloomy and disconnected she felt sometimes, her mother started to sing.

First you get the bowl and it's time to begin
Butter, sugar, flour, the ingredients go in

The big spoon stirs, you must mix well
Cookie-face cookies, so good you have to yell
Round on the pan with lots of lovin'
Twelve minutes later they come out of the oven
Cookie-face cookies made with a smile
Yummy for your tummy with a joy, joy style
A cupful of happiness, a spoonful of glee
Cookie-face cookies for you and me

Through her own memories, it was as though Amara had switched places with Trinette—experiencing her sadness and grief. The emotion was too much for her to bear. Before she knew it, she was smiling at Nettie and humming to relieve the pain. Then the cookie song came back to her as if she'd been singing it her whole life.

Her voice was thin with emotion at first. Then stronger, more buoyant. She bounced with it, made a cookie face, and focused her attention on her silent daughter.

"Sing it again, Mara!" Trina demanded.

"I want to learn it too!" Trinity agreed.

Amara nodded. It was a cute song, she thought. But cute enough for Trinette? "How about it, Nettie? Would you like to sing along?"

Nettie didn't nod. Instead she spoke. "Cookie-face cookies," she sang in a low voice. When she lifted her head, the smile Amara saw on the small girl's face melted her heart. She hugged Nettie tightly and laughed. Suddenly, they laughed together.

"Cookie-face cookies. That's silly," Nettie declared.

"It is silly," Amara said, choking back happy tears. "But they sure do taste good!"

* * *

After that small breakthrough, Amara and the girls spent the afternoon making cookie-face cookies. They made so many that they had enough to share with Shasta and a few of the neighbor kids who came over to play with the triplets.

At that moment, Amara thanked her mother silently for doing at least one thing right in her life and she made a love note in her mind to sing the cookie song with Trinette whenever she seemed especially down.

Ross was gone. So were the girls. They had been in-vited to a birthday party for the daughter of one of Ross's coworkers. Amara was enjoying every bit of their absence.

When Ross had said, "Don't feel like you have to go with us," Amara distinctly heard, "I don't want you to go." So, she'd taken that opportunity to spend some quality time with herself.

It didn't happen that often. On only two other occa-sions had Ross taken the girls and just gone away for a while. Once they had gone to get ice cream and another time they had simply gone for a walk. On those occa-sions, Amara had spent the entire time working furiously to catch up on laundry, dusting, vacuuming, or folding the mountains of clean clothing that had piled up in the laundry room.

But she'd seen the invitation to the party. The activities included lunch at a theme park, a magician and clown show, and a snack at an ice cream parlor. Thankfully, they would be gone for hours.

The first thing Amara did was light some candles and put on some soft jazz. For ten minutes she just sat still, closed her eyes, and thought about nothing. After that, she washed her hair with an all-natural shampoo her aunt Ashley had made for her. While she let her hair air-dry, she took out her bag of cosmetics that was so unused lately, a thin sheet of dust had collected on the top of it. She removed her favorite facial mask and applied it liberally to her face.

As her mask conditioned her face, she ran a tub of water and filled it with hydrangea-scented bath salts.

When the water was ready, Amara slid off her blue satin cloth robe and stepped down into the tub. The water was wonderfully hot and rose to brimming when she settled into it.

"Umm," she moaned, contented to soak for the rest of the afternoon.

She closed her eyes and reflected on her surroundings. No laughing, screaming, arguing, jabbering girls. Nothing falling, breaking, ripping. No skinned knees. No food cooking on the stove for yet another meal. No CNN, MSNBC, CNBC, BET Nightly News droning in the background. No rustling of the *Atlanta Post* or *New York Times*. No angry gruff male voice issuing orders, spouting disappointments, or worse, completely silent.

Just her own breathing, a soft saxophone, and the sound of tiny bubbles breaking in the water. It was heaven.

A heaven she never knew during the hardest part of the day—the evening. Ross typically came home, changed out of his tailored suits, and walked around the house in shorts and a tank top. It was those times when she kept her eyes on not only the girls, but him too. The man had arms the size of logs and they were just as strong. When she and the girls had struggled all day to rearrange the furniture in the living room to make it more open and inviting, he put everything back in its original place in less than an hour.

She didn't understand how a man who looked so good could have such a gruff attitude. She'd done everything she could think of to mellow his harsh mood.

Amara scolded herself for allowing her thoughts to stray and let her excursion in bliss last as long as possible. Then before the water became uncomfortably cold, she washed, got out, and toweled dry.

The air on her skin felt wonderful. She lathered herself with hydrangea-scented lotion and stared at the blouse and matching pants she'd laid out to wear.

Suddenly, she was in no hurry to confine her body in clothing. She couldn't remember the last time she'd felt completely free and uninhibited. While Ross and the girls were gone, she was determined to enjoy her freedom in every way possible. She decided to wait awhile before putting on her outfit.

Soon she discovered that she loved cooking in the nude. Amara had to admit, it held its risks, but if she confined her culinary activities to the counter and the microwave, the potential for heat-related accidents was reduced significantly.

She'd almost forgotten how to cook for one. It had taken her a while to pare down the recipe for chicken casserole, but she'd done it. And in two minutes, by the timer, she'd have a steaming dish of an ooey, gooey poultry delight.

She rubbed the palms of her hands against her forearms. The lotion had done the trick. Her skin felt silky and glistened with health and vitality. She glanced down at her body and a stray thought flashed in her mind. *Ross Hayward, you don't know what you're missing.*

When she turned to retrieve a bowl from the cupboard,

she realized she'd have to retract that statement, because there he was, standing in the kitchen doorway, staring at her with brown-eyed hunger.

He'd been standing in the kitchen doorway for much too long. He knew that. But he also knew that he couldn't move or look away. The woman, and he did mean woman, he saw in the kitchen rendered him incapable of doing anything else but stare.

He'd left the party early. Most of the parents did. There were enough chaperones for three times the number of children at the party. Ross's colleagues had spared no expense and told the mothers and fathers that they could pick their kids up in four hours or so.

Hearing this, he'd dashed home, hoping that Amara wasn't there. If she was home, he hoped like great heaven that he could persuade her to go somewhere, anywhere, visit one of those aunts she seemed so fond of.

His hope of having a quiet evening was dashed the moment he'd come into the house and smelled food cooking. Still thinking he could get her out of the house, he'd headed straight for the kitchen. But when he got there, and saw the naked woman in front of his refrigerator, he stopped where he stood as if he'd been paralyzed in concrete.

She still had the youthful, angelic face he saw every day, but her body was fully grown. It was long with soft curves. It had been so long since he'd seen a woman's naked body, all he wanted to do was take a long visual survey of the woman before him and reacquaint himself.

"Ross!" she exclaimed, and scrambled to cover herself. Finding nothing within reach, she snatched the refrigerator door open and used it as a shield. "What are you doing home and where are the girls?"

"The girls are at the party," he said, not looking away. "I didn't realize it was a drop-off. I came home to relax a little before I go back to get them."

Ross continued his open appreciation of what he could see of her body, swallowed hard, and reminded himself that she was only twenty-two.

Her features maybe. Honey-smooth skin, angular nose, and cheeks. Everything about her was long and sharp, as if her body had been stretched from playing. Too much time hanging from monkey bars, running, or leaping over cracks. But her eyes were those of a much older woman. Wise. All-seeing.

They matched her mannerisms. Her speech. Since the day he'd met her, he'd always thought that she acted and sounded like someone twice her age.

He'd found out later that her mother was a strict disciplinarian and that growing up Amara spent more time around adults than children. For her earliest teen years, she'd been treated more like an adult and had expectations and responsibilities placed on her like those of an adult.

Apparently, she'd rebelled by immersing herself in electronic games. Probably as a way to experience some of the fun she wasn't allowed to have. Brenda had speculated that she could retreat from her mother and play at the same time. Soon the activity became a permanent escape.

That is until she became part of Ross's family.

Hmm, Ross thought. He hadn't thought of Amara as part of his family since they'd gotten married.

Ross's heart was racing. Blood churned hotly inside

his veins. The rise of heat was unfamiliar at first, then Ross recognized it as a slow building lust.

"Why are you naked?"

Amara trembled from the shock of Ross standing there and from the places on her body cooling from the tracks of his heated gaze.

"I, I, I, . . ."

Before she could embarrass herself even further, the microwave timer went off. She stared at it with wide-eyed fear. There was no way she could get her food now. If she could have disappeared into a crack in the door, or into the milk carton, or the box of Arm and Hammer, she would have. Of all the times she'd imagined Ross seeing her naked, none of them were remotely like this.

"Well?"

Why was he pressing this? "I just wanted to relax a little. I didn't expect you back so soon and . . ." Suddenly, Ross's behavior frustrated her. "Why are you just standing there?"

Surprised, Ross realized that he'd been waiting for another glimpse at Amara's beauty. Another second in the presence of her raw flesh. Lust he didn't remember ever having had riveted him to the spot. For those first few moments he couldn't have moved if his life had depended on it.

"I, I . . ." Now he was stammering. "I, uh, I'm going to my room."

From that moment, the man, whose eyes usually had been conveniently buried in a newspaper whenever she entered a room, watched with great interest whenever she crossed the room, or entered, or exited.

Chapter 7

"You look terrible!"

"Thanks," Amara said. Her aunt Morgan was never one to mince words. Amara stepped aside as her aunt entered the house loaded down with sacks and bags. She glanced down at her Kool-Aid-soiled T-shirt, baggy sweatpants, and bare feet realizing what a difference thirty days could make.

Morgan scanned the living room, where it looked as though all hell had broken loose. Toys, books, and half-eaten snacks everywhere.

"Should I come back at another time?" Morgan asked.

"No, no. I'm just trying to get things straightened up before Ross gets home."

Morgan's eyes widened. "You're going to need some help."

"I'll be fine," Amara responded. But her response sounded weak, even to her ears. The truth was, after a month of taking care of the girls and being married to Ross, nothing was fine. The girls were fickle and often argumentative, especially toward each other. Keeping up on the mountains of laundry five people could create was darn near impossible. And the dust bunnies were multiplying just like their live counterparts. And there was still vacuuming, cooking, and teaching to do.

The girls would be starting school soon. Amara wanted to make sure they were ready when they did. Not to mention Ross's demands. He issued orders like a drill sergeant and had precise ideas on how things should be. She was getting used to it, but it still drove her nuts.

If her mother could see how far away from a spotless household she had gotten, disappointment would not be a strong enough word to describe Yolanda Fairchild's feelings. Amara wrapped the long nozzle of the vacuum around one arm and carried an attachment holder in the other, praying that no one in her family would pop over for a surprise visit—least of all her parents. Her mother had certain expectations for a daughter, which had grown exponentially now that she was married. Her mother was not Felix Unger, but she'd always expected her only daughter to be.

While Nettie stared warily at Morgan, Trinity built a multicolored house out of blocks. Trina left Trinity and trotted right over to Morgan.

"I'm going to be a diva!" she said, smiling.

Morgan placed her packages on the floor, then bent down. "How are you, Trina?" Morgan asked, smiling. "Good to see you."

Trina gave Morgan a hug and ran back to her sister—the words "good to see you, too" trailing gleefully behind her.

Amara picked up the sacks and whispered in her aunt's ear. "She's already a diva."

They laughed together.

"Then she's gonna love this stuff!"

"Come on in here," Amara said, entering the dining room. They placed the bags on the long walnut table.

"Girls!" Amara said. "Say hi to my aunt Morgan."

"Hi, Aunt Morgan," Trinity said.

"I already spokeded to her," Trina spewed.

Morgan's gaze caught and held on to the little girl drawing by herself. "Is that Nettie?"

Amara nodded. "I'm really worried about her. Ross says she's just grieving harder than her sisters. He wants to let her work through it on her own—with our support, of course. I just don't know . . ."

"Maybe he's right."

"And maybe she needs a therapist."

Her own words startled her. She needed to change the subject fast. "Girls! Your aunt Morgan has something special for you."

"What is it?" Trina shouted while she and her sisters ran over to the dining room table.

Amara and Morgan placed the three bags where each girl could get to one and stepped back.

As if they'd been told, each triplet climbed up in a chair and peered inside one of the sacks. The ensuing whoops and outcries of glee made Amara feel toasty through and through.

They dug in, grabbing handful after handful of bangles, earrings, necklaces, scarves, and charms. It sounded as if someone had taken a giant box of pennies and emptied it out onto the wooden table.

Amara smiled at their happiness. "What do you say, girls?"

"Thank you!" Trinity and Trina shouted. Although Nettie was silent, the expression of awe on her face told Amara that she liked the present, too.

"Come on," Amara said to her aunt. "I'll make you some coffee."

While the girls oohed, ahed, and played dress-up in the living room, the two women talked over steaming hot java. Now and then one of the girls would come into the kitchen to pose and show off her new look. For the most part, Amara kept watch on them from her seat at the kitchen table.

"Thanks, Auntie M."

"You're welcome, sweetheart. I'm glad I was able to give those things to someone I know."

"There are some nice pieces in there. Are you sure you want to give them all to the girls?"

"Unless there's something in there that *you* want. Otherwise, they can have at it!"

Amara was grateful for her aunt's generosity, but she couldn't help noticing the hint of sadness in her eyes. She knew her aunt had tried for years to make it as a model and had been unsuccessful. Amara wondered if this was her aunt Morgan's way of slowly letting go of that dream. "You didn't give them all of your jewelry, did you?"

"Honey, no! Just the pieces I haven't worn in years."

Amara felt somewhat better and decided to stop dwelling on what *might* be going on with her aunt.

"So what have you made lately?"

Morgan Allgood smiled and picked up her cup. "Your aunt Ashley keeps me busy! Even though her new singing job has her busy, she still keeps up with her belly dancing. I'm in the process of making costumes for her and most of the other women she teaches. Once they found out her outfits were custom-made, the orders came flooding in."

Amara would love to take lessons from her aunt Ashley, or learn to sew for that matter. But now with the girls, there was no time.

"Look-ed!" Trina said, sauntering into the kitchen. She was accessorized from head to toe. And it didn't surprise Amara that everything matched.

"Don't I look good?" she asked in her little girl's voice.

"You look marvelous, daa-ling!" Morgan said in her Hollywood accent.

Amara got up and grabbed the camera from the top of the refrigerator. "Smile," she said, squaring Trina up in the viewfinder.

Just as she'd imagined, the flash brought two other little girls into the kitchen—one decked out from head to toe, wanting her picture taken too, and the other silent, hanging back, seemingly content to watch.

More flashes. "All right, all right! That's enough pictures for now," Amara said, shooing them out of the kitchen.

Trina hung back for a moment. "Miss Morgan, I wanna be a model jus like you!"

As the little girl ran off, both Morgan and Amara smiled broadly.

"You know, this is right up her alley. Ever since the first time she saw you, she's had this idea in her head that she was going to be a model. The other morning, I laid her clothes out for her and she just looked at them. When I asked her what was the matter, she said, "Those aren't cute!""

The two women shared a hearty laugh.

"Now she's into makeup, nail polish, perfume. And I can't keep her out of my pumps. Every time I turn around, she's trying to walk in them." Which was just as well, Amara thought. The only time she went out was to get groceries, to take the girls shopping or to the park.

The women talked about their family for a few moments. Amara was glad to hear that everyone was doing okay and looking forward to the Fourth of July holiday.

Just then Trina, or as Amara called her, the quick-change artist, ran back into the kitchen with a new look.

"This girl changes clothes several times a day," Amara said, shaking her head.

Trina walked in front of the large kitchen counter as if she were a runway model. Amara and Morgan clapped their approval.

"All I need now is cute hair. Who did your hair, Miss Morgan?"

"I did, sweetie!"

"Ooh! Can you do mine?"

Amara touched her aunt's arm in caution. "Be careful how you answer that. If you do one, you'll have to do them all."

Morgan smiled. "Sure! I would love to do your hair."

Shasta Martinez had become as regular in her life as Trinity's wisdom, Trina's posing, Nettie's solace, and the morning sun. Amara had come to look upon their daily coffee time as the only thing she could count on. The girls were nearly unpredictable and Ross was almost invisible.

But Shasta . . . Shasta managed to make her laugh every day. If it wasn't her latest contest-winning story it was just the woman herself, being unique, unusual, and free.

"So when this truckload of venison arrived at my door, I looked at the driver and said, 'Oh, dear!' Get it? Oh deer?"

Amara cracked a smile.

"You haven't heard a word I've said."

"Sorry, Shasta. I was just thinking how lucky I am to have a neighbor like you—a friend like you."

Shasta waved her hand. "Honey, please. I'm just so grateful to have someone to talk to, I don't know what to do. You're good people. Those girls of yours are the cutest little triplets I've ever seen. Now your husband, he's like a lot of the other people in this neighborhood. Reserved. Conservative. Keeps to himself. I'm surprised you agreed to marry him. You two aren't anything alike."

"It was the girls. It would have broken my heart to know they were growing up without a mother and I could have done something about it."

Shasta nodded. "You love them so much."

Amara glanced in the living room where the three girls, her daughters, played with Barbie dolls among a jumble of books, puzzle pieces, and stuffed animals.

"It's funny though," Amara continued. "They smile at me. We laugh and hug together. But there's still something missing. When we sit down to dinner, they fight to sit next to Ross. When Ross comes home from work, they rush to the door so full of love and energy, even though they may have just been arguing with each other or disobeying me. I read them bedtime stories, but they always want their dad to do it. It's like I'm here, but I'm not inside."

"Give them time, Amara. You can't just expect them to love you unconditionally right away, can you?"

Amara rubbed the underside of the coffee cup where the heat wasn't so intense. "Not if I'm being realistic."

"Besides, if you force it, they'll just resent you for it and then you'll have a battle on your hands."

That thought dropped like a dry stone in Amara's stomach. If that happened, she'd have so many things going against her, keeping her promise would be nearly impossible. Right now the only thing keeping her encouraged was the relationship she had with the girls. It had grown a little cold since their mother's death, but if she took Shasta's advice and bided her time, they might eventually come around.

"What do they say?"

"What?" Amara said, blinking out of her musings.

"You were staring into your cup as if it had tea leaves in it. I was wondering what they said."

Amara smiled. "Don't make jokes. My aunt Ashley reads tea leaves, and she's very serious about it."

Shasta laughed heartily. "I like her already!"

Glancing at the short woman at her kitchen table with shiny curls and a Velveeta cheese T-shirt, Amara thought the two unique women would become friends at first sight.

"Hayward!"

Ross's head snapped up. Lawrence Chappell stuck his head into Ross's office and he knew there was trouble brewing. Larry had a way of wearing trouble on his face like some women wear makeup.

"What's up?" Ross asked, wondering what his direct report had cost the company now.

"I thought that you should know," Larry said, entering the office one timid step after another.

Here it comes, Ross thought, and laid his pen down.

"Some of the guys are . . ."

"Spill it, Chappell."

"Going over to La Strata to celebrate!" he said, allowing an uncharacteristic smile to take up residence on his swarthy face. "We ran the test again, and this time, no problems. None whatsoever."

"What?" Ross asked, confused.

"Yeah, we hated the fact that we screwed up so bad

this week. I mean after all that planning, especially the reports that you generated, and for us to be rendered helpless by a simple F-Two tornado. Well, it just wasn't right. So we decided to try it again, this morning, and everything went like clockwork." The smile on Larry's face brightened. "I wish you could have been there."

Ross had run a practice drill to see how the company would hold up in the wake of a tornado disaster. But the disaster had come with the exercise. Obviously Ross had been gone too long. All the contingency planning he'd done for the company before he took family medical leave had been all for naught. At least that's what he thought. For a while, he'd thought they would have to start from square one. As a matter of fact, when Larry had interrupted him, he was hard at work on a proposal for additional training and simulations, to get the contingency planning group back up to speed. He couldn't believe they had taken the initiative to do it again on their own.

"You did it without me?" he asked, still trying to convince himself of what he'd heard.

"Sure did! Braxton is writing the report as we speak and because we did so well, we're going out to celebrate. You have to come with us."

Ross was pleased. He was sure his pleasure showed on his face. "I'll look for Braxton's report tomorrow, but I'll have to take a rain check on the celebration."

Ross knew what kind of celebrating the guys that worked under him did. Cavorting in bars until the darkest dark. Trolling for hotties. He'd lived that life a long time ago, but he wasn't that man anymore. Something told him that one beer would probably be enough to put him under the table with the dust bunnies.

"Sorry, Hayward. We aren't taking no for an answer. This is your victory too."

"My victory? How so?"

"If you hadn't done all of that coaching and delegation, we never would have been able to pull it off. Man, you gotta come."

Ross considered the fact that, unless he had an errand to run, he usually went straight home after work. Maybe he deserved a night out. An evening away from his kids and Amara might be the break he needed to keep his charade of a marriage fresh.

"Ahh!" Larry said, grinning. "Is that a yes?"

Ross felt a smirk coming on and didn't fight it. "Yeah," he said.

Five hours and five beers later, Ross lumbered toward his front door. He'd had a good time with the fellas. He felt refreshed, invigorated, and grateful for the team of guys that he worked with. They were all top notch.

He managed to get the key in the lock without incident and entered the house. The dark and stark silence greeted him. A fitting end to a night filled with questions about his new marriage.

"Congrats on your wedding, man."

"Yeah, man."

"She's good for you, big guy."

At that comment, he'd realized something. She was changing him, in small ways. He was quieter, calmer. More settled. Even though he didn't act like it sometimes. When he came home in the evenings, the pressures of the day stayed behind on the doorstep with his knowing that Amara had taken care of the girls. Knowing that his home would be clean, welcoming. Knowing that she was preparing their meal with her hands and her care made him feel like a king. Like all of the stress he experienced on the job was worth it.

He hadn't felt that way for years.

"I heard the new misses is a pretty young thing. That so?"

"Yeah, I've seen her. She's a looker!"

A looker, Ross thought, feeling his way in the dark. He couldn't believe that Amara hadn't left a light on for him. *Hmmph.* In the past, he'd never thought of her as a looker. Only Amara. But since the other evening when he'd seen her sweet brown flesh, he wondered if there was something about their relationship he was missing.

He doubted it and climbed the stairs, ears still ringing from the music of the live band playing at the club. He could barely hear himself think.

Ross felt trapped between two extremes of opinion. On one side, several of his male friends envied and gibed him for marrying a woman almost half his age. On the other side, neighbors and even some family members looked down on him for marrying so soon after Brenda's death. But Ross knew the reality. He didn't feel lucky to have a "pretty young thing" on his arm, and even though he had loved Brenda until the day she died, it had been over a year since he was actually in love with her.

Her cursed himself for it, but it was the truth. Maybe he'd fallen out of love because her illness had taken a toll on him. Or maybe he'd simply been preparing himself for her death. For the time when he would have to go on without her.

He closed his eyes, knowing something in his life had to change for the better or he would be in a bitter state for a very long time. Or maybe it would just be a drunken state. Kinda like what he was feeling now.

He grunted, wondering when the stairs to his bedroom had gotten so steep.

He thought he'd waited a good while for the effects of the beer to wear off before heading home. At the sudden acute urge to urinate, he knew he was wrong.

"Damn," he whispered under his breath as he rounded the corner to where the door to the bathroom should be wide open, but wasn't. It was closed and the orange-yellow light of the halogens glowed in one golden line under the flash of the door.

"Who's in there?" he asked, sounding a little more desperate than he thought he felt.

"Me," a tiny, sleepy voice said.

He closed his eyes.

Ross shifted his weight from side to side. Unlike the other night, normally he didn't drink. Occasionally, he'd have a beer or two with his buddies. Tonight he'd had five and they'd gone straight through him. He pounded on the door, a little harder this time.

"Trin?" he said. "How much longer?"

"I'm not done," she said. That's what she always said whenever one of her sisters needed to use the bathroom and she was in there. Ross always thought she did that to be mean and make them wait. But maybe Trinity was just that darn slow.

"Aggh!" he said and trotted off to the other bathroom.

Thank goodness they had two. He just hoped, no, prayed, that Amara wasn't in hers.

He trudged down the stairs and stumbled down the hall until he reached Amara's room. He knocked on the door but couldn't wait for her to answer. Instead he twisted the knob and entered.

"Ross, what's—" she asked. He thought she was reading a book, but he couldn't tell. He was moving too fast.

He rushed into the bathroom, not bothering to close the door.

"Ahhh," was all he could say. After waiting so long to relieve himself, the feeling was almost as good as sex. He didn't know how long he stood there, but he figured it was quite a while. He also didn't know how long he'd been moaning from the release, but he figured that to be a good while also. *Oh, well,* he thought. *We live together. There's bound to be some intimate moments.*

Just as those thoughts scurried across his mind, he realized that he was surrounded by bras. Well, maybe not surrounded by, but there were five hanging across the shower bar.

He groaned. "Woman stuff," he said silently.

The thing was, as a man, he couldn't take his eyes off that woman stuff. The bras he saw hanging were delicate. The kind made especially for young, supple, ripe . . .

"Ross?"

How long had he been standing there staring? He didn't know. *It must be the booze,* he thought, and flushed the toilet.

Not wanting to appear inebriated, he collected himself and exited the bathroom.

"Sorry," he said, sweeping a glance over the woman lying on the twin bed. She was wearing a soft yellow pajama set, her nutmeg skin glowing from the contrast. Just then, his imagination played a terrible trick on him. It placed one of those amazing bras from the bathroom on Amara and suddenly, she was wearing nothing else, except a pair of matching panties and six-inch pumps.

He blinked. Hard.

"Ross?" Amara said, rising from the bed.

"No," he said, ambling toward the door. "Don't get up."

"But you need help," she responded.

Yes. How right she was. And if he didn't get to his

room in about twenty seconds, he was going to need help keeping his manhood in his pants.

"I'm all right," he said, deciding to take one more look at her.

Damn. His eyes were still playing tricks on him. She was back into her pajamas, but it didn't matter. She was one of the most desirable women he'd ever seen. He had to stop thinking of her in that way.

"No more beer," he said, and headed as quickly as his intoxicated legs would carry him to his bed.

Ross strummed his fingers against the top of his desk and stared at his phone. Every day, he called his daughters while he was at work. The only time he'd ever broken that rule was when he was away speaking at a conference in Minneapolis. Otherwise, he made it a point to be a part of his daughters' regular routine. He loved hearing their voices.

But today, there was another voice he wanted to hear.

At first, it surprised him. The thought of calling to talk to Amara. To hear her butter-rich voice come through the speaker as it always did. Caressing him without his permission. This time, he would welcome it.

This feeling had been coming on for some time now. He'd noticed it when he'd get up in the morning. Sometimes Amara and the girls slept late, and he would miss their morning prattle and wake-up ritual. He noticed it when he came home and among the three faces he looked for upon opening the door, Amara's mattered more and more.

He could see her now . . . playing with the girls, teaching them, engaging them.

Laughing with them.

She must have two hundred ways to smile, he thought, smoothing his moustache.

Since he couldn't see her smiling right now, he wanted, no, needed to *hear* her smile. He dialed his home number quickly, anticipation flooding his veins.

"Hello?"

"Hello!" Ross said, a little too eagerly.

"Ross?"

"Yes."

"Hold on. I'll call the girls."

"No, wait!"

A heavy silence weighed between them. He wasn't quite sure what to say, but he knew he wanted to speak with her awhile before she turned the phone over to the triplets.

"How are you?"

An even longer pause. And then, "I'm fine, Ross. You?"

"Fine. Well, I'm tired actually. We've had some planning issues here that are taking longer to work through than I anticipated."

"So you'll be working late tonight?"

"No. I . . . just . . ."

"Wanted to talk to me?"

"Yeah," he admitted, glad that it was out in the open. "I guess so."

"Well, it's nice talking to you, Ross. Let me call the girls for you."

"Amara! Wait! I want to ask you something."

"Yes?" she asked. He could already hear the voices of his young children in the background asking if it was Daddy on the phone.

"You finish my sentences sometimes like you live in my head. How do you do that?"

Another long pause followed by, "I know you, Ross. Whether you want to acknowledge it or not, we have a connection. I'm just not afraid to let it show."

And he heard it. The smile he was looking for. It was barely there and a little self-righteous. But it was there.

Ross smiled, too. "All right, kiddo. Put my daughters on, please."

Ross spoke animatedly with his three girls. They had his attention, but something else did as well. A feeling, growing stronger with each day that passed. Ross listened intently and wondered what the hell he was going to do about it.

He didn't go into her room often. Usually, like today, he went to deliver mail, or a message from one of her numerous relatives. But once, he'd gone in simply because the reality of her living with him had a hard time going down.

The moment he'd entered the room, he noticed how she'd changed it. In small ways. Lace curtains on the windows. Flowers in a vase. And everything else in its place. But what he noticed most of all was the clean scent of Amara, or rather her perfume, that clung to the air like a soft whisper. A special secret that he would have to strain to hear.

Grunting, he remembered the task at hand and placed Amara's mail on the dresser. Clustered in the center of the dresser was a bottle of lotion, a case of powder, and a bottle of perfume. Unable to stop himself, Ross lifted the bottle and brought it to his nose. He inhaled deeply. All his life, he would remember this fragrance. The scent of peace coming to his house, of contentment. He allowed the scent to wash into him, and images flooded his brain. Scenes of him nuzzling against the crook of Amara's neck, the bend of her arm. Discovering all the places where she sprayed the haunting fragrance.

He was so lost in his fantasy that the front door closing startled him. He fumbled the bottle in his hands and almost recovered. But instead, it dropped into a small side drawer that Amara had left half open.

Ross groaned with guilt. He shouldn't have been snooping in her things. Quickly, he pulled the drawer open and riffled through its contents. The bottle had rolled between two neatly folded piles of panties.

Does the woman have enough underwear? Ross wondered as he sifted through all the lace, silk, and pastel colors. Just the brush of his fingers against her lingerie made the temperature in Ross's body escalate by several degrees.

I wonder if she ever sprays her panties with this cologne, he said, hooking his hand around the bottle.

"What the hell are you doing?"

Amara's question cut across the room to where he was standing red-handed in her underwear drawer. How was he going to explain this one?

"I was curious," he said, hoping the light perspiration forming on his brow wasn't apparent and grateful that his name was not Pinnochio. He pulled the bottle from the drawer. "I wanted to know what kind of perfume you wore."

Amara leaned against the door opening. "And you couldn't ask me?"

"Actually, I uh . . ." He put the bottle back in its place and scrambled for some good explanation.

"So, what are you doing in my underwear drawer?"

Her arms were folded now. She knew something was up.

"See, what happened was . . ."

He looked up, busted. No sense in trying to make up a lie.

"Okay. You caught me. I wanted to smell your perfume. I like it. It . . . chills me out." He faced her squarely then, but couldn't read her reaction. "When I heard you come in, it slipped from my hands. I was rummaging for it when you came in."

Amara's face remained static but her eyes smiled a little. A victory, he imagined, was what she was thinking. She moved toward him, picked up the bottle, turned it so he could read it.

"White Linen," she said. "I've worn it for years." Then she put the bottle back and pumped some of the lotion out of the bottle and into the palm of her hand. For some strange reason, all Ross could do at that moment was watch as she rubbed her palms together and spread the lotion all over her hands.

"I got it as a free gift. The first time I ever bought a tube of lipstick. I was sixteen then and in love with a boy named Dwayne. I liked the lipstick, but I loved the lotion. I thought it smelled the way a good woman should smell."

Ross agreed. It *did* smell like a good woman. "What did Dwayne think?" he asked.

She smiled then. And her eyes did that thing they did when she was being whimsical or remembering something funny. "Larry thought it smelled like an easy lay. Boy, was he wrong!"

Ross couldn't help himself. He smiled at her. "I'm sorry for invading your privacy."

Amara was silent for a moment and never broke her gaze with him. "No harm done, Mr. Hayward."

Relieved, Ross headed to the door.

"Oh, Ross," she said.

"Yes?"

"What would have happened if it had been me in *your* room?"

He paused, knowing that he would have blown up like a madman if he'd found her elbow-deep in his boxer drawer.

Before waiting for him to reply, Amara breezed past him in the doorway. The scent of a good woman trailing the air as she went.

Chapter 8

She was happier than she'd been in two months. Loaded down with decorations, invitations, and inspiration, Amara finally felt like things were looking up.

The girls were about to celebrate their fifth birthday and Amara had persuaded Ross to go all out for the celebration.

The girls were fond of the Powerpuff Girls and so that was the theme. Powerpuff cups, napkins, plates, place mats, tablecloths. Pink plastic-ware, serving dishes, and envelopes for the Powerpuff invitations.

She'd purchased a new set of Powerpuff DVDs and had ordered a Powerpuff cake with matching balloons. She was sure the girls would adore it.

Best of all, Brenda's family was coming into town to celebrate with them. Brenda's mother was a wonderful woman. Amara had met her before the girls were born and they'd gotten along famously. Tinis Ball was a jet-setting, fast-talking woman who loved life and was determined to live it to the fullest. She was always traveling somewhere, cruising somewhere, on safari somewhere. When Brenda died and Ross told Tinis of Brenda's wishes, Tinis surprised everyone by supporting her daughter's decision and offering to help any way she could. But what meant so much to Amara was the fact that when she and Ross had gotten married, Tinis had come to the wedding and had been behind the union 100 percent.

From the moment they'd met, Tinis had been the grandmother that Amara always wished she'd had. Since her mother's mother had passed away before she was born, and her father's mother lived down South in a small town her family rarely visited, Amara had never known what bonding with a much older woman could be like. That is, until Tinis.

They had taken a liking to each other instantly and were nearly as close as she and Brenda.

Amara knew that she would probably rely on Tinis to get through her new life demands more than her own mother. But she would deal with it.

She had to.

"My Brenda was a smart woman," she'd said. "If she picked you to take care of my granddaughters, then I not only respect her decision, but knowing you the way I do, I support it."

After the turmoil Amara had gone through to convince her family that she knew what she was doing, Tinis's words had been a breath of fresh air and just the bolstering she needed to feel confident in her decision.

Brenda's two sisters, Leeza and Betty June, seemed nice as well, although Amara had only been in their company on two occasions. Once during a Christmas dinner that she'd been invited to and the second at Brenda's funeral. Since they were coming to the triplets' birthday party, Amara was looking forward to getting to know them better.

In preparation, she'd cleaned the house so thoroughly that her hands were raw, red, and blistered in some places. While some people believed in using a mop,

Amara's mother had always taught her that in order to make sure the floor was really clean, you had to get down there with it. And those "wimpy-butt" cleaners, as her mother was fond of calling them, didn't do squat about getting a floor clean. So just as she'd been brought up, she mixed her own batch of cleaner from lye and ammonia. Ross grumbled about not wanting to eat in the kitchen because of the fumes, but she could tell by the expression on his face that he approved of how clean everything was.

She pulled the van into the driveway, grateful for the fact that Ross had agreed to watch the girls while she went shopping. As per their agreement, he would take the girls to the nearby park so that she could bring the presents and decorations in without the hindrance of three excited little girls who would have to touch, handle, and play with everything before it was put away.

Loading herself down with as many sacks, boxes, and packages as she could handle, Amara approached the house. Before she stuck her key into the lock, the front door swooshed open and an angry Betty June stood at the threshold, her round eyes steaming with frustration.

"It's about time you came home!"

Struggling with her packages, Amara stumbled into the house. Betty June stepped aside and let her through with no offer to help.

"Hi!" Amara said, hoping that the woman's outburst simply meant that she was happy to see her. "I didn't know you were coming today."

Amara set the packages down in the entryway and waited for Betty June's expression to change.

It didn't.

"Didn't Ross tell you?"

"Of course he told her," Leeza added, sauntering in from the kitchen.

"Girls! You simply must see what Amara's done with the bathroom! It's absolutely splendid!" Tinis said, emerging from the guest bathroom. "Amara, my dear!" she said, and in a move much too quick for a woman her age, traversed the space between them and enveloped Amara into a remarkable bear hug.

"Hello, Ms. Ball," Amara choked out.

"Hello, honey. It's good to see you," Tinis said, pulling back but still holding on. "How have you been faring?"

Leeza and Betty June looked on from the sidelines and for the first time, Amara realized how much like weasels they looked. Brenda definitely got the looks in the family, she decided.

"I'm doing fine," she lied. As a matter of fact she wasn't doing so well at all. Too many times she wondered why she'd gotten herself into this situation and how difficult it would be to get herself out of it.

Tinis Ball smiled one of those motherly *I can see right through your lie* smiles and patted her on the back.

"We'll talk later," she whispered.

"I just have a few more things to get in the van and then we can catch up," Amara said, trying to squeeze all the unease out of her voice.

"Let me help you, dear," Tinis said.

"Mother, don't you have a phone call to make?" Betty June asked.

"Oh, yes," the elder Ball responded, her blue-green eyes softening in remembrance. "I promised my sister Tula that I'd call when we got here. I just had a few things to take care of first," she said, motioning toward the bathroom. "You know, a woman like me can't stray too far from the commode. But I've made my peace with that," she finished, then took the cell phone dangling from Betty June's hand.

Amara went back to the van to collect the rest of the packages for the party, feeling a bit off center.

Obviously Ross had let them in. They must have arrived just as he was leaving with the girls. Maybe they were too tired from driving to go with them. But exactly how long had they been in her house and why were Leeza and Betty June acting so raunchy?

Yanking the last sack from the floor, Amara imagined that she would find out soon enough. But for some reason, the idea of finding out fell like a boulder of dread onto her shoulders.

Just as she'd imagined, Ross was going out as they were pulling up. Tinis explained that after a round of hugs from the girls, all they had strength enough to do was shower and relax. "We probably would have been asleep if Betty June hadn't heard you pull up in the driveway."

Apparently the drive from Detroit was long and exhausting. Sixteen hours and they had driven straight through. As least Leeza and Betty June had. Driving was something Tinis had never learned how to do.

"When Ross said you would be right back, we thought you would be right back. How long does it take to shop for a handful of party stuff?"

"Leeza! What's gotten into you?" Tinis asked before Amara could respond.

"No, that's all right, Ms. Ball. I can answer the question."

Amara felt something was amiss and she felt a strong

need to fix whatever it was before it ruined the girls' birthday, which was two days away.

"Since Ross is generous enough to foot the bill for the party, the least I can do is be thrifty with his money. I could have gotten everything at the same place or gone to one of those high-priced paper stores. But I didn't. I took sales papers and coupons and gift certificates with me"—à la Shasta, she thought—"and saved about fifty dollars."

Tinis smiled as if she were watching her child just spell a fourteen-letter word correctly during a national spelling bee. Her daughters, on the other hand, looked as though a fourteen-letter word were lodged in their throats and they could neither swallow it nor spit it out. Amara could hear her mother in the background— "y'all ain't go botha me!"—and smiled inwardly.

Food, she decided, would be their conversation piece, and with that, she entered the kitchen and prepared dinner. Tinis offered to help, but Amara refused, knowing what her mother had taught her about respecting her elders. Betty June and Leeza could have pitched in at any time, but they chose to remain at their mother's side and acted as though they wouldn't have the slightest idea how to behave in a kitchen, let alone cook in one. And for the first time in a long while, Amara Fairchild was grateful for the way she was raised.

Over fresh-cut pork chops, butter-tossed vegetables, baked rolls, and mixed salad greens, Tinis and Amara caught up on each other's lives while the other two women in the room rolled their eyes and sulked like three-year-olds. Even the triplets showed more maturity than these two.

Something had happened. They had never seemed this agitated before. But then again, their sister had never been dead before. Amara didn't need to be a rocket scientist or a rocket launcher to see that they resented her place as Ross's wife and the girls' mother. She didn't know which idea they despised more. She didn't care which they despised more. She only knew that before they left, everything would be patched up between them. She would see to it.

By the time Ross and the girls arrived home, things weren't patched up. His presence, however, functioned like a blanket of truce falling over the warring factions. And for the moment, Amara was grateful.

They seemed to grow every moment Ross spent away from them. Even between blinks, he would swear they'd gotten taller, smarter. He loved them so much his heart hurt. Loved them so much, he'd done the unthinkable. And now another woman was in his home masquerading as his wife. Ross frowned.

"What's wrong, Daddy?" Trinity called from the merry-go-round.

"Nothing," he responded and adjusted himself on the thin wooden bench. Just a little more angle and the girls couldn't see his face as clearly in the descending sun, yet he could still keep an eye on them.

The sight of his in-laws had surprised him. He knew they were coming in some time that week, but he'd assumed they would call to confirm the approximate date and time. When he hadn't heard from them, he assumed that they weren't coming.

He assumed wrong.

He tipped his baseball cap a bit. The setting sun was

hotter than normal for this time of year. It had coaxed an inordinate number of residents out of their homes and into the park. Ross recognized many of the families. Most of them had tipped their heads in recognition or smiled uneasily. He knew why. What do you say to a man who buries one wife and marries another within a thirty-day time span? Shasta was kind enough to tell him that word had gotten around of the development of his matrimonial musical chairs and since then it seemed as though people kept their distance more. Gazed at him through disapproving eyes, and urged their children to stay away from his because, well, those girls were going through some changes right now.

The only neighbors who hadn't kept their distance were the new ones—Shasta from next door and Ramona from across the street. Ramona had come over two weeks after Brenda's death. She'd brought a pie that she claimed to have baked, but the perfect crust and pie pan that said Village Inn told him otherwise. He'd thought she might have come out of the goodness of her heart. After a few moments in her company, it was obvious that she'd come for other reasons.

"I'm real good with children," she'd claimed. "*Real* good," as if she were auditioning for a part in the movie *Daddy Day Care*.

Sadly, she hadn't been the only woman to call, stop by, or e-mail with thick words of condolence and slick ulterior motives.

Ross was disgusted by it all.

Amara wasn't one of those women, however. He'd give her that. The way she approached him and the girls was as if they were Humpty-Dumpty and they'd all just suffered a great fall. Daily, she did her best to outdo all the king's horses and all the king's men.

Russ grunted. His backside ached against the hardness of the wood, and he knew Amara would never be able to put the girls, and least of all him, back together again.

"Daddy!" Trina howled. Her little legs pumped like small shovels beneath her as she sprinted in his direction.

"What's the matter, baby girl?" He knew it was nothing serious since there was no fall, crash, or breaking sound of any kind. Knowing his daughter, she probably ripped her cute shirt or popped a button.

"I got bites!" she said, turning around.

Sure enough, three mosquito bites welted up on the back of her neck. They all flashed an angry red in the dimming sun.

He'd forgotten his own admonishment. He always told the girls that the bugs were at their worst an hour before sunset and an hour after. He had tunneled so far into his own selfish thoughts, he'd forgotten about that.

"I'm sorry, Princess. It's time for us to head on home before the mosquitoes make a meal out of you."

He stood and rubbed the area around the angry red blotches. "Come on, girls! Let's go home!"

"Aw!" he heard, and knew it was Trinity. Nettie, on the other hand, walked obediently toward him without so much as a whimper. Every day he grew more concerned about her and hoped that whatever it was that was eating his youngest daughter would work its way out of her system. Otherwise, he'd be forced to do something that could cause more harm than good and that was to take his daughter to a psychologist.

By the time they arrived home, they all had their share of mosquito bites, chigger scratches, and gnat attacks. Ross was more than ready for a hot bath. When he saw the van, caked with road dirt, sitting in front of his house, he grunted and tried to remember how long they said they wanted to stay.

After an hour of Leeza's and Betty June's incessant talking, he was ready for them to leave right now. He didn't remember them ever being so gabby. He and Tinis couldn't get a word in edgewise. And poor Amara. They had practically squeezed her out of the conversation entirely. So much so, he was beginning to think they were doing it deliberately.

"So, Amara . . . now that you're a married woman, how often do you see your family?"

"Well—"

"Oh, I'm sure she doesn't see them as often as Ross would like. There's nothing like spending quality time with your children, especially at a time like this," Betty June answered without blinking and obviously without thinking.

Ross groaned. The last thing he needed was a verbal battle between Betty June and Amara. Although Betty June could talk fast and seemed to have a knack for interrupting people, Ross had no doubt that Amara would win any verbal battle she entered. Not because she was ruthless or fighting back, or aggressive, but because of her ability to cut to the quick of any matter. When he'd first met her, that was the one thing about her that had impressed him. And if anyone asked, it still did.

"Ross, what's wrong?" Leeza asked.

"Wrong?" Tinis said, sliding in a comment. "That looked like a pleasant thought playing in your mind."

Ross shook himself. "It wasn't anything, really. Just . . . thoughts."

Betty June snaked closer to him. The closer she got

the more uncomfortable he became and the tighter the muscles in Amara's face drew. "Well, don't keep us in suspense," Betty June hissed. "Tell us what you think."

He laughed. He couldn't help it. He hadn't heard a word of what she'd been saying for the last fifteen minutes. She no doubt thought he was agreeing to something she'd said. Only he didn't have a clue. It was too funny. His in-laws had always been fun. They'd laughed for hours sometimes on holidays and family gatherings.

Then it occurred to him that he'd never have that kind of happiness again. The thought tore a fresh hole in his soul and his laughter stopped as immediately as it had started. "I think I'll keep it to myself, thanks," he said.

He was glad that dinner was ready when he and the girls had returned home. Although they ate mostly vegetables and then went off to their room, he'd eaten healthy portions of everything and was now feeling the aftereffects. His energy had crashed and he was ready to. Could he leave Amara alone with Leeza and Betty June?

Of course he could. Once a protector, always a protector, he thought of himself. The compulsion to protect Amara felt funny, unexpected. It surprised him. Maybe he was getting just a little bit too used to this arrangement.

Ross excused himself and said his good nights.

Sometimes work would worry his mind before he went to bed. Tonight he knew it would be something else.

They sat in the living room, chatting mostly. About nothing mostly. How did women do that? he wondered. Just drone on and on about . . . everything.

Betty June talked the most—her canary-yellow pantsuit making her look more like a banana than a woman. She was a thick one with an eighties' sense of fashion, a twenties' eye for makeup, and a futuristic bent for hairstyles. The man that snagged her would do well to sit down, shut up, and forget about making any decisions.

Her sister, on the other hand, was obviously trying to be just like her. The trouble was, she was unsuccessful. Leeza always looked as though she were trying out for the Dr. Seuss school of fashion. Or maybe she just looked like she could be a member of the *Simpsons* cast. It would have been funny if it weren't so pathetic.

Tinis, on the other hand, was the epitome of respectability from what she wore, to what she said, and what she did. The eldest Ball had more youth, vitality, common sense, and intelligence than Betty June and Leeza combined. She often gave the triplets a run for their money playing games and just hanging out. It was going to be difficult having her here for the three days they said they intended to stay. Tinis's presence would remind him of the past.

And for the first time since his remarriage, Ross realized what he needed most now was to focus on the future.

Chapter 9

By the time the girls' birthday came around, Amara felt like a pincushion. The evil aunts, as she now thought of them, had verbally jabbed, poked, and needled her for two days. With Ross working during the day, he left her to deal with them on her own. And it wasn't as though she couldn't handle them, it was just that she was tired of defending herself or deflecting yet another round of their inflammatory comments. But she endured it, because she believed that they were reacting to the death of their sister and not to her personally. At least, she hoped that was the case.

Truth was, they went back and forth with her as if they were in a sparring match.

"You're not going to let them wear that, are you?"

"I'm going to let them wear anything that's safe, comfortable, and makes them feel beautiful."

"You really should do something with yourself."

"Can you think of a more important job than seeing to the health and happiness of your three nieces?"

"Ross is used to a certain kind of lifestyle."

"And I'm used to Ross telling me exactly what he needs and then giving it to him."

When she'd made that comment, the evil aunts had looked at her as if she'd suddenly grown two heads.

Then she realized what her words implied. But instead of clarifying her meaning, she decided to let them wonder.

"When Brenda was alive—"

"Well, you know what? Brenda's not alive anymore. She's dead. The sooner you deal with that the better for all of us. Because I tell you what . . . nothing you do or say is going to resurrect her."

But one thing was for sure. If it was a match they were playing, then Amara was going to win every round with superior attitude and power tempered with the personal grace her mother had taught her.

"I still don't understand why you got all this Powerpuff crap!" Betty June said.

"I believe the girls deserve the best. And they also deserve to have their dreams come true and they've been dreaming about a Powerpuff birthday party for months now." In fact, it had only been in the last few weeks that they'd talked about Powerpuff girls. But knowing how much they loved them, Amara decided to indulge them.

The evil aunts' responses had come in huffs, snorts, and industrial strength eye-rolling. But they never seemed to shut up, which was what Amara was hoping.

"Care to give me a hand with this?" Amara asked, wondering if they were ever going to lift a finger while they were there. Ross and Tinis had taken the girls for a walk, which left Amara to contend with Leeza and Betty June. They seemed perfectly content to watch as Amara did all the prep work of cleaning and decorating the living room. As she fussed over chicken nuggets, French fries, and punch, the sisters looked on without so much as a blink in her direction.

Not only were they rude, they were lazy on top of it.

Thank God her mother didn't know they were that way, or she would have come over and given them five or six pieces of her mind.

"Girl, I don't cook," came Betty June's dry reply.

"Well I have been known to cook a little somethin' somethin'," Leeza said, eyes salivating over the hot finger food coming from the oven. But she soon changed her tune after a stern look from Betty June.

Betty June looked mad enough to fry an egg with her eyes.

"Actually . . . I don't . . . don't do much cooking either," Leeza corrected.

"Really? With as much as you two seem to like to eat, I would have thought you'd have learned how to cook."

She said it before her good judgment could call it back. Betty June stiffened and snarled, "I know you are not getting smart with me in my sister's house!"

"No," Amara said. "I'm getting smart with you in mine."

Betty June leapt from the bar stool where she'd been perched like a vulture all afternoon. "Why, you little—"

"Little!" Amara interrupted, knowing very well that at five feet ten, she towered over them both by at least four inches.

Suddenly, she had the strangest sensation—as if someone had put the brakes on time. She placed the chicken and fries on top of the stove and pulled the oven mits from her hands. Then she turned to face Betty June squarely. Leeza's eyes widened to dangerous proportions and Amara readied herself for whatever came next.

But what came next surprised her.

It was Trina bounding in from outside with a crown of dandelions around her head.

"I'm a princess! I'm a princess!" She skipped energetically around Amara's legs, creating a little-girl buffer between her and Betty June. "It's my birthday and I'm a princess!"

"It's my birthday, too!" Trinity insisted.

"Too," Nettie said, too low for most folks to hear, but Amara heard it.

Ross and Tinis entered the kitchen in full conversation, oblivious of the hard tension in the room. But Nettie noticed. Her eyes moved from Amara to Betty June quickly. Amara saw the fear rising in the little girl's eyes and knew she had to do something before her fear got out of hand. Before she could act, a thin squeal of delight jarred everyone in the kitchen.

Trina had discovered the decorations in the living room.

Her two sisters joined her and soon Trinity's squeals joined her sisters'. Although she was silent, Nettie no longer looked scared and a faint smile surfaced reluctantly and shone for a moment on her face.

Ross had invited a few of the neighborhood kids as well as some of the children the girls knew from ballet. They were due to show up any minute.

I guess my showdown with Betty June will have to wait, Amara thought, and tossed the evil aunt a look that said, *We're not finished yet.*

A living room full of screaming brats was the last thing she needed. Betty June swept a glance across all ten of the children screaming damn near to the top of their lungs, and her stomach twisted.

Her nieces were cool. She could tolerate anything they could dish out. But the annoying sounds and antics of those other kids in the room made her want to puke. Or at least spank them all and make them go to bed.

But her nieces, her beautiful, smart, lovable nieces . . . they could stay up as long as they wanted to. And the noise . . . everything they did sounded like music to her ears. She loved her nieces so much, she wished they were her own.

They might have been her own once if Ross had married her instead of her sister. But he had chosen Brenda and she had respected that. Now, however, was a different story. Now, when Ross Hayward could have chosen to marry her if he was looking for a wife so soon after Brenda's death, she would make that little tramp Amara pay. Pay for ever trying to take the place of her sister.

And although Betty June was no longer attracted to Ross and had no designs on him as a mate, she hated the thought of being rejected by him twice. She had every intention of showing Ross what a terrible mistake he had made choosing Amara over her.

"Leeza!" she shouted at her sister, who looked like she was having entirely too much fun watching the kids play musical chairs.

"Yes," Leeza said, eyes blinking slowly.

"Come on outside. I need to talk to you."

By the end of the party, the girls had unwrapped a small mountain of gifts. Powerpuff dolls, Powerpuff CDs, DVDs, and even a Powerpuff Game Girl. They had also gotten pink dresses with white ruffles, books, bead kits, gift certificates, and a total of a hundred dollars in cash.

Amara's mind traveled back to her youth, remembering just how much she would clean up as a child. Her mother didn't go overboard, but her father and aunts certainly did. She had more things than one little girl could possibly play with. And since her mother was funny about other kids coming over to play, she was usually stuck playing with her bounty by herself. Amara was so glad that the girls had each other.

It was hard getting the triplets into bed. Even Ross's typical thunderous commands didn't budge them much. In the end, Ross and Amara had compromised with the girls. They could each take one new thing to bed with them. After that, the girls were bathed, in their pajamas, and in bed in no time. Amara thought it was funny that after their huge protest, the girls were asleep within twenty minutes of going to bed.

And so were Tinis, Leeza, and Betty June. Tinis, Amara could understand. She was older, tired more easily, and needed her rest. But the evil aunts were just trifling and probably took pleasure in going to bed while the living room looked as if the Tasmanian Devil had come to visit instead of the Powerpuff Girls.

Amara's body ached to the bone. "Ah," she moaned softly as she picked up the large garbage bag full of trash.

"I've got it," Ross said, slipping up beside her, taking the plastic from her hands.

She rubbed the back of her neck where a kink was forming. "Thanks, Ross."

"No problem," he responded. He twisted the bag closed and placed it near the back door. Then he gathered up the dishes and loaded the dishwasher. Astonished, Amara watched in shocked silence. She didn't even know he knew how to load the dishwasher.

"You look as though you've just seen an elephant disappear."

"No. Just the man I married."

He grunted and continued his task.

"It's me. I'm trying to show you that I'm grateful. You made my girls happy today. Happier than they've been since . . ."

Amara waited, wanting to hear him out.

"You did a great job with the party today, Amara. Thank you."

Amara allowed herself to sink down into the couch and rest for the first time since she awoke that day.

"If you really want to thank me, hire a maid or let me put the girls in day care twice a week."

He looked up, a serious expression riding his features. "I'm not *that* grateful."

"Hmmph," she said, massaging her temples. "Well, the least you can do is get rid of the evil aunts."

Ross's laughter surprised her.

"I know they've been riding you. They don't mean anything by it, though. They just miss their sister."

"What they're missing is common decency. I'm so glad the girls' birthday is over. I'm not rushing Tinis away, but I sure can do without Ren and Stimpy!"

More laughter from Ross. "You really have got them pegged, haven't you?" he asked, softer than usual.

"Don't you?" she asked, casting her gaze at the disaster that was once a living room.

Slowly she got up, took a garbage bag from a kitchen drawer, and helped Ross with the clean-up.

They didn't speak much at all. Aside from the time they had bumped into each other in the hallway, they each wouldn't have known the other person was there. Except for a kind of presence. Amara felt it in the air, in the atmosphere around her. For just this moment of putting the house back in order, she and Ross had entered a kind of truce. They'd laid down their weapons and agreed not to disagree.

With a common purpose between them, Amara allowed herself to relax a little and to believe that maybe she and Ross could work though the strange tension of their marriage. Maybe, just maybe, they could be happy together.

And the sooner they got Leeza and Betty June out of their house the better.

"You're what!"

"We're staying," Betty June said. She couldn't have been any more smug if she'd just won ten million tax-free dollars.

"But, but, but, but," Amara said, hoping against hope that she'd heard incorrectly.

"That's right. We talked it over with Ross before he left for work today."

"Exactly," Leeza said, trying to sound important. "Mom is leaving, but we are going to stay on for a few more days. We like it here."

"Sure do!" Betty June chimed in. "Besides . . . it will give us more time with the triplets. We don't see them enough as it is." The woman blinked like a sleepy deer, and Amara knew two things for certain. One, they truly were evil aunts and two, if Ross didn't get rid of them, she would.

Ross hadn't realized he'd been laughing until the seven men in the conference room with him stared at him as if he'd lost all his marbles.

"You all right, Hayward?"

"Yeah," he said, pushing back a smile. All morning, he'd been thinking about Leeza and Betty June and wished he could have been a fly on the wall when they told Amara that they were staying a few more days. He knew that she would be far less than pleased. *Yes, yes,* he ruminated and could imagine the look of utter and bitter disgust that would form in her eyes. He could perfectly see the blood drain from her nut-brown face. He had no interest in seeing her suffer, but the way she pouted whenever she didn't get her way amused him. She was truly an only child. But he'd bet if he asked her about it, she would deny that kind of spoiled brat behavior and retaliate by illuminating one of his flaws.

Jeez. When had he started making that many mental notes to himself about Amara? Suddenly, the thought of that was amusing too.

"Hey, chuckles, you wanna join us in meeting land over here?"

Tony Baronni was an Italian guy who looked like Howdy Doody and wished he was John Gotti. He was also vice president of operations and an all-around nice guy. Ross was lucky to have him as a friend. And right now he was being silly in his good friend's meeting.

"Do we gotta call the guys in white suits or are you going to continue to laugh at jokes only you can hear?"

Ross stood. "Sorry, Tony. I'm the one that has to make a call. Please excuse me."

Ross called his daughters every day he was at work. He usually waited until the afternoon, but he wanted to speak with them now. And he realized as he approached his office that a small part of him needed to know how Amara was doing with the news of their company's extended stay.

* * *

Amara couldn't believe that Ross had gone to work and left her and the girls alone with the wicked witches of the east and west. She'd bet that he was amused about the whole thing as if he were getting small doses of pleasure from the thought of her having to put them in their place all day long.

Putting the breakfast dishes into the dishwasher, Amara racked her brain to figure out a way to avoid the two guests in her home until Ross came home and provided some deflection from their constant assault of inappropriate comments and disapproving glares.

A commotion next door jarred her from her plotting.

She rushed from the kitchen to where the girls and their aunts were already staring out the big bay window.

Betty June's face puckered as if she'd swallowed a flask of turpentine. "What on earth?" she asked, voice harsh with judgment.

The semi backing into Shasta's driveway was enormous. The deep rumble of its engine vibrated loudly through the Hayward household. Amara could even feel it in her chest.

She had never ceased to be amazed at the objects and items that arrived at Shasta's home. They came by USPS, Airborne, and UPS trucks on a regular basis encased in boxes of all sizes, shapes, and colors. A month ago, it wasn't a package, but a man that arrived from Thailand. Apparently Shasta had won a husband in an obscure international lottery. With the winnings from an Air Mandalay contest, she promptly sent the young man back to his home country.

But this was something out of the ordinary—even for

Shasta, who was standing on her porch beaming like a lamplight.

When the semi rolled back as far as it could go without knocking a hole into the corner of Shasta's house, two men jumped out of the cab like gorillas on a rampage. Each one of the men looked as though he could carry a piano on his back. When Amara saw what was in the bed of the truck, she knew it would take the both of them to get it out.

"Your neighbor is a straight-up fool!" Betty June bellowed.

The object was perfectly square and was the size of a refrigerator. Its intricate metal design looked ominous and sinister as if a demented genius had designed it.

"Where do you want this?" one of the ape-men asked.

"Right here in the front yard," Shasta directed.

The two bulky men grunted and groaned their way to the middle of Shasta's yard and placed the giant cube on the green lawn with a thud. A small cloud of brown dirt rushed up around the base.

Shasta signed for her unusual delivery while the girls stared on, eyes wide with awe.

"Dang!" Trina said.

Trinity frowned. "Daddy said dang is too close to—"

"Never mind," Amara interrupted.

"I swear, you have a lunatic next door. I'm going to call the city and report her for all that garbage she keeps in her yard."

Nettie's eyes widened even more and she stared in Amara's direction.

"Can we go see?" Trina called, already heading for the door. Her multitude of braids bounced happily on her head.

Leeza jumped as if she'd just been shot by a BB gun.

"You can't possibly allow the girls to fraternize with that koot. She's got a screw loose for sure."

That's funny, Amara thought. She'd seen how admiringly Leeza had gazed at Shasta's yard a few days ago. But now since Betty June spoke of it as if it were a junkyard, suddenly it was a place to be despised.

Amara smirked. The nature of the evil aunts' relationship was becoming all too clear.

"Shasta is as harmless as a hummingbird and as smart as a scientist. She's got an entire system that allows her to—"

"Slack off?" Betty June interrupted, a crooked sneer riding her cartoon features.

Undaunted, Amara continued. "Shasta pays her bills, saves for her retirement, invests in the stock market, takes care of all her basic necessities, donates her winnings to worthy causes on a weekly basis, *and* manages not to judge others who choose to live differently than she does. Now in what way is that slacking?"

Betty June and Leeza looked like two WB characters whose faces had been smashed by an ACME anvil.

Trina started to laugh. Amara shook her head, letting her know that that was inappropriate, and took the girls over to see Shasta Martinez's latest contest prize.

"It's a what?" Amara asked, blinking at the sheer intricacy of the object.

"It's a Borg Cube."

"I don't get it," Betty June proclaimed, standing away from the square with her sister.

Shasta gave Amara a look that said, *We need to talk later,* and then ran her fingers against the rough surface of the square.

"I was in a costume shop—don't ask why—and they were holding a drawing. The winner got to be on the set of the next *Star Trek* movie. Second prize was something called a Borg Cube, and third prize was a bar of gold-pressed latinum—whatever that is. Anyway, I won the Borg Cube."

"Cool," Trinity said, staring up at it. Trina skipped around it and giggled. Nettie held Amara's hand and gazed at her feet.

"It's a model from the movie. I'll keep it on display for a few days and then I'll probably give it to the Children's Museum."

Amara was amazed that the things in Shasta's yard didn't get stolen. She'd had Greek statues, Italian water fountains, doll houses, small clay pyramids, and even a car from a Tupac video. The neighbors were always respectful. They often came out to see the latest addition to the prize garden, but they always left the items alone. Amara admired Shasta's courage to live outside of the box. Not only live, but thrive there.

The way things were going at the Hayward household, Amara wondered if it wasn't time for her to cut her losses, say she tried, and leave her box behind.

After a few more moments of gawking and touching, the Hayward clan went back home with Amara hoping and praying that Leeza and Betty June would decide they need to go for a walk or just plain leave altogether.

Her hopes went unabated.

As soon as they were inside, Betty June turned into someone Amara didn't know or trust.

"Amara," she said, saccharine dripping from her lips, "I'm sorry I misjudged your friend. You're absolutely correct. She is as smart as a rocket and I just want you to know that I believe that."

"Scientist," Amara corrected.

"Yes, whatever," she purred, grinning even wider. "The important thing is, I want us to be friends. I mean, we are practically family."

"Girls, why don't you go into the other room and play?" Amara said. Whatever this turncoat had in mind, Amara didn't want the girls to witness it.

"Aw," they said in their little girl voices. Voices she'd become accustomed to.

"No discussion, go."

Amara didn't trust Betty June as far as she could throw her. But she also knew that she'd mentioned her concerns, not so humbly, to Ross. Maybe, her mind stretched widely around the concept, maybe Ross had said something to her. Maybe she was making an effort to change.

Amara decided to keep her guard up slightly just in case she was wrong.

When Betty June offered to help prepare lunch and actually pitched in and did it, Amara let her guard down just a tad. With the evil sister's help, they had prepared a meal in no time. All the girls' favorites. Grilled cheese and bacon sandwiches, homemade curly fries, with ice cream pie for dessert.

Betty June even got Nettie to talk, which scored big points with Amara. While Nettie explained why her dolls were no longer speaking to each other, Amara listened intently. According to the little girl with the so-sad eyes, the dolls stopped talking because talking made them sick. So in order to keep them all well, they were going to be quiet for the rest of their lives.

Amara didn't need a rocket scientist or a psychologist to tell her that Nettie was projecting her beliefs onto the dolls. Nettie believed that by her being quiet, no one else in her family would get ill. Amara spent the entire lunch wondering where on earth she would get such a notion.

In her reflection, she reconsidered her opinion of Betty June. Everyone had to deal with Brenda's passing in their own way. And if the evil sister could move through her anger and stop lashing out, then Nettie could too. Amara decided her first order of business when Ross returned from work would be to talk with him regarding her suspicions and work out a plan with him to get Nettie the help she needed to get better.

When the two neighbor girls Regina and Bridgette came to see if the girls could come outside to play, Amara was relieved. It would give her some time alone with Betty June to feel her out and talk about what was happening with Nettie.

Before she could bring up the subject, Betty June did as if she were reading Amara's mind. "Trinette isn't doing so well, is she?"

"No, she's not."

Amara had fixed them some tea and they were sitting on the deck watching the girls play hand games. All except for Nettie, who was coloring at a small table especially for the girls.

"At first," Amara continued, "she was just sad. Then she stopped talking so much. Now she hardly says anything and she's not playing with her sisters much anymore. It's as if she's pulling away from them . . . from us."

Miss Mary Mack, Mack, Mack
All dressed in black, black, black

"I think she needs therapy," Betty June said.

Amara sighed with gratitude. Finally. Someone who

was on her side. She let her guard all the way down then. "I think so too!" she said. "But Ross has this friend who's a therapist. He keeps telling us to give it time. But I think it's Ross. He really doesn't want to admit that he has a child who might have psychological problems."

Silver buttons, buttons, buttons
All down her back, back, back

The not-so-evil aunt nodded. "Yeah. And add to the fact that he just buried a wife who was ill. How eager would you be to endure yet another 'illness'?"

"I wouldn't."

"Exactly."

She asked her mother, mother, mother
For fifteen cents, cents, cents
To see the elephant, elephant, elephant
Jump the fence, fence, fence

The girls clapped and recited the singsong verse. They worked in unison. In tandem. Trinity and Regina. Trina and Bridgette. As fluid as a rushing stream. Totally in sync.

Amara wished terribly that she had someone in sync with her. A husband—who shared her hopes and dreams for a family. For the girls. Someone who loved her with common goals.

Someone who understood her. She wished—

"I could talk to Ross, Amara." Betty June's voice came out dangerously sweet. Amara was instantly leery. But she realized that it, whatever *it* had been, wasn't about her anymore. It hadn't been since she'd gotten married.

It was about the girls and their well-being. It was about getting Trinette well. And for that, Amara would do anything. Even trust that the evil aunt could do a good deed.

He junped so high, high, high
That he touched the sky, sky, sky

"Please. Talk to Ross. It's got to be better if he hears it from two people."

"Then I'll speak to him about it as soon as he gets home." Betty June grinned. It was a thin grin. A grin that under normal circumstances would have made Amara uneasy. But these weren't normal circumstances. Her daughter's, yes, her daughter's, life was at stake.

"I only wish you could be there when I talk to him," Betty June said. "Of course that would be inappropriate. He might not open up totally."

Amara nodded. Knowing Ross's stubborn streak, he probably wouldn't.

"Please don't think I'm being unscrupulous here, but maybe you could kind of, oh, I don't know . . . hang around in the shadows. Ross wouldn't have to know." She leaned in. "You could just kind of listen . . . to what we're saying."

The girls were really into the song now. Their hands moved methodically, rhythmically, with one mind.

"I don't think that would be appropriate."

"What's inappropriate about knowing where your, uh, husband stands on getting treatment for Trinette?"

Amara thought about Betty June's question and she knew the answer.

Nothing and everything.

The way things stood with Ross right now, Amara knew he would never confide in her or give her his true feelings. But to someone he'd considered family for years . . . he might be a little forthcoming. And once she knew how Ross felt about it and what his plan was, she would know better how to respond. Obviously, telling him exactly how she felt was getting her nowhere. But knowing exactly how he felt might provide her with answers.

"All right," she conceded. The sound of the girls' hands slapping together resonated in the background.

Betty June's grin broadened, and she clapped her hands together as if she were also playing in the backyard. "Then it's settled. As soon as I'm ready to broach the subject with Ross, I'll give you a signal. Then you make some excuse to leave. But instead of leaving, why don't you sneak into the linen closet and listen to what your, uh, husband has to say? That way, you'll be sure of what you need to do."

Amara didn't think the grin on Betty June's face could get any wider, but she was wrong. The woman was smiling like the Cheshire Cat. Amara was just about to reconsider letting down her guard when Nettie walked up beside her.

From her tiny hand came the picture she'd been so diligently coloring. It would have been beautiful if not for the content.

There were five flowers—roses most likely. They were large and took up a lot of space on the paper. Nettie had carefully colored their petals the darkest shade of red. Their stems and leaves were two shades of a green that complemented each other perfectly on the page. But what concerned Amara was the tears. Each flower was crying. Large blue teardrops fell from the center of each bloom like slow rain.

A pain that threatened real tears sliced through Amara's heart.

And he never came back, back, back
Till the Fourth of July, ly, ly

Amara vowed right then and there to do whatever it took to heal this little girl who was so desperately crying out for help—even if it meant spying on Ross.

Chapter 10

"I think you should go home to Mama."

"What?" Leeza asked, shock lifting her voice.

"Keep it down," Betty June whispered. "I don't want the whole world to know what I'm planning.

"I thought you would be a help to me. Turns out, you're not. I can see it in your eyes. You've got a soft spot for that gold digger. So you best be gone before I lose my patience with you."

Leeza shuddered. Her sister's words came out more in a hiss than a whisper. But she was right. She liked Amara. And as long as Amara loved her nieces and her nieces loved Amara, she didn't see anything wrong with her stepping in when she was most needed. She'd stayed in the guest room that day so that she wouldn't be present to witness her sister's dirty deeds.

Leeza loved Betty June and wanted to keep her sister happy. Usually that meant going along with whatever she said. And just as she thought it, she realized that she would do it again this time. But something inside her had changed. Seeing Amara taking charge of her circumstances and stepping up to the plate . . . she admired her for that. Yes, Leeza would take this time away from her sister to decide what she wanted to do with her life and then, go do it.

And she knew, when she finally discovered what it was, she would call Amara and thank her for planting the seed.

"I knew it. You're thinking too much."

Leeza shook her head. "No, Betty June. I haven't been thinking enough. But getting away from you is a first step."

She could see her comment just bounced off of her sister. Before she could speak again, Leeza turned and marched out of the room, ready to get as far away from Betty June as possible. Too bad Ross wasn't around. She would tell him to be wary. Her sister had something up her sleeve.

And that was never good.

Betty June couldn't stop laughing. She was in the guest room, doubled over, and couldn't wait for her brother-in-law to come home.

Funny how she still thought of him that way. Catching her breath, she realized that she probably always would. And she would do anything to preserve the integrity of her sister's memory. And that meant destroying this farce of a marriage.

Every time she'd brought up the absurdity of this marriage to her mother, her mother would rationalize it and say that it was Brenda's last wishes.

"Forget Brenda's last wishes!" she'd shouted to her mother. "Brenda was dying. She wasn't in her right mind."

Betty June would not see her nieces brought up by someone just old enough to be their sister. And she would not allow the memory of her sister to be usurped by an ill-conceived marriage of convenience. She would rather Ross be a single parent.

And if she had her way, he would be exactly that in no time.

By the time Ross got home from work, he was exhausted. If he had to approve another proposal for the Hot Site, he would burst out of his clothes like the Hulk and smash a building with his bare hands.

As he turned his key in the lock of his front door, a shower, a quiet house, and a newspaper sounded like a good deal to him.

"Daddy!" Trinity shouted. He smiled despite his disposition. Trinity was the eternal greeter. Always the first one to the door. And since she was tall for her age, he had worked hard to teach her not to just open the door when the doorbell rang or when someone knocked.

He bent down for the Trina leap. Another expectation. If Trina was the first one to the door, she often followed that up with a jump into his arms. Trinity was always content with a kiss on the forehead. Nettie used to jockey for arm position, but not anymore.

That concerned Ross. He'd tried everything he knew, and everything his psychologist friend recommended, to get Nettie out of the depression she seemed to be in.

Nothing worked.

He'd made a decision earlier that day to seek out formal counseling for his daughter. She obviously needed help—the kind of help she could only get from seeing a professional.

"How's my angel?" he asked, scooping Trina into his arms.

"Fine, Daddy," Trinity answered.

Always the perfectionist, Trinity thought she was too

old to jump into her father's arms, but not too old to maneuver a comment away from her sister.

Trinette stood in the background watching, her eyes motionless and empty. Ross's entire body ached with remorse. If he could just fix what was wrong with his daughter. He would do anything to take away her pain.

"Ross," Amara said.

He glanced up while Trina slid down out of his grasp.

"Yes," he said, noticing a difference in her. She looked . . . calmer somehow. Settled.

Although he still wasn't keen about her settling in here in his home, he had to admit, whatever her mood, it looked good on her.

"Dinner is ready."

He hugged Trinity. Kissing the spot on her forehead where he always kissed.

"I'm really not—"

"In the mood for a sit-down dinner?" she asked. "I can tell. If you want, I'll fix you a place on the deck. I'll bring you a plate and a glass of water."

There she goes again, Ross thought. *Finishing my sentences and reading my mind. She doesn't know me that well.*

But what disturbed Ross most was the fact that she did. Every sentence she finished, every action she took was right on the money. He couldn't ask for a better companion at this time. It was only his feeling of betraying Brenda that kept him from reveling in the presence of a woman who seemed to know his every need before he did.

What man wouldn't want that?

A man still in mourning for his past relationship, he told himself, and headed upstairs to change.

Before he reached the top of the staircase, he stopped.

"Thanks, Amara," Ross said.

He saw her through the railings. At his comment, she smiled as if someone had just crowned her queen.

And God help him, he liked her smile.

It's amazing what a hot shower and fresh clothes will do to one's disposition. Ross came downstairs with a spring in his step. Between Zest soap and Mennen deodorant, he decided to eat in the kitchen with the rest of the family. He wanted to believe it was the water that changed his mind. But it wasn't. It wasn't having someone like Amara in his house to take care of things.

It was Amara herself.

And just like he knew it would be, dinner was marvelous. Betty June claimed that she helped, but Ross knew. Amara was just being kind. He could tell her cooking a mile away now. Knew it by the smell, the taste, the care in preparation. And her personal culinary signature was all over his plate this evening.

She really could burn.

And she also knew how to handle the girls. He only had to step in on rare occasions when the triplets were in a bad mood or just particularly fussy. Otherwise, like tonight, Amara was right on top of things.

She never talked down to them or was harsh in any way. And they responded to her in a way that Ross felt himself just wanting to sit back and watch.

But he dared not get too comfortable. He still had to keep his mind on his daughters' best interest. And that meant being ready, at a moment's notice, to end this pseudomarriage and take care of the girls himself.

"There's some leftover ice cream pie if you want

dessert, Ross," Amara coaxed. The tone of her voice sounded soft, velvety. Not pent up and under pressure like usual. He found himself fascinated by the sound.

"No, thanks. I'm so full right now, if you poked me I'd explode."

Trinity laughed. Nettie's eyes rounded with shock. Trina stuck her little finger in her father's side tentatively.

"Not for real, silly!" Trinity admonished.

Trina stuck her tongue out.

"All right, girls," Ross intervened before the name calling got any more severe. "Why don't you three go play?"

They frowned and pouted, but for once, didn't protest. Instead they slid off of their seats and headed up toward their room.

Ross knew the sooner they went to their room, the easier it would be getting them to go to bed. Since Amara was in charge of the "getting ready for bed" part of their routine, he hoped this gesture would help her out.

She turned in his direction. Her eyes smiled. Ross swallowed hard, realizing he liked the effect her gaze had on him just a little too much.

"So!" Betty June said, so loudly Ross would have thought she was speaking to someone who was hard of hearing. "Why don't you and I *really* catch up on old times, Ross? We haven't done that since I've been here."

Then Betty June and Amara shared a look. Ross wasn't sure what it meant. *Probably a woman thing,* he said to himself, dismissing the gesture.

"Sure, BJ. Sounds like a good idea."

Amara fidgeted for a moment. "Well," she said finally, rubbing her elbows, "I'll just go upstairs to check on the girls."

"Ahem!" Betty June said.

Amara's face tightened in concentration. "I think I'll read to them. I'll be gone for a while."

"Okay," Ross said, wondering why Amara was acting so strangely.

He watched her walk away and tried to hide his admiration. The guys he worked with often razzed him about being married to a younger woman. At times like this, when something he couldn't fathom compelled him to watch Amara's every movement, he razzed *himself*. Tall. Slender. Soft undulating curves. *All of that young body,* his mind said, as he realized that he would never know what it was like to experience it.

It was also times like these when he was tempted to change that fact.

"I think I'll have some pie," Betty June said.

"I'll join you," Ross answered, needing to cool his libido.

Amara did go upstairs to check on the girls, but instead of staying there and reading them a story, she snuck back downstairs and waited. She and Betty June had agreed upon a signal. Betty June would cough as soon as she brought up the topic of Nettie and therapy. Then Amara would creep into the linen closet, where she would be able to hear every word.

If it weren't for the facade Betty June was putting up, she would be squirming in her seat. She was deliriously happy. Her plan was going so well, she could hardly believe it.

She just knew Amara was in the other room, champing at the bit to know what was going on inside Ross's head. And she would find out very soon. Only what she would find out would be more than she bargained for. If Ross felt about Amara the way Betty June suspected he did, Amara's bags were as good as packed. And then she would be out of her nieces' lives for good. And Ross could get on with the business of raising the girls and finding a proper mother for them—not someone who had been pulled like a rabbit out of a hat from her sister's delirious and cancer-impaired mind.

"So, Ross . . . how do you really feel about Amara?"

Shock and astonishment warred for control of Ross's face. "How am I supposed to feel?"

"Well, you have to admit, you didn't give yourself any recovery time and now here you are married again. You must feel something."

He scooped a spoonful of the frozen treat into his mouth. He probably needed time to decide if he was going to be honest with her. She would give him all the time he needed.

"I'm making it. You know. Adjusting. The girls have someone here," he said. "Which is the most important thing."

Betty June reached over, patted the back of his hand reassuringly. "Ross. It's me. Your sister-in-law. If you can tell anyone, you can tell me. Now I know you enough to know that you're holding back something." She batted her eyelashes innocently. Ate a small spoonful of ice cream. "Now . . . how do you really feel about Amara?"

Ross blew out a breath. "Honestly?"

Got 'im! Betty June said to herself and immediately faked a coughing spasm.

Ross jumped up, pat her on the back. "Are you all right? Should I get you some water?"

"No. I'm fine," she said, suddenly recovered. "So . . . you were saying . . ."

He took his seat across from her at the table, his back to where Betty June knew Amara was listening with eager ears.

"How is she, Ross?"

He shrugged. "She's okay."

"Are you sure?" she asked, voice thick with artificial concern.

"Yeah, I mean, it's really not as bad as it could be."

"But it's not great either," Betty June pressed.

"No. I wouldn't say it was great."

"So what would you say?"

"I would say, it is what it is. I guess I'm okay with it. For now."

Betty June's pie was rapidly disappearing; however, Ross's mostly melted on his plate. It was as if he was in deep reflection. Considering all his answers.

She had to probe deeper. "What about counseling?"

"Counseling! Out of the question!"

"Why?" she asked, blinking like a giraffe.

"It's not like I'm taking this thing seriously."

"Why not?" Betty June asked.

Ross wondered why she was pressuring him. But he knew. She was family and she cared about what happened to her nieces. To her, Amara was a stranger. A stranger who had stepped into her sister's place. And everyone knew, Brenda Hayward's shoes were big shoes to fill.

"Look, BJ. I know where this is going and I want to assure you, I've got my ducks in a row." He finally took a spoonful of his dessert. "I've got a lawyer on retainer. Just in case anything detrimental happens, he can draw up papers for a quick annulment."

He hoped his words would reassure her. But as he said them, they weren't reassuring to him. As a matter of fact, they felt wrong coming out of his mouth.

Betty June couldn't be happier! She'd hoped that by misdirecting Amara, she'd get Ross to plant a seed of doubt in Amara's mind that Betty June would be more than happy to help cultivate. But this . . . this was a boon even she couldn't have imagined.

After hearing this, maybe the silly young woman's bags would be packed tonight.

"An annulment?" Betty June went on. "Why, Ross, what on earth are you talking about?"

"I'm saying that if things don't work out with Amara, I've got an escape route already planned."

As soon as she heard the words, Amara wanted to run from the house. But her legs wouldn't cooperate. The revelation numbed her body from the waist down. Instead of running, Amara lumbered from the linen closet stunned with disbelief.

Ross was talking about her. Not Nettie. He didn't care about her or their marriage. As a matter of fact, he'd made plans to end their marriage at the first sign of trouble.

Which was what? she wondered.

A wrong word? Dinner late? A bad mood? Heaven forbid he come home and one of the girls have a cut or scrape from falling down! Would that be the last straw?

She was finally becoming comfortable in her own skin as a wife and mother and even more comfortable with her surroundings. She'd added touches of rose and other pastels to liven the living space. She'd opened it up by removing a small hutch and table, then repositioning a chair so that the walking space was expansive and inviting, which is exactly what she thought it should be since it was the lead-in to the focal point of the house. And she'd even made peace with that—the kitchen where she performed motherly *and* wifely functions with pride and a sense of accomplishment. Yes, finally when she'd succeeded in making Ross's house feel more like her own and begun to collect fond memories of being a real mother like singing the cookie song with the girls, the unthinkable had happened. The most unfortunate thing ever. Ross had no intention of fulfilling his promise of giving their marriage a chance.

And Amara was tired. Too tired to put up a fight. Tired of putting up with him, questions from her family, accusations from his former in-laws.

She swallowed. Her throat was dry and scratchy. She wasn't sure why but she was sweating. Probably from the realization that she would have to call her mother, ask to move back in, and prepare herself for the moment when Ross decided their marriage should be annulled.

Until then, she would throw herself, her life, full force into the children. She would do the best she could for them with the time she had left.

Ross would pry her away from the girls. They needed a mother. They needed her. And if she was completely honest with herself, she knew she needed them just as much.

She stormed out of the house looking for something to temper her frustration with. To calm her nerves. To keep her from giving Ross any ammunition he needed to fulfill his plan.

Amara tugged the weed with her bare hand, ignoring the gloves and hand hoe. It came up root and all. It looked brown and dry and pathetic in her hand. How could something so thin and frail cause so much trouble? A quick cast of her wrist and she tossed the weed aside to the concrete sidewalk.

She reached for another and then another, pulling and yanking, amazed at the ease with which they lifted from the soil. She tossed them on top of each other and soon a pile of the offending plants began in earnest.

Amara worked quicker, relief and anger propelling her forward. She was relieved to be ridding the garden of weeds and angry that so many remained. In a wave of anger, she tore out a tulip from the soil, and its long root snapped in half like a pencil. Sadness cooled her emotions, but only for a second. In a blinding flash of anger, she tossed the tulip on top of the small hill of weeds and grabbed for the next growing thing within reach.

Her fingers gripped both flowers and weeds. She ripped frantically with both hands. Her breaths came in ragged gulps as she cleared a path in front of her. It all had to go. She couldn't tell the difference between beauty and ugliness. Good and bad. She wanted, needed it all gone. By the time Shasta returned, Amara had clawed her way through the tulips and had started on the begonias. She looked up only for a moment to see Shasta's incredulous expression. But Amara didn't care. She stopped though, panting as if she'd just run circles around the house, and thought, *It doesn't matter*. Shasta would probably win another train load of seedlings to replace the ones she'd ripped away.

One thing was for sure—not since her video game days of Mortal Kombat had she felt so defeated.

Chapter 11

At the sound of the first sneeze Amara knew there would be trouble. She had never known an instance where one of the girls had gotten sick without the other two following suit.

She contacted her aunt Ashley and got a recipe for a potent herbal prevention for colds.

Unfortunately, the girls would have nothing to do with the zinc and Echinachea tea that she brewed. Even when she added honey and lemon, they frowned and initiated a little girl mutiny. So Amara conceded and filled them with megadoses of orange juice and other citrus fruits.

Her efforts were for naught.

Trina was hit first. For the triplet with the most palpable energy, the cold knocked her for a loop. Fever, chills, phlegm-clogged coughing, and sneezing until her nose was swollen and red. And still with all of those symptoms, Amara would have sworn that what bothered Trina the most was not her illness, but the fact that she couldn't change her outfits five to six times per day like she was used to. Instead of "tada-ing" down the stairs like Diana Ross singing "Reach Out and Touch," Little Miss Dress-up was confined to her bed most of the time taking measured spoonfuls of Children's Tylenol.

Over the next few days, each of the other two girls came down with the same cold, although neither of them was as ill as their sister. Trina seemed to carry the brunt of the illness. Trinity and Nettie coughed and sneezed a lot and weren't as energetic as usual, but were still up and around playing games on the computer and putting puzzles together.

But still, Amara could sense a sadness in the girls and couldn't stand to see them listless and unhappy. So she did something she'd been toying with since a week after she moved into the Hayward household. Made some changes.

"Girls, how would you like to do some redecorating?"

"Yeay!" came their weak but enthusiastic replies.

In the span of three hours, they had rearranged furniture, replaced paintings, picked young flowers from the newly blooming garden, and used them to add accents around the house. And on a whim, they drove to a nearby hardware store, picked up a small can of lavender paint, and rag-rolled an accent wall in Amara's bathroom.

By the time Ross arrived home, the girls were happy, exhausted, and seemed to be one hundred times better—colds all but ignored.

Unlike most days when the girls rushed to the door to greet their father, they seemed reluctant to leave Amara's side. But the hesitation only lasted a few seconds. They eventually skipped over to their father and hugged his legs, nearly toppling him. Although Ross's signature smile shined brightly down on his daughters from beneath his moustache, Amara braced herself for the storm she knew was coming.

Ross hated change. When she'd stopped dressing the girls identically all the time, he voiced his disapproval.

When she'd sometimes changed their schedule to play longer, read longer, or just allow them some quiet time, he spouted adamant opposition. And when she'd suggested once—after Ross insisted that the girls clean their plates—that the girls knew when they were full, she withstood a verbal lashing with strength, dignity, and a no-nonsense demeanor, letting him know that he would not intimidate her.

But this, this was big. She was rearranging things that had to do with Ross, without consulting him. As the familiar rise of anger clouded his face, Amara remembered her mother telling her once that it's easier to ask for forgiveness than permission, and braced herself for his outburst.

It never came.

The evil aunts were finally gone. Amara was tired of being civil. Tired of being polite and the only one to make a gesture toward the halfway mark of their agreement. In the past four months, she'd done everything she could think of to try and make their arrangement work. But now she was tired.

Not just physically, but every way possible. Every day when the girls took a nap, she would take one too. Up until the last week, she would always wake up before the girls and start getting things ready for dinner. But the last five days had scared her. She hadn't awakened before the girls. Luckily they hadn't been up much before her. But yesterday, she couldn't tell how long they'd been awake without her supervision. Maybe an entire thirty minutes.

That was not good at all.

Before she let exhaustion, and Ross Hayward, get the

best of her, she'd put up her white flag. Admit defeat before it was too late. Before something happened to the girls or worse.

Amara's eyes felt like bowling balls. They were so heavy and tired that through her vision it looked as though there were six little girls in the room instead of three. If she could just read to the end of the bedtime story, she could go to bed. She knew she didn't have the strength to take her clothes off. She would have to sleep in them.

"And then what happened, Mara?" Trina's bubbly voice broke through the fog in Amara's head.

She opened her eyes wider, sat straighter, but it didn't ease her weariness. Instead it sapped some of the strength she would need to walk from the girls' room down to hers.

"And then," she said, trying to sound as perky as possible, "the big red dragon took his socks to the ball with juice, plaza . . . mermaid . . . glasses."

"That's not how the story goes," Trinity corrected.

Amara's head snapped up. What had she just said? Oh, dear! She'd dozed off in the middle of the story. It seemed the only person *The Big Red Dragon* was putting to sleep was her. She sighed, knowing that the girls slept so much better after having a story at night. She'd been diligent about that, and the last thing she needed was three fussy girls or Ross grumbling to her about something else she'd done wrong.

But she was exhausted.

The girls would just have to understand, and she would deal with Ross if need be.

"Girls, I'm really, really . . ." A yawn caught her midsentence. "Tired tonight. We'll finish the story tomorrow, okay?"

Their moans of disappointment saddened her, but her body felt wrung out. She needed rest and lots of it.

Amara kissed the girls, tucked them in, and vowed to start taking vitamins.

As she walked to her room, she wondered if her iron was low. She also marveled at how inviting the carpet looked right now. With every step a chore, she thought to herself how easy it would be to just lie down right in the middle of the hallway. She didn't though. She used all her energy to get to her room. And just as she imagined, she didn't have the strength to remove her clothes. She fell onto the bed, jeans, T-shirt, and all. She didn't even bother to pull the covers back. Sleep took her instantly.

When she awoke the next morning, it was ten o'clock, Ross was gone, the girls were up, and had been up for hours.

They were playing Hair Train. They all sat on the floor, one behind the other, each with a comb and brush. The goal was to comb the hair of the person in front of you into three neat braids. Amara awarded prizes of extended outside time when the girls were really neat with their work.

Most of the time, the girls' hair was a sight. She and Ross had argued many times about the state of the girls' hair. To him their hair was never neat enough. But combing the hair of three five-year-olds was more than a notion. Amara was so tired these days that she welcomed any kind of activity that allowed her to sit down for any length of time.

Today, Trinity was sitting on a chair behind her, comb-ing Amara's hair. If this little girl could work any kind of miracle and get Amara's straight hair to do anything but hang, she'd be grateful.

"Amara, it's hot over here. I think the heat is coming from you."

"Oh, Trinity," Amara said, swiping a bead of perspi-ration from her brow. "You can be so silly at times."

"The heat is coming from you!" she insisted. "My hands are hot!"

"And you *look* funny, too," Trina said.

"Shh!" Trinity said. "We weren't supposed to say anything about that."

"If you think this is a way for you to get out of the neat contest, you're wrong."

Amara turned to face Trinity, and a wave of nausea weakened her. She steadied herself with a hand on the floor.

"Mara, what's wrong?" Trina called.

Amara summoned what little strength she had to say, "I don't feel so well, sweetie. I'll be right back."

But she wasn't right back. After stumbling into the bathroom, she used the last of her strength to close the door behind her. After that she crumpled to the floor next to the toilet and heaved into it until there was nothing left in her stomach.

Weakened even more, she simply held on to the bowl, shaking, and gasping for breath.

When the girls called her name and knocked on the door, Amara couldn't answer. She could only stare in the door's general direction and say in her mind, *Call your daddy. Please call your daddy.*

It seemed like an hour before the door cracked open. Trinity, Trina, and Trinette peeked in quietly, eyes wide with fear. When they saw her against the toilet bowl, they rushed to her side and began to cry. Without success, they tried to pick her up. She was too weak to help them.

"Call Daddy!" Trinity said.

Trinity and Trina rushed out of the bathroom, while Trinette stood motionless in front of Amara. As she lay there looking up at the little girl she saw the horror building in her face. Large tears streamed down her cheeks and she cried silently.

Despite her weakened condition, all Amara could think about was reaching out to Trinette, holding her, consoling her. Telling her that everything would be okay. She tried to move. Instead of lifting her hand, another wave of nausea hit. She retched and coughed up bile. Trinette screamed and ran out of the bathroom.

Amara's world went black after that.

"We got this, man," Terry insisted.

A thin wire of dread felt as if it were being pulled through Ross. "Are you sure? I don't mind staying. Really."

"We've only got a couple more meetings left today. Then I'm going to make sure everybody leaves on time. These extra hours are getting ridiculous. Especially your extra hours. It's not that deep, man. I don't know why you stay here so late all the time."

Ross knew. And it had nothing to do with reports or deadlines. It had everything to do with putting off going home for as long as possible.

Living with Amara had become nearly unbearable. If it wasn't for his girls, he didn't know what he would do. She was unruly, obnoxious, and inappropriate.

Everything he'd ever tried to teach the girls about being proper young ladies, Amara had undermined. The times he'd come home and the house was trashed and untidy were innumerable. And she had the nerve to walk around in some of the thinnest, slinkiest, most form-fitting nightwear he'd ever seen. It made his blood boil just thinking about it.

Terry hooked up the light box and laptop for yet another PowerPoint presentation. It seemed Ross's world was filled with those lately.

Terry grinned. "After this, man, go home. Go directly home to that young wife of yours. Do not pass GO. Do not collect two hundred dollars."

In a normal world, Ross would have laughed. But these days, his life was anything but normal. He was losing control and things were getting out of hand. He'd been hoping for a reason to get an annulment. What better reason than that Amara was driving him away from his children, changing the landscape of their values, and disrupting their home with her loose ideas on discipline and child rearing? He'd call about it as soon as this meeting was over.

"Wanna run through the presentation one more time?" Terry asked.

"Nah, I think we're good. Let's save the recommendations for—"

The ringing of his cell phone surprised him. Even though he kept it on for emergencies, no one ever called him.

Something must have happened to the girls!

He snatched the phone from its holder on his belt and pressed TALK. "Hello!"

"Daddy . . ." Sobs.

He stood up. "Trinity! What's wrong, honey?"

"No, it's Trina." More sobs.

"Trina. I'm sorry, baby. Now tell Daddy, what's wrong? Is something wrong with your sisters?"

"No, Daddy. It's Mara."

Ross's worry deflated as he reasoned that Amara was probably making the girls do something they didn't want to do. Trina was probably calling to tell on her.

"What did Amara do?" he asked.

"She fell down." Giant sobs.

"What?" he shouted, fresh concern building in his chest.

"She's on the fl-floor. In the bathroom! We tried to get her up, D-Daddy! She's too heavy!"

Now his daughter was crying uncontrollably.

"Trina, you and the girls keep an eye on Amara!" he said, bolting toward the conference room door. "Daddy will be right there!"

He hung up and turned to Terry. "Emergency. Gotta go!" Terry was shouting something behind him, but Ross didn't hear. Within minutes, he was out to the parking lot, in his car, and dialing 911. He gave the operator his address and explained the situation as best he could.

He beat the ambulance by five minutes.

He couldn't believe it, but his hands were shaking. He could barely get the key in the lock. When he did, he rushed in, leaving the door open wide.

"Girls! Amara!"

"In here, Daddy!" two voices shouted in unison.

The scene in the bathroom was worse than he'd imagined. Amara was unconscious. Her breathing was shallow and there was vomit everywhere. He was sickened by the sight, but a large stroke of fear drove him to pick her up and take her to the living room.

His girls were a mess too. Their faces were wet with tears and from runny noses. Their faces were pale with fright.

"Don't worry," he said, trying to reassure them as well as himself. "Amara's going to be fine."

A disheveled Trinity spoke the words that had been floating around in his head. "That's what you said about Mommy."

Before he could respond, a small fire truck and rescue unit parked in front of the house. The rescue workers wasted no time in getting to the front door.

"You called for—"

"In here!" he shouted.

The paramedics rushed to where Amara lay, pale and fragile, on the couch. Ross's heart knocked hard in his chest. Unwilling to leave her side, he was assured by the man and woman paramedics that it would be better if he stood back and let them take care of her.

"She allergic to anything?" one of them asked.

"I don't know."

"Is she on any medications?"

"I don't know."

"Does she have a history of fainting?"

"I'm not sure."

"Is she pregnant or being treated for diabetes, high blood pressure, asthma?"

"I don't know. I don't think so."

"She your baby-sitter?"

"No. She's my wife."

The girls huddled around him. He hugged them, patted their heads. Tried to say comforting words. But he realized that he was as concerned as they were. He would never have believed that the thought of Amara falling ill would cause so much turmoil inside him. But if he didn't hear a reassuring word from the paramedics within the next few seconds, they would be having another sick patient on their hands. Him.

Another duo in yellow jackets came in with a stretcher. The girls wailed.

Ross stepped forward. "What's wrong with her?"

"Can't say for sure. Looks like stomach flu. But it's too late in the year for that. My guess would be a virus of some kind."

After they got her onto the stretcher and lifted her up, the other paramedic spoke up. "She seems to be coming around now. Her vitals aren't too far from normal. We'll take her in. See if we can find out what made her sick, why she passed out. Do you have a hospital preference?"

"Hospital?" He'd spent days trying to block his last hospital experience out of his mind. He couldn't take going back to Atlanta Medical. There was too much pain there and memories of chemo treatments.

"East Side General," he said, thinking that was where the girls were born. His memories would be better there.

"All right," the woman said. A smile reached her lips as she glanced at the girls gripping their father's pant leg for dear life. "Don't worry. We'll take care of your mom. Let's roll, guys!" she called and headed outside.

"She's not their—" Ross began, then stopped himself. As he knelt and hugged his girls to him, Shasta burst into the house.

"Oh, Ross, what happened? Are the girls okay? Where's Amara?"

"They're taking her to the hospital. Can you stay here with the girls while I follow them to East Side?"

"Of course."

* * *

The rhythm of Ross's heart finally settled into a regular pulse. He'd been at the hospital for over an hour and watched helplessly as doctors and nurses fussed and rushed over Amara's debilitated body.

They took her temperature, her blood pressure, her blood. They poked her, prodded her, listened to her lungs, stuck in IVs, clipped something on her finger, and shined a penlight into her eyes. Ross fought like a lion with himself not to throw everyone out of the room to give Amara some rest. How could she possibly get better if people wouldn't leave her alone?

But finally things had calmed down. And so, it seemed, had he. He didn't realize, until he sat down, how on edge he was. How keyed up.

How worried sick.

Amara stirred and it was the first relief he'd had since the phone call from his daughter.

"Where are the girls?" she asked, voice weak and strained.

"Shh!" he said, getting up and moving to her side. "Rest, now."

"Ross, I'm sorry. I didn't mean to—"

"Now look. You're worse than the girls."

A weak smile pursed her lips. Her eyes sparkled just for a moment. The sight sent of a flicker of happiness through his body.

"I'm glad you're awake."

"How long was I out?"

"About an hour."

Amara frowned and closed her eyes. She winced as if in pain.

"What's the matter?" he asked, taking her hand. Some of the earlier panic reminded him that it was still there just below the surface.

"The bathroom," she said. "It must be a mess."

He released a deep sigh. "Is that all? I thought you were in pain."

Amara's thoughts cleared just enough for her to realize that her only pain was being married to a man that didn't love her. Next to that, this passing-out incident was mild.

"What's wrong with me? Did they say?"

"No," he said, stroking her hair. "But I know you're going to be fine."

She looked so vulnerable lying there. So fragile. So . . . beautiful. *God, please don't let anything happen to her.* Please . . .

He felt himself drawing near to her face and the lips he suddenly wanted to kiss.

"I think we've got it," the doctor said, approaching. "Or that is, you've got it." She whisked into the room, her white coat trailing behind her like a superhero's cape.

"Why's she sick, Doctor?"

"Looks like pneumonia. More specifically mycoplasma pneumonia, which most people pass off as a cold or just extreme tiredness. Most folks keep on keepin' on until it busts them down like it did little miss here."

Ross squeezed Amara's hand tighter.

"I don't have a crystal ball, but I would bet dollars to doughnuts that she's been feelin' poorly for a while and has just been ignoring it."

"Amara . . ." Ross said, wondering if his insistence on having the house and the girls in perfect order had anything to do with her illness. He'd been relentless recently and knew that Amara had been struggling to keep up with his demands. Something told him his demands could quite possibly have gotten out of hand.

Ross's cheeks puffed out as he blew hot exasperation from his mouth. He felt horrible.

"We'll keep her tomorrow. Maybe the next day, just to get some fluids in her, build up her strength. We'll also start her on an antibiotic to fight the infection in her lungs. I'd give her about two weeks. She should be back to normal."

The doctor rubbed the back of Amara's hand, patted Ross on the shoulder, and headed out of the room. "A nurse should be here in a few minutes to give you a Godzilla-sized dose of penicillin. Call me if you need me."

"Thanks, Dr. Connor," Ross said.

"Yes, thank you," Amara echoed.

Ross's mind filled with memories of being beside hospital beds. Praying that the woman he cared for would get better, receive a miracle. If his bullheadedness had anything to do with Amara being in the hospital, he'd . . .

"Amara," he said, still stroking her soft hair. "I'm so sorry this happened to you."

"It's not your fault," she said, struggling to breathe. "People get sick."

"Yes, but . . ." He wasn't sure what he wanted to say.

"Ross?"

"Yes?"

"I want to talk to the girls. Will you call them for me?"

"I don't think you should talk on the phone."

"Please. I'm worried about them. And they're probably worried about me."

"Amara . . ."

"Please. It would make me feel better."

At those words, he relented and dialed the number for

his home. Shasta answered in the middle of the first ring. "Ross?"

"Yeah, Shasta. It's me. Amara's got pneumonia. But she's going to be okay. Are the girls around?"

"Yes, just a moment."

After an earful of shifting and fumbling, the voice of his eldest daughter came on the line. "Daddy?"

"Hi, sweetheart. Somebody wants to talk to you. Hold on."

Not wanting her to waste her strength, Ross held the cell phone up to Amara's ear. "It's Trinity," he said.

"Trinity?"

He heard his daughter's squeals of joy from where he stood.

"Hey," Amara continued. Ross could tell she was putting on a brave and happy front. "I'm fine. I'll be home in a couple of days, so you be good for your daddy until I get back. Now let me talk to Trina."

She spoke to each of the girls with the same bright enthusiasm. Ross was amazed. He knew how ill she was. And he knew that Trinette probably wasn't saying much if anything at all. But that didn't stop Amara. She'd already promised to bake cookies and sing something called "the cookie song" to her as soon as she got home.

His heart melted.

When he took the phone back, he saw Amara sink down into the bed as if the mattress were swallowing her. His heart quickened. "Shasta, can you stay with the girls tonight?"

"Of course."

"Good. I'll make other arrangements tomorrow. I've got to go. Thanks for everything."

With that, he clicked off his cell phone and moved closer to the frail woman lying on the bed.

"Amara? Are you okay?"

She nodded, but it was obvious all her strength had been used up in her conversation with the girls.

She closed her eyes. Her breathing was labored, and in a few minutes, she'd drifted off to sleep.

Ross pulled up a chair, took Amara's hand in his, and watched over her all night.

Amara was having the most wonderful dream. The man she loved also loved her and had told her so several times throughout the night. He'd stroked her hair, kissed her, held her hand, and told her that from now on, he was going to be the man she'd always dreamed of. Then the light of day pierced her eyes as she opened them. She struggled to breathe. Her chest hurt as if an elephant had been sitting on it. And she was so tired, she felt queasy. Somehow she managed to turn her head. Ross Hayward sat beside her, smiling gently, holding her hand.

At least *part* of her dream was real.

"How ya feelin'?"

"Not good," she managed. "What time is it?"

"Twelve."

"Noon?"

"Yes."

He was wearing the same clothes as last night. He hadn't changed. Hadn't moved from the uncomfortable-looking hospital chair.

"Thank you for staying."

"You're welcome," he said. "And before you ask, I spoke to the girls this morning. They're fine. Shasta's still with them. They send their love."

"Okay," she said, stretching to sit up. "Who are you, and what have you done with the ogre I married?"

Ross's smile broadened. "I've, uh . . . made him go on vacation. At least until you're better."

"Is that so?"

"It is."

"Well, if I'd known that, I would have gotten pneumonia the day after we were married. It would have saved me a ton of grief."

"Oh, yes," he said, patting her hand, "you're feeling much better."

It started out as a laugh, but ended in a coughing spasm. Afterward Amara's throat felt raw and cut open.

"I'll get you some fresh water," Ross said.

He stood, lifted the plastic pitcher, and headed toward the door. "Be right back," he said.

Although she couldn't remember feeling sicker in her entire life, she couldn't remember feeling so happy either. And it *wasn't* a dream. Something in Ross had changed, given in, made a compromise. He'd walked toward her and was offering an olive branch. And she knew one thing with all her heart.

She would take it.

For the first time since Brenda's death, Ross had looked at her with care instead of contempt. She felt better just thinking about it, breathed better just remembering the look in his eyes. The brown eyes that she'd memorized every golden fleck of had softened for her. The reflection she saw in these eyes was one she recognized. One that did not hurt her feelings or crush her heart.

Maybe he would never love her. But she believed now that he could like her and respect her for what she was trying to do for him and the girls.

"How's your throat?" he asked, returning with the water. He reached over to her bed table, picked up a cup, poured the water.

"Here's a straw," he said and held the cup to her lips so she could drink.

Amara took in the water slowly—just as slowly as she took in this new Ross Hayward. She knew if she drew the liquid in too fast, it would do more harm than good, choke her, and make her cough again. She took her time letting the cool water trickle down the back of her throat, coat the rough places there.

She stared into his eyes. He stared back.

He placed the cup back on the table. "I called your folks. They're on the way to see you."

Amara garnered enough strength to smile. It felt good. "Thank you, Ross."

"You're welcome, Amara," he said, stroking her hair.

She closed her eyes and swallowed slowly. Maybe they'd be okay, she thought. Maybe they would be okay after all.

Chapter 12

The rest Amara was supposed to get was finally coming. After a long day of questions and concerns from her parents and another long day of visits from all of her aunts, she was finally released from the hospital. The only thing that kept her sane during that entire hectic time was her frequent calls from the girls. Knowing they were all right made Amara's recovery go much faster.

"You're awake," Ross said, coming into the den.

"Yes," she said, sitting up. "It was good to sleep in my own bed. That hospital bed was too hard. And the sheets were too thin. I don't know how they expect you to recover in a room that's so cold."

"Well, I'm just glad you're feeling better. Can I get you something?"

"No, don't bother. I can get Shasta to help me. I don't want you to be late for work."

"I'm not going to work."

Amara frowned. "Why not?"

"I took some time off. To help out while you get better."

A thrill of appreciation rumbled through her veins. "Ross, you shouldn't have done that."

He leaned against the doorway. "Why?"

"Because we don't do well in the same room together. I don't want to even *think* about being cooped up with you for a few days." Actually she did want to imagine it. But more than that, she wanted to experience it. Live it. Try it on for size.

"The girls are already up. We had cold cereal together. They've been begging to come in here and wake you up. I wouldn't let them. Why don't I ask them to come in and keep you company while I make you something to keep your strength up? And they've given me their word that they won't wear you out."

Amara felt as if the sun were rising inside her. She couldn't wait to see the girls!

"Thanks, Ross," she said, propping herself up.

He opened the door to where three little ragamuffins had obviously been huddling on the other side.

"Mara!" their shouts came. The children she'd come to love as her own tumbled onto the bed with her and covered her with kisses. At least Trinity and Trina. Trinette stood still beside the bed and fumbled with the bedspread. Her eyes were brimming with sadness.

"I missed you, Mara!" Trina said.

"We all missed you," Trinity said.

Trinette edged closer but remained quiet.

"I have to finish your hair," Trinity cooed.

"Can we have some cookies now, Mara?"

"Hold on!" Ross's voice thundered from across the room. "Amara has to rest for a while. Several days in fact. So you girls have to be on your best behavior."

"Okay, Daddy."

"Now have a seat and tell Amara what you've been doing for the past few days. I'll be back soon."

As soon as Ross left, the girls settled down, but only a little.

Trinity and Trina babbled on about all of the games they'd played with Shasta while she was gone. They also had stories galore of Burger King and Happy Meals. Somewhere in the back of her mind, she remembered that Shasta didn't cook.

"We made you something, but Daddy told us to give it to you later," Trinity said.

"It's a college," Trina whispered, intent on spoiling the surprise.

"No, no. Not college. It' a col—col—" Trinity struggled.

"Coll-*age?*" Amara asked.

"Yes!" they shouted, throwing their little hands in the air as if to say, *Eureka!*

Amara laughed. "I can't wait to see it."

Moments later, Ross came in with a trayful of hot breakfast food. Oatmeal, toast and jelly, apple juice. He placed the tray across her lap.

"Thank you," she said.

"Don't mention it. Come on, girls. Let's let Amara eat her breakfast."

"Okay," they said with sad voices. Trinity and Trina walked over to where their dad was waiting. Trinette still stood next to the bed.

She was looking down at her hands. For as long as Amara could remember, she and Trinette had been meal buddies. No matter how much food Trinette had or ate, she would always want some of Amara's food too.

Amara cut a slice of toast in half and offered it to Trinette. The little girl didn't move, at first. Then slowly she reached up and took the bread. Without looking at Amara she walked over to her dad.

"You're welcome," Amara said, smiling. Things really were getting better.

For a long time now, Amara had felt her love for Ross diminishing, fading away like the last star at midnight. But just this small gesture of attention reminded her of why she'd been so taken with him. If her love didn't return, at least her respect and admiration had returned in full force.

She smiled through the pain in her chest.

"How many days do you have off?" Amara asked after her third day of royal treatment.

"Several," Ross responded. "Family medical leave is a beautiful thing."

"Family?" she said, then stopped herself. *Don't look a gift horse in the mouth,* she could hear her mother saying.

Ross had stepped in and taken over her household duties and the girls had been on their best behavior. But Amara feared that wouldn't last for long. After the girls became accustomed to their father being home during the day, they would turn back into their normal, wonderful, curious, irking, mischievous, arguing, cuddly selves. She also wondered how long it would take for Ross to become tired of housework.

Amara was amused by his initial claim that cooking and cleaning weren't tough jobs at all. She'd give it two more days and see how he felt about it then.

"How are you feeling today, kiddo?"

Amara chuckled, the soreness in her chest reminding her not to overdo. "You haven't called me that in years."

"Not since you were eighteen," he said. "After that, Little One seemed . . . inappropriate. But looking at you now, it seems to fit you again."

Amara threw the covers off and swung her legs off the side of the bed. "Well, not for long. I plan to make a full recovery and be stronger than ever. Thank you very much!"

Trinity skipped into the guest room, followed by Trina and Trinette. They'd lost the individuality Amara had allowed them and were once again dressed in matching outfits and sported identical hairstyles.

"We came to help you get dressed, Mara!" Trina's bright and cheerful voice proclaimed.

Trinette huddled close to her sisters, looking slightly agitated.

"It's time to get you ready for the day," Trinity said, echoing Amara's morning words to the girls.

"I see you're in good hands. Want some breakfast?"

Amara let the girls help her up. "Sure."

"It'll be ready by the time you get back."

The delight of motherhood surged through her veins as she basked in the care of the three little girls whose actions showed how much they cared about her.

The triplets were interested in dressing up not only Amara but themselves as well. In no time, the four of them were dressed like debutantes going to a ball. Even Trinette joined in the fun. She still wasn't saying much, but Amara was grateful for her energy. Their individuality shone through in the results of their escapade. Trina walked like a tiny Mae West. Trinity was more conservative in her choice of dress, preferring a baseball cap to the feathered headdress of her sister. Trinette created a hodgepodge clash of styles with long white gloves and thick-soled tennis shoes. By the time Ross came back to check on them, they were all giggles and all decked out.

Ross was not amused.

"Girls!" he chided. "What do you think you're doing?"

Their made-up little faces turned to their father in surprise and worry.

"It's okay, Ross. I've missed playing with them."

"And they've missed getting away with anything they want."

"You know what? You really should let the girls be girls."

"I have no problem with them being girls. I just don't want them getting out of hand."

Amara turned and shook her head. "No chance of that."

"What was that?" Ross asked, frustration in his eyes.

"Nothing," she mumbled and gathered the girls to head to the kitchen.

Breakfast was uneventful. Aside for the occasional dip of clothing into the food, anyone standing outside looking in would have believed that they were the typical American family sharing a meal. Amara knew that Ross was making a special effort at being nice. She decided to make a special effort as well. She would focus on getting well and try not to butt in on Ross as he pitched in on his days off.

By day five, Big Ross Man was movin' mighty slow. Not only that, but his appearance didn't have the usual immaculate grooming he was famous for. Amara couldn't resist commenting on the change.

"Everything okay, Ross?" she asked, one evening while he came into the den with a cup of tea.

"Fine," he said, handing her the steaming liquid.

"Are you sure? You don't seem fine."

"Just a little tired."

She could see the frustration warring in his face like he wanted to go on with an explanation, but wasn't sure.

"It's just that . . ."

"Yes?" she said and sipped her chamomile.

"The girls. I can't believe how unruly they are today."

Amara laughed so loudly and so strongly, her chest hurt and she thought she was going to spill her tea.

Ross sat down, thankful that his daughters, whom he had recently dubbed the three terrors, had mercifully gone down for a nap. Just getting them organized to play one game of Candy Land had taken the whole morning. He'd barely had time to fix lunch. So the laundry he'd planned on doing while the girls were playing had had to wait. His entire day had been knocked off schedule.

Ross hated being off schedule. "There's nothing funny about this. I'm beginning to think there's something wrong with them."

Amara's laughter increased. "Ross, the girls are just being themselves and you're finally getting a full dose of it."

"Please. I know my children."

Amara set her tea aside. "No, Ross. You know the sweet triplets that you come home to at six P.M. and put to bed at nine P.M."

Ross bristled. "What are you trying to say?"

"I'm saying that the darling little girls that you see are on their best behavior when they're around Daddy. But now that you're here all the time, their best behavior has long since worn off. What you see now is your daughters keepin' it real."

Ross blew a quick breath of disbelief through his lips and wondered if any part of what Amara was saying could be true.

"The next time I tell you the girls are a handful, you'll listen, won't you?"

Her self-righteousness irked him. There was something attractive and sexy about a woman who knew she was right.

"Aw, take your medicine, why don't you?"

Suddenly the room was illuminated with their laughter. It was as if a rainbow had burst above them and was showering them with wondrous colors.

Amara grabbed her stomach. Ross moved quickly to her side.

"Are you all right?" he asked, placing an arm around her.

For the first time since she'd known him, Amara considered lying to him. *No,* she wanted to say, *I'm not all right,* in hopes that his touch that warmed her skin would linger. Would he stroke her hair again like he did in the hospital? Touch her skin? *Taste* her skin?

"Amara?" he said, voice soothing and chock-full of concern.

Oh, God, it's still here, she realized, turning away. *All that love I've felt for so long.* She thought it was gone, whittled away by challenging circumstances and brittle tensions between her and Ross. But it had not worn away. It had been there all along, simmering just below the surface like lava waiting for the precise moment when the pressure was too much and it would overflow.

She gasped for air, being overwhelmed by her rapidly churning feelings.

"What's the matter, kiddo? What can I do?"

Love me, she thought. *Like I love you.* "Ross, I . . ."

"Yes?" he said, closing the distance between them.

"I . . . think I should lie down."

"No problem," he said, and scooped her into his arms. He carried her doll-like to the bed and laid her down, and covered her with a sheet.

"Thank you," she said.

He brought her a cup of tea and placed it on the nightstand. Then he swept a few stray strands of hair away from her face. His fingers brushed the side of her temple and she trembled inside. His eyes caught hers and for a moment she allowed herself to think he would kiss her. She waited, hoped, prayed.

Nothing happened.

Instead he straightened and walked toward the door. "I'll get you some water for your pain pills. Be right back."

Ross's heart thumped loudly in his chest. How could someone so young and demure, and ill even, be so beautiful and seductive?

The way the left side of her mouth curls up when she laughs, Ross thought and knew he had been milliseconds away from drawing the lip into his mouth, sucking on it, nursing at it until the aching in his heart vanished and the tension in his loins eased away.

Suddenly, he was concerned about what he would say if he opened his mouth, or worse, what he would *do*.

Laundry, he had to do the laundry or something— anything to take his mind off of the woman lying in the den, whose curves he'd unwittingly committed to memory, whose sweet breath he was dying to taste.

After returning with her water, he left the room without a word, marched upstairs, gathered the baskets brimming with clothes, and hurried to the basement.

In a moment of calm, the girls had helped him sort the laundry—colors and whites. After that they'd gone back to being the obnoxious triplets he barely recognized as his own. Ross dumped the load of whites in the washer, thankful that other thoughts were helping to cool his lust.

He was not ready to ruin his plans.

Just because they'd recently proven that they could be civil to each other and maybe even enjoy each other's company was no reason to abandon his plan. He'd continue to gather evidence, any evidence that Amara was an unfit wife and mother. Although he could all but taste her body in his mouth and wanted her badly, he wanted this annulment more.

And nothing would stop him from getting it.

Memories of bachelorhood flooded his mind. Before he got married, he'd been what he would consider a successful bachelor for years. He'd learned to take care of himself. Cook. Clean. Wash clothes. He'd never been a slob. His apartment was always orderly and immaculate. Everything in its place. He'd rely on those skills again now and they would get him through to when she was healthy again.

Looking at his watch, he imagined that the girls would sleep for another hour and then he would get them up and read to them.

Taking a much needed break, Ross took the newspaper from the mail stand in the entryway, flopped onto the couch, and put his slippered feet up.

No sooner had he opened the paper to the sports section than he heard a voice that made him cringe.

"Daddy, I want to play with the puzzles."

It was Trina. She was rubbing her eyes and holding her Rafiki doll. She'd changed her clothes. He noticed she did that a lot, as if she were a fashion model.

If it had been either of the other two girls, he would have nothing to worry about. He could have coaxed them back to bed and not disturbed the other sisters. Trina was different. She wasn't comfortable doing things alone. He'd seen evidence of this over the past several days and noted that whenever Trina had the opportunity, she'd pull her sisters into whatever she was doing.

She'd never be satisfied assembling a puzzle alone. Or with him for that matter. She would fuss or laugh loudly or let out a high-pitched bree that would surely wake up her sisters. He was sure of it.

Right now, he was too tired to put up a fight.

"Go wake up your sisters," he said. "I'll get the puzzles."

"Yeay!" Trina cheered, and skipped off to do what she had every intention of doing in the first place.

Ross's day went downhill from there. It started after the puzzle was finished and when the girls got into an argument over violet blue. For some reason, no matter what they were coloring—a leaf, a squirrel, a sailboat—it had to be colored violet blue. No other color would do and Trinity wouldn't share. Ross had watched with dismal despair as Trinity tried to reason with her sisters. Reason! Explaining how leaves and squirrels couldn't be violet blue, but sailboats could. She told them that there were seventy more crayons in the box and that some of them might even be better than violet blue. What she failed to realize was that the more she tried to lure them away from her crayon, the more they wanted it.

Ross's first instinct was to speak to them in his "father" voice, threaten to take the crayons away, or worse, make Trinity share. But he'd discovered days ago that his "father" voice was losing its potency. Punishment meant enforcement—which with so many things to get done around the house was difficult—and forcing any of his daughters to do anything meant screaming.

"What is going on out here?" Amara asked, looking sleep-deprived and frustrated.

A cacophony of explanations erupted from the children. Even Trinette spoke up.

"All right, that's enough!" Amara said and moved slowly to where Trinity sat defiantly on the floor.

"Let me have the crayon," Amara demanded.

"Mara . . ." Trinity pouted.

"Now!" she insisted.

Reluctantly, Trinity handed over the crayon.

Amara blew a puff of frustration between her teeth, snapped the crayon into three pieces, and handed each child a section.

Ross's jaw dropped.

Amara patted him on the shoulder. "You gotta keep them guessing," she said. "Now I'm going back to bed. Can you manage to keep the peace for a little while so I can get some rest?"

She didn't give him time to answer. Instead she headed back to the den, leaving Ross with three contented little girls.

Contented for the moment, he thought.

The last straw of the afternoon came when Ross went to take the white clothes out of the washing machine and put them in the dryer.

When he opened the washing machine he let out a deep rolling groan. Instead of white clothes, they were all pink.

"What the—" he said, digging around in the load. Trinette's Laugh&Love doll had somehow gotten mixed up in the wash. Laugh&Love's red dress was faded to a meek pink. She looked as if she'd walked through a storm and didn't quite make it.

Ross's heart plummeted into his stomach. "Trinette

loves this doll," he said out loud. It was the only thing that made her smile these days.

Could one of the girls have put it in the wash on purpose? he wondered, then dismissed that idea. They were a handful, but they weren't malicious. Trinette must have set it down and it got scooped into the basket with a pile of clothes.

He looked at the string hoping against hope that the doll still worked. Hair could be fixed. He could buy a new dress, but . . .

He pulled the cord.

"Ha . . .ha . . . ha . . . I . . . love . . . you."

The doll sounded like Darth Vader on downers.

He'd just have to buy a new one and replace this one without Trinette finding out.

The ear-piercing scream behind him told him that he was too late.

Ross immediately scooped his daughter into his arms and went upstairs with her. He was frustrated beyond belief. Not only did he need to console his daughter, but he needed to console himself.

Everything was out of control.

The girls, screaming, yelling, disobeying, behaving like cute little monsters. Out of control. The breakfast dishes, ruined laundry, and dinner that would be late. Out of control. His feelings for Amara running rampant and unchecked. Out of control.

It was crazy. It couldn't be this hard to run a household. To take care of the girls.

Could it?

"I'll buy you a new Baby Laugh&Love," he said. No sooner were the words out of his mouth than his other two daughters chimed in.

"I want a new doll, too!"

One more week of this. Just one more. He was exhausted already. If he had to take vitamins, hit a punching bag, and drink a gallon of Poweraid a day, he would do whatever it took to get through this in one sane piece.

The girls piled onto the couch where he sat with Trinette. There was no relief. They were everywhere, all the time. His thoughts reminded him of a day a few weeks ago when he and Amara had had a huge argument.

Things had not gone well at work. The disaster recovery drill was a debacle and he was left to figure out exactly why. That meant long, tense hours at work. On one of those days, he'd come home at seven P.M. The moment he'd walked in the door, Amara lit into him.

"Can you take the girls for a walk or something?"

He couldn't help it. After the kind of day he'd had, her words were the straw that broke the strong black man's back. "Damn, can I at least get in the door good?"

She'd only glared at him, which fueled his frustration even more.

"Unlike you, who gets to stay at home and have fun and play games all day with the girls, I've been working. And now, I'm dog-beat tired. Now I'm going to go upstairs, change my clothes, maybe take a shower, eat, read the paper, and watch CNN. In that order. Then maybe, just maybe, I'll take the girls for a walk."

And just because he was so angry, he'd added, "That is, if I feel like it."

Bill Cosby had talked about his wife having a conniption during one of his stand-up routines. It was one of Ross's favorites because of how far-fetched he'd thought it was. Until that evening with Amara.

He didn't know a twenty-two-year-old could say such things. But after she'd insisted that the girls go upstairs to their room and close the door, she'd let him have it. Five ways from Sunday, his mother used to say.

And even after that stiff tongue-lashing, he still hadn't understood what the big deal was. But now? Now, he'd pay somebody good money to come and take his girls for a walk. He loved them with all his heart and soul, but good Lord in heaven, he needed a break.

Over the next week, Ross did a lot better with taking care of the kids, Amara, and the house. Although he never reined in a schedule he felt 100 percent comfortable with, he learned a valuable lesson: nothing will ever go exactly as you plan it, so the best thing to do is go with the flow. A hard lesson to learn for a guy who all his life had worked to control the flow.

Another thing that happened was that he gained more respect for women, for stay-at-home moms and all they did for their families. More specifically, his admiration grew for Amara, who had stepped into a ready-made family and handled it for months better than he did for a few weeks. He didn't know how she did it. But he was grateful. Something that was hard for him to admit to himself. Could it be that this arranged marriage was not such a bad thing after all? As he and Amara made the transition back to their roles as breadwinner and caregiver, he wondered.

But things never did go all the way back to the way they were. Ross wouldn't let them. For the next few weeks he stayed only his designated eight hours at work, came home, and spent more time with the girls, more time helping out around the house, and more time with Amara.

They'd become a team and whether he liked it or not, it felt good.

"I want to thank you," he said one evening.

Amara smiled. He loved her smile. Loved the way it made him feel. Like all was right with the world.

"Thank me for what?" she asked, loading the dish-washer.

"For . . . everything. You didn't have to do it, you know. Marry a man you don't love, take care of his children, run his house. You didn't have—"

"You didn't have to either. You didn't have to marry someone you didn't love, allow her to care for your children, live in your house."

She stood straight and took a deep breath. "We both loved Brenda. Still love her. And there isn't anything that she could have asked that we would have refused. Even this."

Ross didn't know what possessed him. The sincerity in her eyes, the emotion in her voice, or the fact that his body had been craving her touch for a long time. But he went to her. Wrapped his arms around her. Held her tight. Tighter still.

He released a deep breath when she held him back. Sank into him, and squeezed. They stood like that for a long time. It was as though they were taking strength from each other and giving strength to each other at the same time. It felt . . . like they were meant to hold each other like that. It felt soothing and bolstering and weakening. It felt . . . like magic and healing, and a promise.

"I asked Shasta if she would watch the girls tonight," Ross said, peeling himself away.

"What? Why?"

"I want to take you out to a nice restaurant. Have

someone cook for you and wait on you. I want to show you my gratitude."

"I don't know what to say," she replied. But her smile said it all.

Chapter 13

Amara wasted no time getting ready. Her aunt Morgan had taught her well. She knew exactly which outfits made her look good. Which blouses accentuated her full bosom. Which skirts showed off her round hips. She knew which dresses sent the message that she was a woman with a total package.

She chose one of those.

Her aunt Morgan had also shown her how to put on makeup. She'd hardly had occasion to use her skills lately, but she decided that all that was going to change starting with tonight.

Although what she applied to her face was what her aunt told her was a glamour look for nighttime, she also knew how to apply a natural look for day wear, something she would apply on a regular basis starting tomorrow.

She checked herself in the mirror and liked what she saw.

It had been a while since she'd gotten "all gussied up," as her mother would probably put it. And she felt good. Even down to her underwear, which was sheer and sexy. Not that Ross would ever see it. But what mattered to her tonight was that she liked it. She felt sexy wearing it and that sexiness showed on her face. She smiled wondering how Ross would be able to resist her. Knowing that he would, but that she darn sure wouldn't make it easy for him.

She waited to make sure that he was in the living room waiting for her. Then she strolled out of the den. Her aunt Roxanne had taught her about walking, and the way a woman could walk with elegance, grace, and sensuality at the same time. She tried it and liked the results.

Ross's eyes all but popped out of his head and rolled around at her feet.

Amara one, Ross zip!

She did have to admit that he looked good as well. Tailored blue suit. Did he remember that blue was her favorite color? She wondered, but would not let herself dwell on the fact that he looked like the man she'd conjured in all her fantasies. The man that whispered sweet nothings in her ear and kissed her every chance he got. No, she was too busy focusing on what her aunt Ashley had taught her about men. Energy. Her aunt Ashley said that all creatures respond to the energy around them, most without realizing it—especially men.

She said that all creatures emit energy and that humans have the power to control the energy they give off. Right now Amara focused on sending off energy to Ross Hayward that said, *You want this. You want this.*

By the evidence of his breathing and the fact that he hadn't spoken or taken his eyes off of her since she entered the room, she believed that her efforts—all of them—were working.

Finally he smiled and licked his lips. "You make a brother want to stay home for the evening."

Then his eyes widened in shock and he shook his head. "I'm sorry. That was inappropriate. Please accept—"

"It's okay, Ross. It's good for a wife to know that her husband finds her attractive."

It was the first time that she'd been bold and put their marriage out there like that. She stiffened, waiting for his reaction. All she got was a grunt and the extension of his hand to her.

"Shall we?" he said.

She smiled. Amara two, Ross nada, she thought. As she strolled closely past him and caught a whiff of his cologne, she decided to give him a point for his "stay at home" comment.

Harrison's wasn't just an exclusive restaurant. It was the most exclusive restaurant in their part of the city. Amara had heard that they were only open one night per week, they served a ten-course meal, and they booked reservations a year in advance. She also heard that they only served couples and the small but elegant space only had room for ten couples. Before they arrived, Ross confirmed all that she'd heard.

"How did you get a reservation?" she asked.

"Shasta. She won a standing reservation in one of the many contests she enters. When I told her I wanted to take you out, she suggested I use it."

Amara felt special already and they hadn't even arrived at the restaurant yet.

When they finally got to Harrison's, Amara felt as though she'd left reality and stepped into a movie or a fantasy. The opulence went beyond anything she could ever have imagined.

They were escorted to their table by someone who acted as though he'd been trained by the Queen of England. His service and attention to detail were flawless. Except for one thing.

"Where are the menus?" Amara asked.

"There aren't any."

She blinked back confusion. "Why not?"

"Because everyone gets the same thing. There's no choice. In order to be served you must arrive before eight P.M. After that, they lock the doors."

"Amazing," Amara said truthfully. She was utterly amazed by it all.

If you would ask her later how the food was, she would remember that it was good, but not much beyond that. What she would remember was the conversation, the way her insides tingled when Ross looked at her, the way their laughter mingled and harmonized to make the most beautiful sound she'd ever heard.

She would remember Ross openly discussing his work, his desire to start his own company, and how he truly believed he was making a difference in the world.

She would remember how he listened without judgment to her discussing her love for children—something she'd gotten from her parents—and how she'd love to one day have her own day care center. She hadn't shared her dream with many people, but she'd shared it freely with Ross. And he'd nodded thoughtfully, like he was considering all the ways in which she could make that happen.

Each course brought a new delight between them. Soon it was Amara six, Ross six. Then Amara seven, Ross eight. Then Ross nine. Ross ten. In no time, Amara had to stop herself from slumping over the table, resting her head on the backs of her fingers, and staring nonblinking at her husband.

Husband.

Every day he felt more and more like her husband. And she more and more like a wife.

The dessert came. It was the most delectable chocolate cheesecake she'd ever eaten. Almost more mousse than cake. But the sweetest thing about it was not the taste, but when Ross said, "I've been fighting something all night and I'm tired of fighting it."

"What's that?" she asked, apprehension going off like tiny firecrackers inside her.

"This," he said, taking her fork. He sliced a small sliver of cheesecake onto it and lifted it to her lips. She took it slowly, sensually, gratefully. She closed her eyes and imagined that it wasn't the chocolate of the dessert that was in her mouth, but the chocolate of his skin, melting, blending, mellowing. She savored it. Even moaned in disappointment when it was all gone.

Ross's reaction was stunning. He simply stared, licked his lips, and said, "It was good for me, too."

That's game, she thought, and couldn't wait to get home.

When the champagne came, Amara knew she didn't need it. She already felt bubbly, sparkly, and just plain intoxicated from the wonderful evening she was having. Perfection would not describe it. Heaven wouldn't do. Everything was going so right. As if she'd fashioned it from one of her many dreams.

For the first time that evening, Amara really noticed the people dining with them.

The couples.

They were all laughing, grinning, smiling, basking in the glow of their partners, just like her and Ross. But something was different, too. They all seemed to be celebrating something.

The younger couples she imagined were celebrating engagements or first anniversaries. The couples in their thirties and forties were probably celebrating birthdays, or promotions. And the other couples—the older ones who looked like they'd spent a lifetime finishing each other's sentences and who had already begun to look like each other—looked to be honoring lifelong commitments and milestones in their relationships. Amara was suddenly saddened by it all. She sipped her champagne slowly, tentatively wondering if she really deserved it.

A quick glance at Ross told her that the champagne had sobered him as well. They hadn't been together as long as the couples in the restaurant with them, but she knew what he was thinking.

He was thinking about all the toasts he would never have with Brenda. All the celebrations. The anniversaries, like their tenth coming up in a few months, that they would never celebrate. The glasses that would never clink in their honor. She could see it in his eyes. She could feel it in the energy he was sending her.

She took several deep breaths. The sadness was palpable.

"I do so much for the house and for the girls. I'd like to do something for you, Ross. What can I do for *you?*"

"What you're doing is enough. I couldn't ask for anything more, really."

Amara nodded, knowing that her feelings for Ross were stronger than ever. If he did ask for anything, she doubted if she would be able to refuse him.

"What's the occasion?" a waiter asked, filling their flutes.

Amara stared into Ross's eyes, knowing his pain, feeling his emptiness.

"No occasion," she said, forcing a smile.

"We're here . . . just because."

"Just because?" The waiter brightened. "That's even better. Enjoy!" he said.

They sipped their champagne in silence and avoided

eye contact. Amara sighed. No matter what they did, no matter how far they came, Brenda would always come between them. What was and what might have been would always be a dark cloud in their sky. She might as well get used to it.

She had to get away for a moment. She couldn't stand to be in Ross's presence with this much tension between them.

"Excuse me," she said and headed toward the ladies' room.

Amara stared at her reflection in the mirror for a long time. Her makeup was still flawless, her dress still accentuating. The same face her aunt Marti pinched and said, "Doesn't she look just like me!" But inside, she'd changed tremendously. Grown up. Her outlook on life had completely changed. She saw the world with the eyes of a woman with responsibilities. And tonight she started to think about the future.

Her marriage to Ross had taken care of an immediate problem. But would they be able to build a future together? Would they create the kind of family with milestones and celebrations and significant events to toast, birthdays, anniversaries, graduations?

It was all too overwhelming to contemplate at once.

She decided then and there to celebrate in her heart every day she had with Ross and the girls. Each day would be something to toast and to be thankful for.

The hope of that thought gave her the strength she needed to go back into the dining room and face Ross again, and whatever else the evening held for them.

"Everything all right?" he asked when she came back to the table. "I was beginning to think I'd have to send in the troops."

"I'm fine, Ross," she said as he got up and pushed in her chair.

"Thanks for tonight," she said when he was seated. "It's really meant a lot to me."

He gazed into her eyes. A simmering blaze could be seen below the stare. "Me too, Amara."

His cold shower the night before hadn't done any good. He'd needed another one as soon as he opened his eyes this morning. Last night was a test of will he hadn't experienced since his college days when some girls would only let him get so far.

The water gushed from the showerhead. Ross stood beneath it nearly immobile, just allowing the cold wet to wash over him, bring down his drive, cool his libido.

She was getting in, he admitted. Sneaking in quietly like a thief after his heart. And he'd done everything to prevent it.

Stayed away from her, argued with her, disagreed. Tried not to listen or to deliberately agree with anything she said.

Nothing had worked.

In the end, it was him and the woman, yes, woman, he saw before him.

She was so much more than the child he'd made her out to be or convinced himself that she was. She was strong, responsible, and new life to heal aging, aching wounds.

Ross listened to the water gush for a while. Tired of listening to what his heart had been trying to tell him for days.

He wanted Amara.

At first, he'd wondered if it was just proximity. If the

reason he'd been drawn to her was simply that she was around. Simply that over the weeks and months he'd grown accustomed to her.

"Time and opportunity can make any woman attractive," one of his buddies had said.

But that wasn't it at all. It was all the things about her that flickered across his memory like flames licking him with a soft warmth. Her hair. Her long hair that he wanted to sink his fingers into. Her eyes that looked at him sometimes with an innocent hunger that jarred him. Her mind that worked like a steel trap, especially when it came to the girls.

The girls.

She was perfect for them. She fit like she'd been made for this family. And knowing Brenda the way he did, maybe she had.

Ross lathered a washcloth, stroked it across his chest and arms. He had to make up his mind. The final battle started here. Either he would remain celibate and fight to keep his feelings and needs in check or he would do what his mind was consumed with, what his body demanded.

A hard pang of guilt closed Ross's eyes. He couldn't believe he was even contemplating making love to another woman. Brenda was still in his heart. Still a living memory in his home. They had meant so much to each other. How could he betray her memory this way? This soon?

And then he realized that what he was feeling could be his mind's way of rushing through the grief. Making him think that he was attracted to Amara, simply as a way to get over Brenda.

He wondered if it was true. His gut told him it wasn't but he had to be sure.

Stepping out of the shower, Ross grabbed a towel from a bar and dried himself. His heart was on the line as well as the hearts of his daughters and Amara. He couldn't rush into anything, no matter how much it pained him to be in her presence and not be inside her presence.

Shasta perched on the bar stool at the kitchen counter and leaned on her elbows. Her stare and smile were unwavering.

"What?" Amara asked.

"You must really be feeling better."

"Why do you say that?" Amara asked, putting some water in a teakettle to boil.

"Because you look great! The outfit you're wearing is too cute for words. And you've lost weight."

"My aunt Morgan made this for me. She says I've become too friendly with sweats. She thinks I should wear something more fashionable. But I keep telling her that stay-at-home moms don't need to be cute, and as dirty as I get during the day cleaning and chasing after three girls, I'd ruin anything trendy."

"Well, every now and then you need to treat yourself. I never knew you had such a cute shape."

Amara removed large white porcelain cups from the cupboard and grabbed tea bags from the pantry. "I didn't either, until I got sick. I lost nine pounds."

"Not that you were overweight from the get-go. But now, you look . . . toned down. Cut."

"Believe me, my aunt Morgan can sew clothes to make anyone look good. Even me."

Before Shasta could respond, Ross came into the kitchen. Amara already had a pot of coffee made for him.

"Morning, ladies."

"Mornin.'"

"Hey, Ross."

"Amara, I'm running late. I'll probably be at work until seven tonight." He grabbed a Styrofoam cup from a shelf.

Amara walked to the refrigerator and pulled out a pan of cheesecake. Ross stared. What was she wearing? Damn if she didn't look good. No, better than good. Downright sexy. Something stirred in Ross. Something just below his abdomen, reminding him that he hadn't had sex in a long, long time.

He licked his lips and stared some more. The polite thing to do would have been to look away. Pour his coffee like he'd started to. But he couldn't. He could look at her forever.

She was prattling on about waking up early, making dessert, and how he should take a slice with him. Her words barely registered. Only her movements. She was busy cutting, wrapping, looking eatable. Suddenly he couldn't tell which was the dessert, Amara or the cheesecake. She was looking mighty sweet.

One last look, he told himself, then turned his attention back to his coffee. He told himself that he didn't have anything to be ashamed about. After all, she was his wife. Even if it was in name only.

She handed him a paper bag. "I hope you like it," she said.

He took the offering and headed out the door, before telltale signs of his heightened state became much more apparent.

"I like it," he said.

"You haven't even tasted it." She chuckled.

"I meant to say thank you." He had to get out of there before he dry-humped her right then and there.

"I'm out," he said.

Amara frowned. "Bye."

Shasta shook her head. "I thought I was going to have to excuse myself so that you two could have an early morning session."

Amara put the cheesecake back in the refrigerator and turned off the heat beneath the kettle. "What kind of session?"

"The kind of session that husbands and wives have when the husband wakes up horny."

"I told you about our arrangement, Shasta. Sessions are not included."

"You better tell that to Ross. He looked like he could have eaten you alive and not left a crumb."

"You're crazy!" Amara said, pouring the boiling water into the cups. But she felt as if she were the one coming to a boil and not the water. The thought of Ross even considering her like that made her warmer than the fever she had had when she was ill.

Shasta dipped her tea bag up and down into the cup. "I'm telling you, girl, the man wants you."

Amara shook her head, unable to believe.

"And speaking of wants . . . you're married to a man you don't have sex with. So, what do you do when you get hot?"

Amara's face flushed with embarrassment. Her eyes widened and her hands shook. Many times she'd looked at Ross and felt the lust stirring within her. She'd fantasized about them together so often the images ran like a tape in her mind. Because she was still a virgin, she wasn't sure if what she'd imagined was accurate, but it helped her through those rough times. And if all else failed, she'd reach for one of her favorite romance authors and live vicariously through the lives of the heroines in the stories.

"I read," she said, finally.

Shasta sipped her tea. "Really? And what do you think Ross does?"

A jolt of uncertainty stiffened her. She'd never considered that. Never thought that he might be suffering too.

"Do you think he's getting his needs met elsewhere?"

"No! I don't know," Amara admitted.

Ross had never seemed like the kind of man that would step out on his wife, even a pseudo one. From what her mother had told her about sex, men needed it more than women. Thought about it more than women. Had it more often than women they were involved with. If that was true, then maybe she should do something about that. Ross hadn't accepted any of her gestures of appreciation when she'd tried to thank him for taking care of her. Maybe, just maybe, he'd accept this.

"Shasta, will you watch the girls tonight?"

Her neighbor nodded and smiled.

By the time Ross made it home that evening, he was exhausted. He'd worked hard, partially because his major project was near completion and he was eager for it to come to an end. The other reason he'd worked so hard was to force the images of Amara from his mind. He'd been more successful at one than another.

Amara in the outfit. Amara naked. Amara under him. Amara on top of him. Amara bent over the couch, legs spread wide apart, hair hanging sexily down the side of her face, hips gyrating, and . . .

Oh, Lawd!

He slammed his car door shut, thinking, *Cold shower. Cold shower now!*

When he walked in, his first thought was that he'd entered the wrong house. First of all it was quiet, clean, and smelled like someone had been cooking all day.

"Anybody here?" he called, wondering if Amara had taken the girls to the mall.

"In here," Amara called.

He entered the kitchen and the sight before him made him gulp, swallow hard, and lick his lips.

It wasn't the fact that dinner was not only ready but waiting for him on the kitchen table. It wasn't the fact that all his favorite foods were piled high on the good china and piping hot. It wasn't even the candles burning and the neat and orderly way the table had been set. And it wasn't even the fact that his daughters hadn't accosted him before he could get into the house.

It was Amara.

She was stunning. It was what she was wearing—a silvery white dress short enough to show off long shapely legs and snug enough to accentuate a thin waist and ripe bosom. It was what she wasn't wearing—long-sleeved sweatshirt, sweatpants, and house shoes.

No, this evening her feet were clad in sandals with thin white straps wrapped several times around her ankle. And her skin. There was so much of it. Brown, luscious, tantalizing.

Suddenly he remembered he needed to breathe to stay alive.

"Would you like to change before dinner?"

Dinner? he thought. He gave her a once-over, knowing that the last thing he wanted to do right now was eat . . . food, that is.

"You look . . . better than that food," he said. "And I'm a hungry man, Amara."

She blinked, shuddered a little.

"Why are you doing this? And where are the girls?"

"The girls are staying with Shasta tonight. And, Ross . . . I just want to say thank you for taking care of me. And besides that, you're a man, and men have needs. I don't want—"

So that's what this is about, he thought. "Don't worry about my needs, Amara. I can keep my needs in check as long as you . . ." He stopped himself. What was he going to say? *As long as you stop looking so beautiful? As long as you don't brush up against me? As long as you keep your distance?*

It wasn't her problem, it was his. He'd agreed to marry Amara, but he hadn't agreed to bed her or consummate their marriage in any way. If that happened, his out—his annulment would be difficult, if not impossible to get.

For a moment, he'd let his hormones get the best of him. That was stupid.

"I'm going to take a shower first. If the food is cold when I come back, I'll pop it in the microwave for a few minutes."

"Ross—"

"I'll eat in my office," he said.

His shower wasn't cold enough. He'd dressed, come back downstairs, nuked his food, and still felt the aftereffects of knowing what his "wife" was offering.

This was the hardest battle he'd fought yet, he thought, not tasting his food. Why hadn't he considered what living in the same house with an attractive woman would do to him? And the way she looked at him sometimes. Her eyes so full of admiration and need. He'd turned away from that look for weeks, but now it was so much harder.

He'd actually come to like so much about her. Her smile, her devotion to the girls, the way she stood up to him, matched him wit for wit. Her determination to make things work despite everything he'd put her through and all the ways he'd tried to discourage her. Inside, he'd hoped that she'd be the one to give up, throw in the towel, and say enough is enough. But she hadn't. In the end, she'd been the one to call all of his bluffs and even take it one step further.

He had no doubt that if he called her now, she would come to him, disrobe, and allow him to possess her.

"What's wrong with me!" he asked, pushing the rest of his food away. He couldn't eat. Not with this turmoil in his gut. What would his lawyer say to this one? "Hendricks, I need to get an annulment because I want to hump my wife crazy." That didn't sound like adequate grounds. He didn't think a judge on earth would hear that and rule in his favor.

He didn't hear her come in. But he felt her presence. He looked up and took a sharp intake of breath. His loins ached for her so badly, he nearly doubled over in pain.

She was wearing a nightgown. A short one. It was translucent as hell. As if she were wearing a cloud. His heart boomed in his chest and his blood went hot with desire.

"You don't give up, do you?"

"Not easily."

Her gaze caught and held on his erection. He didn't try to hide it. There was no use in that or giving her what she wanted.

"Leave me alone, Amara."

His words deflated her. Her shoulders slumped and her head bowed slightly. She didn't move for what seemed like an eternity. When she finally turned to go, he said her name again. Or rather moaned it.

"Amara." It came out like a sultry whisper of smoke. He hadn't meant it to, but he couldn't help it. She'd gotten to him.

"Amara," he said again and she turned around.

"Come here," he said.

Nervousness, fear, excitement, and desire flickered wildly inside her like the head of a sparkler. She walked toward her husband, legs weakened from the desire in his voice. Add that to the lust in his eyes and she hoped she knew what she was getting into.

She stopped in front of him. He remained seated and slid his hands from her knees slowly up her thighs. His touch burned her skin. She gasped from the heat of it.

His hands continued their sensual ascension beneath her gown, lifting it up until her panties and bare stomach were exposed.

He moaned and pulled her close. Before her next breath, his lips were on her skin, sucking, licking, nibbling, traveling. Amara had never felt a sensation so incredible in her entire life. Shaking like a leaf, she wondered what Ross would do next.

His hands continued upward, blazing a trail of heat on her sides and on to her breasts. His touch was perfection. Nothing she could have imagined could compare to the flames of passion ignited within her burning out of control and the mere flick of his fingers against her nipples.

"Ooh," she crooned, knowing any moment now she would no longer be able to stand.

The pleasure was overwhelming. She wasn't sure how to respond. She wanted to throw her head back and bask in his attention. But her inexperience left her wondering if she should be touching him as well. Bringing him the same pleasure he brought her. And how could she, if she wasn't sure exactly what to do to please a man?

He pulled her down into his lap. His arousal pulsed hard and strong between her thighs.

"Kiss me," he said, voice thick with lust.

He didn't have to say it twice. She couldn't wait another moment to do the thing she'd wanted to do for more years than she cared to admit.

Amara lowered her head. Their lips met, tentatively at first, and then the intensity built with each second they pressed together.

Ross emitted a low growl and flipped her onto the couch. "What are you doing to me?"

Amara was too stunned that she was in Ross's arms to speak.

She could only lie relatively still while he removed her gown. In one quick movement he snatched off his shirt and threw it in the corner.

The muscles that she'd admired beneath his clothes every day hovered over her in 3-D. She couldn't help reaching up to touch the body that was now hers to touch. She ran her fingers over the soft skin and hard physique beneath. He was magnificent. He felt better than anything she could have imagined. And she realized that she could not stop touching him. She'd never be able to stop running her hands across his body.

He sat up a little. "Help me," he said.

When she realized what he was referring to, a thin ribbon of fear cut through her. He wanted her to help him out of his pants.

The thought of seeing Ross naked was so compelling, she began quickly undressing him by herself.

"Wow!" she said when he was finally naked. Amara hadn't meant to sound so astonished, but it was the first time she'd ever seen a naked man up close. And for that man to be Ross Hayward, and look as good as he did, she couldn't control herself.

He looked fashioned out of clay or chiseled out of granite or stone. Perfect as if an artisan, a female artisan, had experimented with perfection and created the man lying next to her.

"I don't know what's come over me," he said, nuzzling her neck, nipping at the base of her jaw. "But I like it."

When he took her mouth again, she moaned uncontrollably. On his lips, she tasted the sweet nectar of ambrosia. She was intoxicated with it.

Here, she thought. *He's going to take me right here.* Amara wasn't sure if she liked the idea of her first time being on a couch, but if it was with Ross it was perfect.

His fingers singed her flesh and they moved across the outside of her thighs. She squirmed when he hooked his hands into the elastic of her thong panty and slowly pulled it off.

He froze for a moment upon seeing her nakedness. "Beautiful," he whispered. He lowered himself on to her. "Like an angel."

With that he kissed her and Amara braced herself for what was coming next. Ross's manhood pressed against her leg, then her inner thigh, then her innermost core. She squeezed her eyes shut and waited for the pain she'd heard her friends talk about.

Ross's breathing grew heavy and his erection pushed into her farther, then farther still.

She winced at the discomfort and Ross's body stiffened. He pulled back and stared at her in wonder.

"This is your . . ."

"First time," she finished, voice winded with excitement.

His erection faded. Her hopes went with it.

He sat back. "I didn't know."

"It's okay," she said, feeling the magic slipping away and praying they could get it back. "Ross, I want to."

He shook his head and stood. "I won't," he said. "Put your clothes on. Go to your room."

Amara gave a startled gasp and blinked back her disbelief.

He turned away, feeling the shame burning in his chest.

A virgin!

The thought echoed in his mind like a bullet ricocheting in a canyon. He couldn't let her give herself to someone that didn't love her. She deserved better than that. Her transition to womanhood should be guided by someone who wanted more from her than to simply quench his lust.

Ross ran a hand down the front of his face, closed his eyes, grunted, reined in his libido. Desire raged within him like a caged lion, a lion that had tasted freedom and wanted more.

"This was a mistake, Amara. I'm sorry."

"Ross," she said, reaching for him.

"I gotta get some fresh air," he said and after yanking on his clothes, he left, leaving Amara baffled and disappointed.

It was several moments before she was able to gather her clothes and go to her room. She couldn't imagine a more unromantic first encounter than the one she had just experienced. Was the thought of her being a virgin that disturbing to him that he'd retreated as if he'd seen a ghost?

Maybe he *had* seen a ghost. The memories of a previous marriage were alive in her also. She felt them lingering in the air sometimes, watching, judging. Amara put her nightgown back on, went back to the den, and crawled under the covers, hoping that tonight didn't cause more friction between her and Ross. Whatever barrier he'd erected between them seemed to be falling—that is until they faced the most difficult barrier of all—themselves.

Ross drove around the block believing that getting some distance between him and Amara would help to clear his head.

It didn't.

Instead he was faced with the same feeling that had been building inside him for weeks—he wanted Amara. Wanted her badly.

He'd always found her attractive. The moment he'd laid eyes on her when she was sixteen, he thought that she was a cute little teenager who would probably grow into a woman that would drive men crazy.

He was right.

She had matured into a beautiful young woman who was driving at least one man crazy—him.

Ross pulled into the parking lot of a drugstore knowing full well what his intentions toward Amara were ever since he'd seen her in the kitchen that evening. Discovering that she was a virgin had taken him aback and reminded him of how serious an action he was taking— *they* were taking. He was shocked, that's all.

He stepped out of his car knowing that what his mind, body, and soul wanted to do could change his life forever.

He hoped he was ready for it.

Chapter 14

Maybe it was her smile that had gotten to him, or the way his children smiled when they were with her. Maybe it was the way she smelled, her dogged determination to make their house a home. It could have been his realization of everything she did to keep their life functioning regularly or the sexy way she looked in that short nightgown. He thought it might even be the fact that his body felt as though he hadn't had sex in decades and that Amara was, after all, his wife.

It could have been any of those things. And in fact, it was probably all of those things. But more importantly it was the fact that he'd fallen in love with the young woman who had come into his house like a fresh breeze. Despite all of his efforts, she'd cracked his hard exterior and gotten inside. And the part that floored him most was that he liked her there.

He sat in his office, surrounded by papers and a laptop, pretending to work. What he wanted more than anything though was to take Amara up on her generous offer, to cash in the rain check he'd taken in his mind, to possess her fully.

Since that night, they'd gone through the motions of a family with none of the emotions of a family. Both he and Amara refusing to acknowledge the awkwardness of their brief encounter but both of them knowing the simmering desire just one taste of each other had caused.

Slamming his fist down on the desk, he released a groan of anguish. The tension was killing him.

For several nights since, he'd kissed the girls good night, Amara had put them to bed, and then he'd retreated to his office and she to the den. The nighttime brought with it the hot pulse of lust. They both felt it. Only she was willing to do something about it. At the risk of her own virtue.

And he'd kicked himself for putting her in this position. Where her first time would come from a man who for months had no intention of consummating their relationship. If he'd stayed in that frame of mind, they could have ended this charade and she would be free to find a man worthy of her love and innocence. But now? Now the thought of her giving her virginity to another man tore him apart. If he took her now, he'd take her forever. Not just to subdue the lust boiling between them, but to symbolize his feelings.

To declare his love.

What he needed to do was talk to her first. Make his intentions known and give her a chance to refuse. He rose from the place where he'd sat for the last hour in pain and torment and headed for the den.

Amara stared up at the ceiling. She fingered the sheer fabric of her nightgown and sighed. If she couldn't wear her new purchases for Ross, she'd wear them for herself. Only it wasn't as exciting. She knew once and for all that Ross didn't want her. Didn't find her attractive. Not even to sate his lust. He'd turned away from her. She was ashamed.

It was all she could do to hold her head up in his presence. What man would turn down sex with his own wife?

The kind that doesn't want you as a wife. The kind that has someone else, a shrewd voice hissed.

Amara closed her eyes as a single tear tracked down the side of her face. She was too weak with sadness to wipe it away.

A faint knock and then the door opened. "Amara?" Ross's voice called, breaking the night silence.

"Yes," she said, sitting up slowly. She didn't bother to cover herself. She knew it didn't make any difference one way or the other.

"We need to talk," he said, coming in. Her beauty halted him. Even in the faint streams of moonlight siphoning in through curtain parts, she mesmerized him. He forgot his words and why he'd come. All he knew was the woman before him and the loneliness inside him. The one eclipsed the other.

"Amara," he said, almost whispered.

Why had he come? To make sure she knew her place, which was definitely not in his bed? Was there something wrong with the girls?

She sat straight up. "What's wrong?"

"Nothing," he said, too quickly. "No, that's not true. This is wrong."

"Us?" she asked as a brilliant bolt of fear surged through her. Was he asking her to leave?

"Yes. No! Damn it, Amara. You can't sleep here anymore."

Amara hung her head, deflated. Defeated. She'd lost. The only man she'd ever loved and the children she cared for as if she'd given birth to them herself. Tears stung the corners of her eyes. Lost in her own pain, she barely noticed Ross kneeling beside the bed.

He lifted her face. "Come to my bed," he said, half above a whisper.

Before she could question, his lips caught hers and drank slowly.

She jerked with the shock of it. Welted from the sheer pleasure of it. Sighed from the relief of it.

After kissing for what seemed like all too brief a time, Ross pulled away.

"Let me take you to my bedroom . . . our bedroom."

Amara nodded quickly before she could wake up from her fantasy. But Ross's strong arms around her, lifting her, told her that it wasn't a fantasy at all. This was the real thing. And Ross Hayward, the only man she'd ever wanted to make love to her, was about to do just that.

One hundred times, maybe a thousand, Amara had imagined what it would be like to be in Ross's arms. To kiss him, to hold and be held by him. She'd rehearsed every movement, every word. But now, lying before him on his bed, she couldn't move. Couldn't speak. No, that wasn't right either. She was moving.

Trembling.

"It's okay, Amara," Ross said, removing his shirt. "Don't worry. And don't be afraid."

She couldn't stop shaking. And when Ross removed his slacks and boxers, finally standing naked before her, she trembled even more in awe of his raw masculinity.

He moved in slow motion. The touch of his hand against her cheek calmed her a bit.

"Are you cold?" he asked, brushing his lips across her temple, then traveling further to the crook of her neck.

"N-no," she stammered.

His hand stroked her arm. His fingers hooked inside the top of her nightgown and pulled it down.

Her eyes bored into him. She was actually going to do it. Out of all the times she'd been in compromising situations with boyfriends, she'd never let them get any further than deep kissing and serious rubbing. But this time she was actually going to go through with it.

He removed her nightgown as if he'd been doing it for years. When she lay naked before him, a rush of embarrassment warmed her face. Totally self-conscious, she moved to cover herself. Ross held her hands.

"Don't," he said. "You're beautiful. Don't hide your splendor from me."

She relaxed a bit, but was still a bit shaky.

He scooted closer. The heat from his body scorched her skin. He leaned against her. She smelled the remnants of aftershave that had been applied hours ago, Paradigm cologne, and something else—desire!

He bent to kiss her. Her eyes widened and then closed as the hot softness of his mouth covered hers.

Instinctively she reached up, draped her arms across the back of his neck, parted her lips to receive him.

He took his time, tasting her, learning her, committing her to memory. She breathed quickly to keep up with the sensations rushing inside her body. Flicks he made with his tongue inside her mouth affected her elsewhere. Her spine tingled, her toes curled, her soul soared. It was so much so soon. His mouth tasted like peppermint, coffee, and her own perfume. His hand slid across her waist, back, then down to her thigh. She melted into him, felt herself drowning.

She had to come up for air.

Sensing her tension, he pulled away. Her eyes held an

alluring mixture of desire and shock. And there was something else. Fear.

"Just say the word, and I'll stop," he said, all the while thinking, *Please don't ask me to stop now. I'm not sure I could.*

The next four words from her lips were the sweetest he'd ever heard. "Ross, I want to."

He moaned deeply in response, donned protection, and sank against her.

His weight surprised her. Would she be able to hold him? Would he crush her? When he moved with it, slid his hips across her thighs, she had her answer. Yes!

Lifting himself slightly, he slid his hand down the middle of her body. She tensed, anticipating his intimate touch.

"I'll be gentle. I promise."

His fingers slid inside easily, though not all the way. Slowly, carefully, delicately he began a slow massage. He stroked in circles. The sensation thrilled and frightened Amara. Fear must have shown in her eyes.

Ross kissed her forehead. "Trust me," he said.

They both watched as he continued his rhythmic caress. The same rhythm, but a different feeling. The pleasure she felt grew stronger as if something wonderful was being pulled steadily to the surface.

Amara relaxed with it and let go of her fear. Her breathing increased. She moaned. It was a sound she had no control over. It simply came from the pleasure. She was starting to feel blissful, drunk, weightless.

"Yes, let go," he said. He kissed her again. More this time. Softer this time. The moans came again.

Her hips moved. She couldn't control them either. They just moved. Matching his slow attention stroke for stroke.

Another wave of pleasure hit her. As if she were being carried up a ladder of sensation. The closer she got to the top, the greater the feeling. She went with it, ascending and not looking down.

She wanted to fly.

"Ross," she whispered, feeling herself reaching the apex.

She was close. He could see it in the rapture on her face. He could feel it in the hot moisture on his hand.

At the very second when she shuddered through her release, he entered her.

Amara stiffened and gasped at the hot snap of pain between her legs. It felt as if she'd been stung by a bee.

Once inside her, Ross was still. He stroked her hair and stared into her eyes. She was frightened again.

"Okay?" he asked, barely able to speak. The sensation of being inside a woman again was almost too much for him. Every fiber in his sex-deprived body yelled for him to take her quickly, hotly. Now there was no turning back. He needed to come. Had to come. He closed his eyes and searched for restraint.

When Amara leaned up and kissed him, he moved.

Amara closed her eyes, feeling full and connected and one with Ross. *This is what it's like to be joined with someone,* she thought. *This is what it's like.*

She wanted to experience it all, feel it all, see it all. She inhaled deeply, amazed at the aroma of their lovemaking. Her hands kneaded and caressed Ross's back. Her fingers worked the hard muscles. Her eyes swept around the room. What she saw sent a jolt of guilt sailing through her body.

She was in Brenda's room.

Her things were still here. The curtains she'd made, the walls she'd decorated, the bed she'd slept on.

The man she'd loved.

Oh, God. Was Ross thinking about Brenda? Comparing her to Brenda? Wishing she was Brenda?

As her husband moved carefully in and out of her, the pleasure Amara derived from it shamed her. Yet she was powerless to stop it.

Until this very moment, she hadn't let herself fully realize how much she missed her friend or how hard it was to fill her shoes. Did she do the right thing marrying Ross? Trying to be the girls' mother?

Her pleasure grew along with her guilt, her remorse, her love for Brenda and Ross. It was overwhelming her.

She began to sob.

Looking up, she saw fresh tears in Ross's eyes and anguish. He felt it, too.

With every second he came closer to climaxing, the grief over his wife's death increased. He hadn't allowed himself to grieve for Brenda, and no matter how much he tried to prevent it, he was doing it now.

He grieved for her companionship. For her as the mother of his children. For the anniversaries they would never have.

Most of all, he grieved for himself without her. He'd become someone he didn't know after her death. A person that deserved from this moment on to be buried.

A tear dropped from his face on to Amara's. The power of their lovemaking compelled them to move together. The force of their grief compelled them to cry together. The strength of their love made them come . . . together.

When their tears subsided, Ross kissed Amara deeply. She lay limp while he kissed, petted, and stroked her until he was hard again.

A fresh condom, and he entered his wife again. To

the questioning look on her face he said, "That was about anguish and lust. Now, let me show you about love."

"Yes," Amara said, voice thick from weeping, and surrendered to her husband.

Amara knew that her aunt Ashley was an extremely healthy eater, so she'd prepared a special lunch for the both of them. Organic bean curds on a bed of fresh dandelion greens, a bowl of sliced papaya, guava, and plantains, tall glasses of rice milk with a side of alfalfa tea cakes, and for dessert, frozen strawberries dipped in carob. She wanted to know all of her aunt's tricks, and so showing her that she not only appreciated her dietary choices but could prepare them as well would go a long way to making her aunt happy *and* talkative.

When the doorbell rang she was ready—she thought. But when she opened the door, nothing could have prepared her for the sight on her porch. Not one but all of her aunts had showed up. A lump of dread sank to the bottom of Amara's stomach.

"Aunt *Ashley,*" she said, pouting.

"I know you didn't expect me to do this alone," Aunt Ashley said, smiling.

"Hey, baby girl," Marti said, grinning.

Morgan sauntered in. "Hi, sweetheart."

"Amara, you look happy, honey," Roxanne said.

Her aunts came in and bestowed their greetings as they entered the living room. Amara closed the door behind them, knowing exactly what she was in for. Instead of getting a one-on-one question-and-answer session with Ashley, she would have to sit and be quiet while her aunts talked on and on about what they knew, experiences they'd had, and lessons they'd learned. These "shut up and listen" sessions all ended the same way, with one of her aunts saying, "Do you understand?" Most of the time, the answer was no, but Amara would always smile and say yes to make them feel good. They could talk for hours sometimes. Remembering that shooed the feeling of dread away as Amara realized that this time they would be talking about sex. Maybe this wouldn't be so bad after all.

"Since I didn't know you all were coming, I just made enough for me and Aunt Ash."

Roxanne swung an arm around Amara's shoulders. "When you have a big family like ours you learn how to stretch things. Let's just see what we're working with."

When the women reached the kitchen, the groans of their disappointment filled the room. Ashley, however, was elated.

"You did all this for me?" she asked, squeezing past her sister to hug Amara. "I love you," she said, and kissed the middle of Amara's forehead.

Amara thought the frown on her aunt Marti's face was comical. "Is there a Popeye's Chicken near here?" Marti asked, holding up a dandelion leaf as if it were a bug. "If I eat another meal with a name that I can't pronounce, I'm going to scream."

Amara's youngest aunt's husband had lots of money and from what she could tell was not afraid to spend it on the best of everything—which apparently included food.

"There's a food court at the mall." Rutgers's Outdoor Mall was only four blocks away from her house. Very convenient for shopping and picking up a fast food meal when necessary. Amara was just about to suggest that they walk over when there was another knock on the door.

"That must be my neighbor," Amara said. "She stops over from time to time." Before she could respond to her aunt Morgan's "I don't think so" remark, she opened the door. At the sight of her mother standing on her porch, the lump returned to the pit of her stomach and grew larger. Amara thought she was going to be sick.

"I know you didn't think you were going to have this discussion without me, did you?"

Yolanda Fairchild entered her daughter's home to moans of disappointment.

"Okay, I'll eat the food. Just make her go away," Marti said.

"Aunt Ashley!" Amara shouted. "How could you!"

"It wasn't me this time. I only invited the cool-spirited people."

"Morgan told me and I'm glad she did!" Yolanda said, chest heaving and arms flailing dramatically. "If anyone's going to school my baby in the ways of the bedroom, it's going to be me!"

Amara hung her head. All she wanted to do now was dissolve into a corner where no one could see her.

Roxanne Allgood-Storm snapped at her sister, "Morgan, how could you do that? You know how Yolanda is. She'll scare the poor girl into never having sex."

Amara retreated into the kitchen, determined to let them duke it out for a bit. She busied herself by looking in the refrigerator and cupboards for something she could whip up that they all could eat. By that time, her aunts would have worked some of the tension out of their system and she would try to gain control of the situation. After all, they were in her house and she was not some naive teenager that needed to be shushed out of the room during "grown folks' talk." She was a married woman now. A married woman who had every intention of keeping her husband satisfied, whether she got advice from her family or not.

"That girl ain't scared to have sex. And she never will be again," Yolanda said, taking a seat in the largest chair in the living room. Her younger sisters followed her into the room and took seats on the couch and on the love seat.

"What do you mean?" Morgan asked.

"I mean, my baby's not a virgin anymore."

"What!" came the cries of astonishment from the aunts.

"Everything okay in there?" Amara asked from the kitchen.

"Yes!"

"Um-hm!"

"How do you know?" Marti asked in a lowered tone.

"A mother knows. And besides, you see the way she's walkin'? That's the walk of a fully grown woman. And by that little bounce, I'd say she likes what she's getting."

When Amara emerged with a tray of iced tea and lemonade, the room fell silent. All eyes were on her and she felt self-conscious immediately. She looked from relative to relative, not wanting to know what was on their minds but feeling she had an idea. "I'll be back with some sandwiches," she said, placing the tray on the coffee table.

The moment she stepped into the kitchen, the living room erupted.

Amara ignored the sound, and smiling, grabbed the bread from the box to make sandwiches.

"Well, then, maybe she doesn't need us. Maybe she can teach us a thing or two."

"Hush. My baby is liking it, but she's a little scared. That's why she called witchy woman. She wants to know all those tricks you use on men."

"I beg your pardon. It's not a trick. It's tantra. And it's based on normal body energy. And besides, it's not men, it's man. I do have a *man* now."

More whoops!

"She sure does! When are you and Gordon going to belly dance down the aisle together?" Roxanne asked.

"As soon as our schedules allow. We're thinking about a fall wedding."

"This fall, Aunt Ashley?" Amara asked, returning with a trayful of cold sandwiches. *A cold meal is just what a hot July day calls for,* she thought. The sisters smiled and dug in.

"So what do you want to know, sweetie?" Ashley asked with a mouthful of salad.

Amara glanced at her mother. A twinge of embarrassment moved through her, but she suffered through it. She'd taken on the responsibilities of a husband and three daughters—a ready-made family. Certainly she could handle discussing sex with her mother in the room. She swallowed hard, determined to get the most out of what her aunts knew.

"I want to know how to get Ross off and I mean really get him off. He . . . that is, I . . ."

"Told you she likes it."

"Mom!" So it wasn't going to be as easy as she thought. Well, she was determined to get through it. "I need some advice."

Morgan spoke first. "What kind of man is he? I mean he seems like a take charge kind of person. Almost military."

"He sure does," Roxanne agreed.

"He likes things a certain way. He has an idea of the way things should go and he gets frustrated if they don't go that way."

"Control freak."

"Mom!"

Yolanda leaned forward in her chair. "If you're going to shout *Mom!* at me every time I say something, then I'm leaving."

"Good," Amara said. A few of her aunts looked quite pleased with the idea of their eldest sister leaving.

"Please," Yolanda said. "You couldn't pry me away from this house with a pair of ten-foot pliers."

"Well, at least try to be more supportive," Roxanne said.

"All I'm saying is that if the man likes to be in control, then what he needs is to be tied up."

The room fell silent. Jaws dropped. Amara couldn't believe that her mother, the queen of prim, proper, and upstanding behavior, was talking about tying a man up.

"See, y'all thought I was wrong. I invited Yolanda for a reason," Morgan said, smiling.

After that, the conversation was on. Amara nearly faded into the background while her aunts, and from time to time her mother, spoke freely about sex, making love, and what they'd done to turn men on. A lot of the things they spoke about, Amara had never heard of. Sometimes she would have to stop them and have them explain things to her like positions, toys, and aphrodisiacs.

They described different ways to touch a man. They all had funny names like the Washing Machine, the Jackhammer, and the Cake Decorator. They mentioned something called a *kegel* muscle and told her it was important to keep it fit. They stressed using protection and birth control.

For a while she just listened and tried to commit everything to memory. After a while, it became difficult to keep up with everything her aunts were saying. The ideas were coming a mile a minute. So she got out a pad and paper and took dictation as if she were a secretary in an office building.

"One time I made a man come so hard, he had a bowel movement at the same time," Morgan proclaimed.

"Ugh!" they all shouted unanimously. When their cries of disgust quieted down, Amara asked with a hushed voice, "How'd you do it?"

"Well, just at the moment when I knew it was gettin' real good to him, I slid my finger into his behind and—"

"Ugh!" came a louder response.

"Don't knock it. If you rub the spot just right, you will send your man into orbit. I'm telling you, you can make a brotha cry!"

Amara could feel the look of shock on her face. "So, did he . . . on your finger?"

"Oh, no!" I could feel that he was about to have the big O, I'm talkin' the big, big O. So, I pulled my finger out just in time. Ol' boy was cryin', comin', and dumpin' all at the same time!"

Roxanne shook her head. "Don't believe her! She's making that up."

Morgan threw up her hands. "I swear it's the truth!"

The room filled with bright happy laughter.

"Now if you really want to make a man cry, beg, plead, and promise you the world, there's only one thing you've got to be good at."

Shouts of agreement reverberated in the room.

Amara's curiosity was piqued. "What?"

"If you want him to beg, you've got to get on your knees."

Amara's eyes widened again. As the image grew in her mind, her face drew up as if she'd just bit into a lemon. "I thought black women didn't do that."

"Yolanda, what have you been tellin' this child?" Roxanne asked.

"The truth!"

Roxanne took her niece's hand. "Honey, it's a wonder your father is still with your mother."

Amara shook her head while her aunts chuckled softly.

"I don't want to do that," she said.

"Well, just in case you ever change your mind," Morgan said, "let your aunties give you a few pointers."

Amara's mother huffed and turned her head while Roxanne, Morgan, Ashley, and Marti proceeded to give her an in-depth session that could easily have been called Oral Sex 101. She got information on methods, styles, and techniques called Hoover, Kirby, the Black Hole, and something called the Swish and Flick. Amara took copious notes . . . just in case.

Soon after that discussion, Amara noticed her aunt Ashley fiddling with the collar of her blouse. "What's wrong, Aunt Ash?"

"Oh, I'm just feeling a little warm. My red chakra is swelling and turning." She squirmed at bit. "This conversation is . . ."

"Making me hot," Roxanne said, fanning.

"I *mean*," Morgan responded.

Marti popped the gum she'd been chewing. It sounded like small firecrackers going off. "I think I need my husband."

"That's right," Yolanda said, rising. "You all just take

your hot tails on home, filling my daughter's head with all of your stories and instructions."

"You started it, with your tie-him-up idea!" Marti said. "Don't get mad at us because we finished it."

Yolanda smiled. "I must admit, that tie-him-up idea was a good one. And if he's used to giving orders, he'll still want to do that. So, let him. Tell him you're going to be his love slave and anything he wants, you'll do. He just can't use his hands or move around to help. Now depending on what he asks for, you might have to . . . uh . . . try some of that vacuum stuff. But only if he asks for it!"

Amara watched as her mother grabbed a napkin from the table and fanned herself with it. "What?" Yolanda asked. "I'm just having a flash."

But everyone in the room knew better.

Seconds later, her mother and her aunts all made excuses to leave. She knew it was because they'd talked themselves into a state of need and it was time to try out some of the things that they'd talked about.

At the door, Amara noticed that she was feeling a little tingly, too. She couldn't wait to try out some of the things on Ross. It would be such a turn-on to her to get him turned on. She told her aunts good-bye, kissed each one of them, and thanked them for coming and being so open and generous about their advice. Her mother was last to leave, as she knew she would be.

"If you really want to know what your husband likes, just ask him, sweetheart," she said.

Amara kissed her mother on the cheek. "I'm glad you stopped by, Mama. Even though I'm embarrassed beyond words."

"I'm glad I stopped by, too, baby. Remember, you keep your man happy, and he'll keep you happy."

"Okay," she said, watching her mother get into her car and drive away. She realized she still had a long way to go before she thought she was a good wife and a good mother. But her mother had been married to her father almost twenty-five years. So, she had an example of how to keep a marriage together. And although she and her mother didn't always agree on everything and had had their moments, Amara knew that no matter what, her mother would be there for her, even when it came to something as intimate as keeping her husband happy. With a support system like that, Amara felt she was ready for anything.

Chapter 15

When Ross came home from work, he knew immediately what was wrong with his wife. The girls ran to him, and yipped like puppies to be held and picked up. Amara stood over the kitchen sink, nearly trancelike, drying a few dishes and staring at him. Her eyes registered wonder, hunger, and just a hint of fear. It stoked the fire of his ego and swelled his chest. He'd turned her out. He was sure of it. He watched her carefully as she fidgeted over the sink and shifted her weight back and forth. She was hot. He could see it in her eyes. *Uh-huh. Turned out.*

He didn't mean to do it. Well, in a way that made his ego feel damn good, he had wanted to give Amara pleasure beyond her wildest fantasy. What man wouldn't? He just hadn't imagined that creating such pleasure could also cause such a challenge.

She wouldn't let him sleep. Every night, several times a night, she would wake him up with kisses, strokes, or just an out-and-out shove. He loved making love to her. But doing it so much was starting to affect his job, his strength. And his back was killing him.

Yesterday, he remembered embarrassingly, when Amara had nudged him at five A.M., she said she wanted to give them plenty of time to "do it" before the girls woke up.

"Baby, I just got to sleep a few hours ago."

"I know," she purred. "But I miss you when you're gone."

He turned over. "I have to get some sleep."

"I have to get some of you. Please, Ross. Please."

He hated it when she begged for it. It always made him horny. No matter what.

She draped a luxurious thigh over his leg. She'd showered quickly after their last tête-à-tête and smelled fresh and alluring.

"Please, Ross. It feels so good when you do it to me. Make me feel good again, Ross. Baby. Make me feel good."

His soldier was in full salute then. Going without sex these past few years left him with an abundance of pent-up sex drive. Add that to the fact that he was giving it to her good and he couldn't resist making her cry again or taking her so deeply she bucked like a bronco in response.

He turned over and touched her lightly on the shoulder, the arm, a nipple. She was trembling already.

He pushed her down upon the bed and rose above her. Putting on another in a long succession of condoms, he was determined to give her the kind of loving she'd pleaded for. The kind that would last her through the day.

His eye caught the cobalt garter belt on the nightstand. Amara watched ardor flicker like golden tongues of fire in his eyes. Her skin prickled with anticipation.

Ross picked up the lace garment and knelt beside her. "I know I'm supposed to be taking this *off*," he said, the words sliding out like tender caresses between lips licked and eager. *But under the circumstances,* she thought, finishing his sentence in her mind.

Small sweet gasps escaped her lips as heat from Ross's fingers singed her flesh and made her crazy with desire. A rash of tiny explosions went off inside her, each taking her deeper and deeper into Ross's sensual possession.

His hand rose up her thigh, raising the garter higher. The gesture of her husband putting her garter belt on mirrored their relationship. How they'd come into it backward by getting married and *then* falling in love. And just like the shape of the belt, they had come full circle as a couple, finally finding their way back to each other. Finally creating a love of their own.

"Oh, Ross," she moaned, welcoming him. Her warm arms crossed around his neck.

"Amara," he whispered, knowing he wanted her as much as she wanted him. And for making him feel like a king again in his own castle, he would love her the right way, for a long, long time.

By the time they'd finished making love, he was already late for work. Rushing in, he'd made it just in time to attend his first meeting of the day. When he arrived in the conference room, he sat down among his colleagues and listened while one of the employees continued on a half-hour-long brainstorming session. Ross only participated in the first ten minutes. After that he was out like a light. No one even bothered to wake him until the meeting was over.

This morning was a repeat of yesterday except that he'd run out of the house without shaving, and it was his own meeting that he'd fallen asleep in. Midsentence he'd drifted off. When he went to the men's room to splash cold water on his face, he saw a man who looked like he hadn't slept or eaten in at least a week. And nothing he wore matched. Not even his shoes. People were beginning to talk.

Something had to be done.

"Hello, Amara," he said.

"I've been playing with the girls all day," she said. "We played so hard and so long that we skipped a nap, didn't we, girls?"

"Yep," Trinity said, "and I'm tired."

Ross smiled knowingly. "Why don't you girls go play in your room? Daddy needs to talk to Amara."

"Okay," came the youthful chorus.

Before the girls were up the stairs good, she came to him. Like a moth to a flame, she touched him, rubbed him, humped him.

"Hey, hey, hey. Slow down," he said, holding her hands, which had been roaming all over his body.

"Ross, I feel so . . . so . . ."

"I know," he said feeling the heat rise. He nuzzled her neck, tasting its sweetness. "I know."

"I can put the girls to bed; then we can—"

"Hold up," he said. "It's just six o'clock. We've got all night."

"Please, Ross," she said, freeing her hands and caressing him again. "I need to . . . feel like last night. Please . . ."

Yep, he thought to himself. Turned all the way out. She needed to come now or they'd never have dinner or put the girls to bed properly.

"Turn around," he said.

"Don't you want me to take my clothes off?"

"No," he said. "Just turn around and stand against me."

She did as he instructed her and he walked her over to the cabinet. With her back to him, he reached around, placing one hand across her breasts and reaching down into her pants with his other hand. Just as he thought, she was hot and dripping wet. His erection grew. She moaned.

Quickly, he found the orb of her pleasure and stroked it. With building intensity, he rubbed it, flicked it, and teased it. Her moans grew louder. He shushed her.

"The girls are upstairs," he whispered. "Try to control yourself."

"I can't . . . can't help it, Ross," she hissed.

"Daddy?" came a small voice from behind them.

Ross continued to pleasure his wife knowing that his bulk hid her body from his daughter's view.

"Yes, Trina," he said, without turning.

"Can we watch TV in your room?"

"Yes," he responded, hoping that Amara wouldn't cry out or moan loudly.

"Okay," she said.

Just when he thought the coast was clear, his daughter spoke again. "What are you doing?"

"Helping Amara get something. Go watch TV, okay, sweetpea?"

"Okay, Daddy."

At the sound of little footsteps retreating, Ross felt Amara shudder and burst open like a damn. Female ejaculation could be just as forceful as male ejaculation, as she came all over his hand. He smiled, proud of his work. He turned her around.

"Better?"

Her face was still drunk with passion. She panted, "Yes," and collapsed against him.

He held her and was reassured by the thought that Amara's sex drive was so strong, it would easily match his own. But as much as he loved making love, he knew that with three small children, quenching that sexual thirst wasn't always going to be easy. In fact, he knew it would be a challenge. Especially if he had to travel.

He looked her in the eye, wondering just how much of a virgin his virgin was.

"Next time, you might have to take care of this yourself, while the girls are napping."

Amara straightened her clothes and Ross washed his hands in the sink. "I mean masturbate. You do masturbate, don't you?"

"No!" she said, a look of shock sending her eyebrows into the hairline of her forehead.

Ross realized that he had his work cut out for him.

That night, when the girls were asleep and they were in bed, he brought up the subject again.

She'd come to bed wearing nothing but her birthday suit and had been pawing him since the moment he'd lain down.

"Amara, I think it would be a good idea for you to spend some time with . . . yourself."

"What do you mean?"

"I mean you need to get to know you. What you like, what you don't like. Your sexual responses. Your G spot—"

"That's what I have you for," she said, kissing his hands.

"I'm serious, Amara. The other night was your first time, and from your response it was good for you. But it can be so much better than that."

"Better?" she asked, sitting up.

Her breasts bounced on her chest and Ross thought he would explode at the sight of them.

"Yes, better," he said, redirecting his thoughts. "But I can't make it better by myself. You have to know you.

You have to be comfortable with you. You have to teach me what you want and how you want it.

"I'm not a mind reader. And although I will admit I know a little somethin' somethin' when it comes to the bedroom, every woman is different."

"But that's so nasty," she said, slumping down on the bed. She looked so disappointed and rejected.

"Who told you that?"

"My mother."

"Your mother grew up in a different time, and has a different set of values. You have to create your own values."

Ross snuggled close to Amara and stroked her cheek. "Now if you try it, and I mean give it an honest try, and you don't like it or don't learn anything about yourself, then fine. We'll just have to fumble through it together. But if I'm right, and you learn some things that you didn't know before, then you've done our union a great service and you won't feel so pent up and in need. And more importantly you won't wear a brother out!"

At that, he brought a smile to Amara's face.

"Tell me, how did you feel all day today?" He traced a finger across her chest, feathered his fingers over her nipples, and began a slow descent down the center of her body.

Amara purred. "Like I was chained up and I needed to be freed."

"Really?" he said, dipping his fingers into her feminine core.

"Yes," she whispered. "It was painful, Ross. I wanted you so badly."

He pushed his fingers inside and slid them out until she moaned with abandon. Just when he had her where he wanted her, he stopped.

"What are you doing?" she asked, eyes snapping open.

"I'm giving you a chance to . . . explore the unknown."

"Ross!" She all but screamed his name.

"Nope. You'll get no more from me until you try it yourself." He licked his lips. "I'll watch, though."

Amara's shoulders slumped. She looked so sad, it pained him. He lifted her chin and stared into her eyes.

"I can show you some things that you can do while I'm at work that will cool your urges—help you get them under control. Do you trust me?"

She nodded.

"Then trust that I would never force you to do anything you didn't want to do. But I can help you find some relief when you need it . . . at least something that can tide you over until your man comes home."

"My man?" she asked, shock heightening her voice.

"That's right. Your man. Now are you down or what?"

The next night, while the girls were asleep, Ross gave Amara her first lesson.

"The first thing you have to realize, know, and accept is that this is *your* body. You can do anything with it that you want. As long as you are not hurting yourself, hurting someone else, or doing something immoral like French-kiss a pig. Understand?"

"Yes," she said.

"Okay. Now take your right hand and stroke your left arm."

A knot of awkwardness tightened in Amara's stomach, but she did as he asked.

"No, not like that. Imagine that your hand is my hand. Now touch your arm the way you would like me to touch it." His gaze bored into her eyes. Into her soul. She shuddered.

"Touch yourself the way you want me to touch you right now. Close your eyes if you have to."

She did as he asked and imagined that it was Ross's hand on her skin, stroking, caressing, kneading.

"That's right," his voice crooned. Now move your hand . . . my hand . . . anywhere on your body you want me to touch. Show me where. Show me how. Guide me with your mind. Make me touch you."

Amara took a deep breath and went with the sensations. She wanted Ross to touch her so badly, she ached. And he was touching her, wasn't he? Caressing her. With not one hand, but two? Couldn't she feel him stroking her? Everywhere?

Her arms. Her sides. Her thighs. Her stomach. Her breasts.

"Yes," he whispered. "Let me touch you, baby. I want to touch you. Open up, so I can touch you."

She did. She spread her legs wide and let his hands roam freely. His fingers dipped inside her and she cried out.

"Does that feel good, baby?"

"Yes," she responded, feeling her heat rise, her emotions culminate, her need grow.

"Can I make you feel better? Let me make you feel better, baby. Let me take you there."

"Yes!" she shouted, as his hands caressed her breasts and stroked her core. It was building, just as it had before. That maddening sensation that made her feel as if she were flying apart and coming together at the same time. He was taking her over the edge. She couldn't hold on any longer. His hands felt too good. Oh, God, so good! So . . .

"Ah!" she cried out as waves of ecstasy crashed over her. Amara's body shook with each one, jerking like a mighty pulse.

She peeled her eyes open to see her husband's smiling face beside her. Another glance saw her hands buried between her legs.

She smiled, too.

"I love you," she said, revealing for the first time feelings that she'd felt for years.

He kissed her mouth fully, then pulled away after a few moments of heated tongue exchange. "I love you, too, Amara."

Quickly, he yanked off his pajama bottoms, put on protection, and straddled her.

She gasped and smiled.

"My turn," he said, and entered her slowly.

For the next six days, Ross surprised Amara with a new "lesson" every night. He warned her that he was going to tempt her with a variety of things. What she liked, he would continue and also encourage her to experiment with. What she didn't like, he would never approach her with again.

For lesson two, he brought her something she'd seen in many magazines as a back massager. When he touched her at her most sensitive spot, she knew it to be much more. With that device, he taught her what it was like to be multiorgasmic. She'd never known such pleasure was possible and now knew that most of her friends were lying when they'd described their escapades. Until then, she'd felt like an outsider and like she'd been missing out. But now that she knew what it was like, she knew what her friends had described wasn't the half of it. She and Ross had taken turns with the massager until she'd had more orgasms than she could count.

"No more," she said, huffing. "My legs will never stop shaking."

"Wait until tomorrow," Ross said. "You ain't felt nothin' yet."

The next day, he brought home a straight-up vibrator. Except that it wasn't straight up. It was curved.

"Where do you get this stuff?" she asked.

"That's in my advanced class," he said. "You're not ready for that yet."

"Oh," she responded.

"Women are phenomenal creatures," he said, laying her down and undressing her. "You all can have all kinds of orgasms. Clitoral, vaginal. I can't even name them all. But this," he said, closing in with the brown, hooked, rubber thingy, "is designed for the G spot."

After that remark, he kissed her, stroked her, and invited her to touch herself in preparation for that night's lesson. Amara abandoned herself to all of her husband's requests, trusting him implicitly. And when she was fully aroused, he proceeded to show her exactly where her G spot was and how pleasurable it could be having it stimulated. It felt so good, she thought she might urinate on herself. Afterward, Ross explained that that sensation was normal and that she should not let it interfere with her pleasure.

"How do you know all this stuff?" Amara asked, quaking after her climax.

Ross stared at the ceiling and without hesitation said, "I loved Brenda very much and made sure she was satisfied in every way possible."

At that moment, Amara remembered that she was in Brenda's bed, making love with Brenda's husband. Clouds of remorse and betrayal darkened the room.

"Don't," Ross said. "Don't shut down. And don't feel guilty."

Amara turned to him with tear-filled eyes. "Is this wrong?" she asked.

"No," he said, holding her. "It's what she wanted. Don't you see? It's what she wanted," he repeated as a single tear tracked down the side of his face.

His tear washed with Amara's in a mixture of sorrow and elation. Someone they loved and cared about deeply was gone forever. And out of the ashes of her death rose their love. They were fated. Even as they rocked and consoled each other, they knew in their hearts that a force beyond their control had brought them together.

And they were thankful.

On the next night, Ross did not disappoint her. Although her day had been filled with tending to the house and taking care of the girls, in the back of her mind, she thought of the night and what new experiences it might bring.

"Let's take a shower," he said.

"A shower?" she said, letting her disappointment show through in her voice. "I thought I was going to get another lesson."

"You are," he said. Then he led her into the bathroom and proceeded to show her the wonders of water pressure and a carefully aimed handheld showerhead.

"What do you think?" he asked, when they were both drenched with water.

"I think you are wearing me out!" she said, barely able to stand.

"Just hold on," he moaned, kissing her face, lips, and

neck. He licked the water from her skin and Amara dissolved at the sensation of his tongue against her skin. "You've got three more days," he whispered, then made love to her while the showerhead whipped around in the tub below them.

By the fifth day in her "schooling," Amara felt like a new woman. She had more energy with the girls and Shasta mentioned how joyous she seemed.

"What's gotten into you?" her neighbor had asked. "You are strutting around here like you've just won the Powerball. What's going on?"

Amara mashed her lips together to prevent a cheese-eating grin to give her away. But she was too late.

"Oh, I see. Ross has been taking care of his husbandly duties. Am I right?"

Amara picked up some of the girls' toys that were scattered throughout the living room. "No comment," she replied.

"No need," Shasta said. "It's all over your face . . . and your arms, and your legs, and—"

"Okay. I'll just say that life as a wife definitely has its perks."

"Service on the regular," Shasta responded. "I really miss that."

At that moment, Amara wanted to ask her an extremely personal question. But she felt she didn't know her well enough. She just wished she knew if what Ross was saying about women "handling their own business" was true.

"I guess from here on out, it's going to be *self*-service for me," Shasta said.

Amara's eyes widened in shock and then the two women shared a laugh and went to the kitchen to make tea.

* * *

When it was time for lesson number five, Amara was ready. But it seemed her husband was not. She was already in bed wearing nothing but a T-shirt. However, Ross was sitting up, pajama bottoms still on, and he was reading the paper.

"Honey . . ." she cooed, tugging at the red silk on his legs.

"Hmm?" he said, seemingly oblivious of her need.

"What about tonight? Do I get another lesson?" Amara slid her legs against each other, already feeling tingly. And the aroma of Ross's cologne didn't help much. He'd showered before getting into bed and he smelled like something eatable. Something she wanted in her mouth right now!

"Ross!"

He leaned over and gave her a peck on the cheek. Then he scooped something off of the nightstand and stood. "I have some work to do before I go to bed. I'll be in my office. I won't be long."

Her heart plummeted. He couldn't leave her like this. Not after she'd been waiting all day. Well, that wasn't altogether true. While the girls were asleep, she'd tried that battery-operated thing. It wasn't bad. But it wasn't her husband. "Ross! What about—"

"Shh. You'll wake the girls." He stopped at the door, his handsome muscle-bound frame filling the doorway. "Don't I always take care of you?"

She nodded.

"Then don't worry."

She watched as the man she loved sauntered out of the bedroom. Amara gnawed lightly on a knuckle, hoping that Ross would come back soon so that the aching between her legs and in her soul could be quenched.

Reluctantly, she lay down and closed her eyes. Maybe she would sleep until he returned. But it would be difficult. She marveled at how easily she'd become accustomed to not sleeping alone. At first it was strange having someone in bed with her. Another person, a man, breathing beside her, taking up space beside her. But the warmth he generated next to her comforted her. And because he weighed so much more than she did, she found her body tipping toward his. But even that just felt right. Now that her bed was empty, she felt empty.

The ringing phone didn't give her a chance to wallow in her thoughts any longer. She answered it quickly so it wouldn't wake the girls.

Who would be calling this time of night? she wondered. "Hello?"

"Hey, baby."

Just the sound of Ross's voice launched shivers from head to toe. She smiled. "Where are you?"

"I'm in my office. Where are you?"

"I'm in the bed, silly!" She chuckled.

"Really? Are you lying down?"

"Yes. Ross—"

"What are you wearing?"

"You know I'm wearing your T-shirt."

"Umm," he said. "Take it off."

"What?"

"You heard me."

"Why?" she asked, but she was beginning to get the picture.

"Because I want you naked, like me."

"What! Ross? What if the girls catch you like that?"

"I locked the door. I suggest you do the same. Now what are you wearing?"

Amara locked the bedroom door, flung off the T-shirt, and whispered, "Nothing."

At first she felt awkward, and a little embarrassed, as Ross's deep voice whispered sweet sensual things through the receiver. He told her how beautiful she was, how desirable, and how he would spend the rest of his life keeping her satisfied.

"What are you doing now?" he asked, voice husky with arousal.

"I'm throbbing, for you," she said, lightly touching all the places on her body that wanted him.

"Know what I'm doing?" he asked.

"What?" she responded, breathless, barely coherent.

"I'm brushing the back of my hand against your neck."

Her fingers moved automatically to the place on her neck where she felt his touch. And for the fifth night in a row, he became her teacher. Even across phone lines, he helped her explore her body, gave her a guided tour of her own sexuality. She realized in this escapade of learning more about herself, she was also learning about Ross. Trusting Ross. Building a strong bond with her husband—one she hoped would never be broken.

She didn't know such closeness was possible.

He continued to murmur to her, urging her along the journey to ultimate satisfaction. And she went gladly, freely, turning herself over completely to his urgings.

His words alone were enough to take her over. He told her repeatedly how much he cared for her, wanted her. Loved her. Words she'd waited years to hear. She sobbed with elation.

She knew then that even as she was alone on the bed, she was not alone. As long as she was Ross's wife, his presence would always be with her. To protect her and do the things a husband is supposed to do for a wife.

"Oh!" she moaned.

"It feels so good when I'm inside you," he whispered.

His words seeped in through her pores and took her up.

"I love making love with you, baby," he said, panting. "I love, ah, come with me baby," he coaxed.

"Yes," she muttered, flying apart.

"Come . . . with . . . me!"

"Yes, Ross! Yes!" she said, as love for her husband burst inside her and broke her into pieces.

Totally spent, she dropped the phone to the floor and lay against the bed immobile and heaving for breath. She heard Ross shouting her name from the receiver, but she couldn't move right now.

A few short moments later, Ross pounded on the bedroom door. "Amara! Are you all right? What happened?"

She peeled herself from the bed and managed to unlock the door. He stepped inside and scooped her into his arms. Carefully, he placed her on the bed and stroked her hair.

"I love you," he said, and placed delicate kisses all over her face. "Do you know that?"

He glanced up for a moment. A distant shadow covered his features for a moment. Then he turned back to Amara. "I didn't think I would ever say those words again. But it's true. I can hardly believe it myself. But I want *you* to believe it."

His hot gaze bored into her eyes and seared her soul. "With all my heart, Amara. I feel like a husband, again. A father, again." He took a deep breath. "A man, again."

And Amara, in all of her twenty-two years, felt like a fully grown woman.

Chapter 16

The sun rose lazily over the Savannah horizon. It came up in a warm yellow glow on a sweet September morning. The temperature was seventy-five degrees and Amara and Ross had slept outside all night long. But *slept* wasn't a good word to use to describe their evening. For the better part of the night, they did everything except sleep. They ate, talked, laughed, played, drank, and made love. For Amara, the experience was more perfect than the word *perfect* could define, explain, or ever represent.

The girls were spending the weekend with their aunt Marti and uncle Kenyon. The way the girls had fought over who was going to get to hold Kenyon Jr. first still played cutely in Amara's mind. Marti had her hands full. And if she knew her uncle Kenyon, he'd probably hired someone to assist them in taking care of the triplets. He had lots of money and had no problem spending it.

When Ross first brought up the idea of a weekend getaway to Savannah, Amara thought the idea sounded like he was spending a lot of money. And with only one person in their household working, that was money that would be better spent on the girls or bills. But Ross explained that he'd mentioned to Shasta if she ever won a free vacation, he'd be glad to take it off her hands. When she finally did, he'd offered to compensate her for it, but she wouldn't take anything. Just said that she wanted her two favorite people in the world to go away and have a great time.

And that's exactly what they'd done.

Amara didn't want this time with Ross to end. She loved the girls and loved taking care of their household, and yet there was something special about spending time alone with her husband. Something she treasured with all her soul.

"Do we have to go home today?" she asked Ross. She'd been snuggled beside him for the past few hours and could tell by his breathing that he was no longer asleep.

"We can do anything you want to do, kiddo."

"Can we make love again?"

Ross laughed and pulled her closer. "You sure know how to make a man feel like a man."

"And you," she said, sitting up a little, nuzzling his neck a little, "sure know how to make me feel like a natural woman." She sang the last few words.

He slid his arm beneath her, lifted her onto his chest. His eyes, still languid with sleep, bored into hers. "What do you know about being a natural woman?"

She shuddered, surrendering to the power of his very glance. "Everything my mama told me and everything that my husband has shown me."

"Well, then, kiss me and prove it."

Her mouth descended upon his with eagerness. She remembered all the lessons he'd taught her last night. But most of all, she'd learned the lesson of love. He'd taught it to her when they were in the middle of discussing the new direction of their relationship and she just couldn't keep her hands from roaming his body.

"I brought you here so that I could share with you the most important lesson of all."

"What?"

"How to make love."

Amara frowned with confusion. "Ross," she said, stroking his thigh, "we've been making love for weeks now."

"No we haven't. Not really. We've been having sex." He stopped her strokes by grabbing her hand and kissing her fingers.

"What's the difference?"

"You've been focused on sex because of the way it feels. Now it's time to focus on love because of what it means."

Amara trembled. Maybe anticipation caused it. Maybe fear. Or maybe it was the truth in what Ross was saying and the implications of that truth.

The way she felt was indescribable. She felt like rain. Like a sun dream. Like an emerald. Like open sky. Like some be-bop blues on a Coltrane day. Like a misty morning bathed in possibilities. Like three sunsets splitting a purple horizon. She stroked her arm and felt randy and new born. Her eyes felt heavy-lidded. She couldn't get enough of what she'd wanted for so long. Now that she had it, she wanted to bask in it, savor it, experience it over and over and over until she was sure it was real.

She'd never had so much attention in her life. She wanted to soak all of it up. Take it into her pores until it became her—a permanent part—like a tattoo on her very soul. Like DNA, she wanted it to be part of the very fabric of who she was. Her love for Ross and the girls. Their love for her. If it had been liquid like water in a pitcher she would have turned it up and gulped it down.

She felt like orange blossoms in spring. Like the sun splitting on the horizon. Like a song. Like a smoky bar full of jazz riffs and spoken words. She felt free and bendable. Like a new day. Deep like the set of Ross's eyes. She loved seeing her reflection in his dark browns. Loved the taste of herself on his lips. Ripe like a fruit. Like a night in Jamaica. A bird soaring. A ship sailing. A star falling.

Like a woman truly happy.

"Umm," Ross said. He'd been watching her. Staring. Studying. "Please tell me I have something to do with that expression on your face. And with the way you changed just now. The way your body just softened. The way your breathing deepened. The way your spirit settled."

She looked up. The sun shining behind Ross bathed him in a warm orange glow. He looked as though if she touched him, her fingers would melt.

She touched the side of his face anyway. No longer afraid of the fire or the change she felt in herself.

"You are . . . a little."

He stroked her hair. Planted a kiss on her forehead. "Just a little?"

She smiled. "I've got to give myself some credit. It takes two to tango, you know. Besides, I've grown a lot since marrying you. I've allowed myself to grow. I've forced myself to grow. And yes, you helped me with that." Amara laughed. "You should have come with a label. 'Warning: can become habit forming.'"

"Sounds like a good thing to me," Ross said from the crook of her neck.

How drastically her life had changed, she thought. Looking around, she realized it would be easy for her to forget her past while surrounded by expansive beach, and warm sand, strong breezes, and blue water gulf. The sounds of the water lapping, lapping was enough to make her forget everything she had been before her wedding day.

"What?" Ross asked, seeing a flicker of pain in her eyes.

"I was just thinking," she said, sitting up, "I've got to put all this in perspective. I mean, it's nice, don't get me wrong. But back in the real world I've got some issues I need to resolve."

Ross sat up then, his face a ball of concern. "What kind of issues?"

"With my family mostly." Amara waited a beat, then swallowed hard. "With my mother mostly."

Ross remembered when he had first met Amara. Based on what Brenda had told him about her, he'd expected to see a depressed young woman. Although she was far from that, there was still a sadness in her eyes. The same sadness he was seeing now. Maybe if she talked about it . . . "Tell me about your mother."

Amara turned to him, face serious. "My mother is a unique person. I think self-absorbed would be a good way to describe her. She's a mother when it suits her, which isn't very often.

"How much do you know about when I was in high school?"

"Some," he said.

"Well, so I won't bore you with the details, I'll give you the microwave version. When I was sixteen, I pulled away from people. Everybody. I think I was trying to avoid being close enough to people so that they couldn't hurt me. If I'm not close to anyone, I can't have expectations of that closeness or start creating crazy notions in my mind of relationships. Heck, my mother never did anything I expected, like care about me in any kind of deep, obvious way, so why should anyone else?"

"What about your father?"

"My father loves me. But he also loves my mother. So much that he doesn't think straight half the time. She has no idea how to appreciate a man like that.

"Anyway, I just stayed in my room and played video games. I didn't go out. Didn't talk on the phone. Stopped hangin' out with my friends. My friends became Zelda, Lara Croft, and Parasite Eve.

"They were all on quests for treasure and I guess in a way, I was too. A quest to find the treasure of my mother's love."

She looked up to the sky. Felt a tear trickle against her cheek. "Brenda saved me. She taught me that I can love myself despite what others think, say, or do. She taught me that some people have a hard time expressing how they really feel or sometimes express how they feel in unique ways. But most of all, she taught me how to save myself.

"So did you have something to do with the way I feel today? Yes. You did. Brenda did. But mostly . . . I did."

The morning was warming up fast. If they didn't get inside soon, they might run the risk of actually burning their skin. "Ready to go inside?" Ross asked.

Amara nodded. For the first time in her life, she felt like she was ready for anything.

She was sleeping so peacefully, she would have sworn that she was floating rather than lying on a bed.

Somewhere between twilight and being awake, Amara felt Ross's hands caressing her stomach, kneading his way to her chest and breasts.

She came to a little, but only a little. She was still nestled inside that sweet place where the best dreams manifested themselves. Ross's attentions became more deliberate, methodically, exploratory as his fingers slid in circles over her breasts. At first she was in heaven, deliriously happy that her husband wanted to make love again after such an active night of sharing each other's bodies and souls. But the more her consciousness awakened, the more she realized that he wasn't being amorous. He was being something else entirely.

Her inner smile faded and she opened her eyes.

"Ross?"

He was quiet. His eyes flickered with bright intensity in the early morning light. His fingers continued their circular path.

"Ross . . . don't."

He didn't look at her—only the place where he examined her like a highly trained physician.

She placed her hands over his. "Ross . . ." she said again, more quietly this time, the realization of his actions sinking in, deepening her love for him.

She raised her arms above her head, giving him full access.

"Will you let me do this for you . . . every month? I have to make sure, babe. I can't . . . go through—"

"Thank you," she whispered, basking in his love for her. "I promise. Every month. I must admit though, I am disappointed. I thought I was about to learn another lesson."

"Disappointed?" Ross said, swinging one long,

muscular leg over her. "Here's my promise to you. You will always leave our bed happy."

Amara's entire soul smiled. She threw her arms around his neck and knew with her entire soul that Ross Hayward would keep his promise.

Wind in her hair. Sun on her skin. Ross by her side. Amara felt dipped in love the way some strawberries are dipped in chocolate. She thought back to their passion of the last few nights and closed her eyes. She didn't know if Ross had done it or if she'd allowed it, but all she knew was that her desire had been set like a thermostat. All of the feelings and emotions that raged inside her nearly unchecked for the past few months were now at rest. It was as though they'd finally found the right frequency and would no longer drive her crazy.

She remembered wanting so badly to confess to Ross. To tell him that she'd loved him since she was sixteen. That she'd always loved him. That she'd felt so guilty for so long for loving him. That she still felt guilty sometimes. Like she was doing something wrong. She knew if she told him, that he'd make it right. That getting it off her chest was her absolution.

But the words wouldn't come.

They were naked on the beach. He'd been on top of her. Kissing her, stroking her, caressing her. And she'd been wound up like always, but steadily uncoiling to his tenderness.

"Ross," she whispered, looking up at him. "There's something I have to tell you. Something . . ."

He kissed her eyelids, ground his hips hypnotically against hers.

"Ross, love . . . I've loved you . . ."

"Shh," he said, brushing his lips against her jaw, the nape of her neck. Lingering there nipping, moaning. He kissed his way to her mouth and covered it with his. She couldn't have felt anymore drowned than if she'd jumped into the gulf and plunged at that very moment.

Then he let her breathe. Ross ran the pad of his thumb over her lips. "Don't tell me with this," he said. He stroked her arm, her hand. "Tell me with this."

He rubbed her breasts, her chest and stomach. "With this," he said, voice lowering with need.

He kneaded the flesh of her thighs, strummed his fingers against her calves. "With these," he urged.

From her calves, his hand traveled slowly up the center of her body and stopped at her core. "With this," he said, then settled himself once again on top of her and kissed her senseless.

The waves of the gulf lapped to their kiss. The wind blew in gusts in time with their kiss. Even the radiance of the sun seemed to shine to their rhythm.

And being a good lover, Amara did as she was told.

Thinking back on it now, Amara realized she'd done things with her body last night that she hadn't known were possible. And she'd made sure that with every movement, every gesture, every undulation, touch, flick of her tongue, press of her lips that she sent Ross the same message over and over. *I love you. I've always loved you. I'll love you for the rest of my life. I'll never love anyone the way I love you. No man will ever come close. I love you, my husband.*

Ross's reaction to her declaration was beyond anything they'd experienced before. She'd turned the tables and driven her passion in him. In the end, all he could do was lie beneath her, quivering and moaning into his climax.

* * *

"Amara, Kiddo, why did you do it? Why did you agree to this marriage?"

His question pushed the effects of the relaxing waves away from her psyche. Her stomach jumped nervously. The one thing she hadn't admitted out loud was the fact that since the moment she'd seen him, she welcomed the chance to be his bride.

The more she thought about it, the more the sense of dread tightened her stomach muscles. And then she realized that that wasn't it. The reason she married Ross had to do with her past, not her future as his wife. Something inside her wanted, needed to be for those three girls what her mother had never been for her. Her soul, like Brenda's, would not rest unless she knew the girls she loved with all her heart received all the love, affection, attention, encouragement, and support they deserved. She would never have forgiven herself if she hadn't done everything possible—including marrying Ross—to ensure their happiness.

She loved them too much not to. And she told him exactly that.

Chapter 17

The life of a wife and mother truly had its ups and downs. After experiencing so much of the upside of that life, experiencing the down took Amara by surprise and drained her.

Ross was working on a Saturday again, so Amara decided to take the girls on an all-day outing. Shasta had given her several mall discount coupons and gift certificates. She'd saved them for a special day like today. But when Amara had tried to awaken the girls, none of them wanted to get up. When they finally did, they were grumpy and argumentative, and they refused to do anything cooperative.

The girls gave new meaning to the phrase *children will be children*. Between their toothpaste wars, screams, and shrieks of "Mine! Mine!" over blouses that were nearly identical, and refusing to eat their favorite breakfast, Amara's reasons for assuming the job as mother were being thoroughly tested.

Why did it sound like such a wondrous privilege to stay at home, play with the girls, go to the mall, and be a day lady? The reality of the lifestyle was much more demanding than Amara had ever imagined. Now she understood fully why her mother and aunts had asked her repeatedly if she was sure about what she was doing.

"Girls!" she shouted, exasperation raising the volume of her voice. "You are going to put your jackets on, we are going to get into the van, I'm going to drive us to the mall, we're going to spend money, and most of all, we're going to have a good time! Do you understand me!"

Three girls, who looked more like Ross with each passing day, were stunned into silence, which was surprising since they'd been yelling all morning.

Their facial expressions were priceless. They stood side by side, six eyes as wide as saucers. The scene was almost comical until Amara realized that this was the first time she'd ever raised her voice to them.

She could tell they were trying to decide if they wanted to cry. Amara knew that if Trinity started, the other two would follow suit.

"Come on, girls," she said, changing the intensity of her voice. "Let's get going. We can stop at Popcorn Palace first and get rainbow popcorn balls."

It didn't change their expressions, but they seemed to relax a little. She couldn't help thinking that they looked as though they'd been frightened by one of the monsters in *Monsters, Inc*.

She couldn't stand the thought of the girls thinking of her as a monster. She vowed never to raise her voice so severely again.

On the drive to the mall, the girls were unusually quiet. Aside from occasional whispers among themselves, Amara hadn't heard a peep. She couldn't remember one van ride with the girls where there wasn't at least one incident of hitting, pushing, singing, shoving, screaming, giggling, or crying. There was always something. She'd come to expect van-drama as part of the rhythm of her children, and it frustrated her to no end. But this silence was much, much worse. They were punishing her for going overboard.

"Anybody wanna sing the cookie song?" For a brief second, she saw a light in Trinette's eyes. But it faded and she was back to her typical morose self.

"Mara? Can we go to Toys R Us?" Trina whined.

Amara knew instantly that if she said no, the next sound from Trina would be high-pitched and excruciating.

Before she could say yes, Trinity butted in. "It's *A*-mara, Trina. How many times do I have to tell you?"

"You're not Daddy!" Trina snapped.

Trinity crossed her arms. "I *know* I'm not."

"Then stop talking like that!"

Their bickering pushed Amara to the end of her rope. "Okay! Okay! Girls . . . settle down or so help me, I'll turn this van around and go home. And when we get there, there will be no TV, no toys, no outside. Understand?"

The expression on their faces said that they'd temporarily forgotten how mean she'd been to them earlier, but now they remembered. Now they understood. Amara hoped that they wouldn't test her. She really needed some time away from the house. It would be a shame to ruin the first nice day they'd had in a while. It had been raining for a week. The forecast called for more rain. She would hate to miss an opportunity.

On the flip-side, Amara was exhausted. If she wasn't careful, she'd be ill again. Ross had advised her against doing too much. He asked her repeatedly if she needed help. Brenda's mother called at least once a week to see if Amara needed anything. She was so used to having to be independent and responsible that it was hard for her to recognize when she needed help sometimes.

When she parked the van, she thought, *Not anymore. After today I'm going to take everyone up on their offers.*

As they entered the mall, a panhandler approached them and asked for spare change. She was an old woman, her skin dark and leathered from too many days in the elements. The dress and shirt she wore over it were on their way to being rags. She smelled like a sewer in summer.

The girls grabbed on to Amara's leg and held tight, their eyes once again large with alarm. Amara wanted the woman gone, and fast. She rustled inside her jacket pocket, grabbed the change she had there, and handed it over to the woman. The old hag grinned. Three decaying teeth smiled at Amara, and then the woman scuffled off toward what Amara imagined was her next victim.

"Come on, girls," she said, making sure her voice was full of reassurance. "Let's get inside."

Apparently, Amara was not the only one who wanted to take advantage of a break in the weather. The mall was packed.

"Remember what I said," she told the girls. She'd made them promise to hold hands and stay close. And there was to be absolutely no running off.

"What do you think? Food? Or shopping?"

"Shopping!" the three squealed in unison.

Just to get it out of the way, Amara maneuvered them through the throng of people and into Toys R Us. If they got a toy in their hands, maybe they would be good for the remainder of their outing. The plan was toys, clothes, a meal, and then home. In addition to coupons and certificates from Shasta, Ross had given her a hundred dollars. They were going to have a ball!

For identical triplets, they couldn't be more different. Trinity wanted a Harry Potter book. Trina wanted a fairy princess wand. Nettie chose a Blue's Clues puzzle. Even with their different choices, Amara wondered how long it would be before they were swapping toys and fighting over who had what. Ross's solution would be to purchase three of everything, but Amara was determined to teach the girls compromise and respect.

When they left the toy store, they ran into a clown dancing a jig in front of a new store's grand opening. They stopped to watch. After a quick and humorous performance by the clown, the four of them laughed their way to the clothing store. For the peace it gave Amara, it was like skipping down the yellow brick road.

The afternoon turned into something wonderful. The girls were a delight, trying on dresses and picking out shoes. They spent every one of the coupons and certificates Shasta had given them. They even spent half of the money that Ross had given them. Within the span of three hours, they were loaded down with packages.

Energy bubbled inside Amara. The only thing that could have made the afternoon more perfect was if her husband had been there with them. But spending hours shopping was not Ross's idea of fun. Just then Amara decided to buy Ross a present. She would take the rest of the money that he had given her and do something for him that he would never think of doing for himself—buying something nice.

Amara threaded them through the crowds until they made it to the men's department at Von Maur. They weaved in and out of the traffic of customers eagerly sifting through sales racks and discount displays. The store was having a huge clearance.

When they made it to the notions department, Amara was pleased with their selection of leather wallets. The girls fidgeted at her side while she slid her thumb across the soft eel skin and leather of each billfold.

"Mara, I have to go to the bathroom," Trina declared.

"Can you hold it for a second, pumpkin?"

"Okay," she said weakly.

Amara scanned the selections quickly, intent on finding something special. Most of the billfolds were 50 to 70 percent off. There were so many choices, it was hard for her to decide. She decided to take Trina to the rest room and then come back and make her purchase.

When she glanced down at the girls, all thoughts of a gift for Ross vanished.

Trinette was gone.

Trinette had been trying to get away from her sisters all afternoon. The harder she tugged, the tighter her sister Trinity held her hand.

It made Trinette so mad, she almost said something. But that would be bad. Talking was bad. When her mom first got sick, her daddy had told her how important it was for her to be quiet. So she was quiet, but she hadn't been quiet enough, because her mom had gone away.

But Trinette believed that her mom would come back if she was very, very quiet.

And she'd been practicing for such a long time. She wondered how much longer she would have to not talk.

Her sisters talked too much. They made her want to talk. She'd been trying to get away again when the best thing happened.

She saw her mother!

She was walking down the hall outside the store, wearing a soft pink sweater and a blue skirt. Pink and blue were the colors Trinette knew. She was glad her mother had chosen to wear those colors.

With one hard yank, she pulled away from her sister and took off toward her mother.

Everything around Amara blurred to gray. Her maternal instincts took over. She grabbed Trinity and Trina by the wrists and sprinted through the crowd. Her eyes darted from child to child—searching frantically for a glimpse of the lavender and powder-blue fabric on Nettie's dress.

She couldn't have gone far, she thought.

"Did you see where she went!" she shouted at the girls.

"No," they said, voices quivering with alarm.

"Why did you let her go! I told you all to hold hands!"

Trina's tears spoke for her. But it was the look of terror on Trinity's face that jolted Amara to the core. Maybe Nettie hadn't just wandered off.

"Did anyone bump you, brush up against you, try to hold your hand?" she asked, all the while praying that the answer was no.

"No," Trinity said, as they dashed down aisles, between customers, and around displays.

Desperation and fear collided and crashed inside Amara like a mighty thunderstorm.

"Nettie!" she called. "Nettie!"

"Nettie!" the girls echoed.

"Stop playing, Nettie!" Trinity shouted.

Fear rose in Amara's throat and left a flat metal taste in her mouth. People stepped back and shifted out of the way as her search became more and more desperate.

And more bold.

"Have you seen a little girl, three feet high, wearing a blue and purple—"

"No," a woman said. And a man, and another woman and another.

"She looks like me," Trinity said, choking back tears.

Oh, dear God, Amara moaned to herself. Why was she wasting time describing Nettie, when Trina and Trinity looked just like her!

Because she couldn't think! Couldn't breathe.

She stood shaking at the entrance of Von Maur, scanning the area in all directions for any sign of Nettie. Her stomach turned over like an icy lump.

"Mara!" Trina shouted and pointed to two small bags beside the wall. The three rushed over. Inside the sacks were Nettie's things, untouched.

Gone, Amara's mind whispered.

Suddenly it was as though a cold fist were closing over Amara's heart. For a moment, she thought she would be sick.

"Ma'am! Ma'am!" a male voice shouted, but it was too late. Amara plummeted to the floor as if a trapdoor had opened beneath her.

The police had given them a ride home. Amara barely remembered it, or the face of the officer that kept asking her questions.

All she remembered was the questions flashing through her mind like warning signs. *What if a stranger has her? What if an evil person is poisoning her? What if she's hurt? What if she's sick? What if she's being molested? What if she's . . . she's . . .*

A dizzying wave of terror spun her again. As she settled the girls into their beds, her eyes didn't miss how their faces were stricken with fear.

Amara drew up courage she didn't know she had to reassure her daughters.

"We'll find her," she said, voice unusually calm. "You know how your sister is—always fascinated by colors. She probably saw balloons and went to play. Now you two go to sleep. I'm going to do everything I can to make sure your sister is home by the time you wake up."

She hoped the half smile on her face was enough. She hoped the weak conviction in her voice was enough. She hoped her unsteady hand smoothing their hair, tucking them in was enough.

She prayed to God, *Please let it be enough*.

Amara would not be able to deal with her own fright, panic, and hysteria if she had to deal with the girls' too. And right now, she had to use every resource available to her if she was going to get Nettie home safe. She thought she'd heard somewhere that in the case of a disappearance, the first twenty-four hours were critical.

She sank into a couch in the living room and hadn't realized until then how much sheer determination was holding her up. It certainly wasn't strength. That had drained out of her the moment she'd seen Nettie's packages at the store entrance.

Von Maur store clerks conducted an extensive search of the store as well as stores nearby, and came up with nothing. The store manager had taken Amara and the girls into an office area and offered them something to drink. The ordeal became a blur after that. She knew that the police had been called, and that they'd come and asked her some questions. She thought they said something about searching the mall and not finding anything. What she knew was that from that moment on, she clutched the girls tightly to her chest and did more praying than she'd ever done in her life.

The next clear memory she had was that of being walked to her door by one of the officers who'd shown up at the store.

She sat in the dim of the room marveling at how everything there was in its place. It seemed like over the past few days, she'd gotten some kind of rhythm to her role as wife and mother and she was doing a much better job at balancing her responsibilities.

The knickknacks on the shelves were freshly dusted, the floor vacuumed.

Not a sofa pillow, wall hanging, or house plant out of order. The place looked like the living space of an ordinary happy family. How could this be when the world had suddenly gone wrong?

Then the memories hit her.

Faces of women, of families with children all going about their normal lives shopping, laughing. Existing. How dare they look so regular when the sky had fallen and a beautiful little star from that sky was missing?

As the sheer magnitude of Nettie's disappearance tore at Amara's insides and brought her to tears, Ross Hayward walked in the door.

Chapter 18

"What did you say?"

He'd approached Amara tentatively. As soon as he'd come through the door, he saw her crying in the dimly lit living room. And she'd looked up at him, eyes painfully miserable and swollen a deep red.

He thought she'd said, *Nettie is gone*. But that couldn't possibly be right.

"What did you say, Amara?"

He watched as the woman he'd grown accustomed to needing like air—the young woman he'd seen in just a short period of time blossom into a full-bodied wife and mother—dissolved before his eyes into a tearful, shaking, crying child.

The gravity of what she'd said brought him to his knees at her feet.

She was hysterical. He had to get her to tell him what was wrong.

He clasped her arms firmly. "Amara. Honey. I need you to tell me what's wrong, baby." A hard rock of anxiety burst inside him. "Now, it sounded like you said—"

"Nettie is gone," she repeated, as her tears flowed like rain down her cheeks.

His grip tightened. "What do you mean gone? Gone where?"

She looked up at him. Eyes as sad and long as a wino's weekend. "She's missing."

Ross bolted upright. "Nettie!" he hollered, sprinting toward the stairs. A crazy form of anger and desperation propelled him up the stairs and into his daughters' room.

"Nettie!"

Trinity and Trina lay tucked into their beds. Their heads popped up, a groggy expression on their faces.

"Where's your sister?" he asked.

Their mute response chilled his veins like ice. He headed back to Amara, leaping down the stairs in groups. She was at the foot of the staircase waiting for him.

"We, were shopping . . . at the mall and . . . and one moment she was there and . . . and . . . the next, she was gone. We searched . . ."

Anger and shock warred for control within him. He moved to the sofa table and grabbed the phone and dialed 911.

"What are you doing?" she asked weakly.

"I'm calling the police."

She touched his arm. The caress of her hand felt like cold snakes against his skin. He pulled away.

"I've already spoken to the police. They came and searched the mall. They brought me and the girls home. The police—"

"I'm calling them again!" he shouted.

Amara recoiled from his outburst like a whipped puppy. What had she done? Ross wondered. How had she managed to lose Nettie? How long did she look? Did she say something to make Nettie run away? Did she strike her? Did she refuse to buy her the toy she wanted? What was the trigger? Nettie would not have just gone off or run away without being prompted. What had Amara done?

For months, he'd asked the Lord to send him a sign—give him some indication that this marriage was wrong. Each time he'd prayed that prayer, he'd gotten just the opposite. Something would happen to show him how good Amara really was for the kids. Then things changed. He began to see how good Amara was for him. He'd forgotten all about his annulment plans.

Now, in the wake of his daughter's disappearance, he remembered fully what he'd promised himself: if it turned out that Amara's presence in the girls' lives was in any way detrimental, he would end their marriage.

This was no accident—no par-for-the-course parentage. This was a sign.

He loved Amara with his whole heart. But he loved his girls with his whole being. He would do anything to protect them. Anything. Even if that meant divorcing Amara.

When the police arrived, Amara recounted her story for the benefit of the new officers on the scene, but more for Ross's benefit.

He was afraid. She could see it in his eyes. But his words and actions represented those of an animal, recently released from his cage, and ready to pounce on unsuspecting prey.

Amara had never seen him in such an enraged state and she hoped she never would again.

There was something else that frightened her. In addition to the fear she felt from Nettie's disappearance, the man she'd first married had returned. The man who'd gazed at her with disdain and resentment.

Ross marched across the living room as though he were trying to wear away the carpet. She had tried to approach him, to touch him, talk to him, but he wouldn't let her. Neither had he tried to console her or accept her consoling. Amara felt as though she'd just been tossed into a freezer—cold, cut off, and alone.

The turmoil of the next fifteen minutes swallowed Amara whole. Between questions from the police officers and Ross's frantic ranting, she thought her soul would explode. She could not just sit back and wait for news of Trinette's whereabouts to be brought to her. She had to *do* something.

"Ross, I think—"

"Shut up! I don't want to hear what you think."

The veins in Ross's neck were drawn tight like cords. His words stung like a lash against her skin.

"You're not being fair."

"You *lost* my *daughter!*" he shouted, his voice loud enough to shake the furniture.

It shook something else. Amara's resolve. She snatched an umbrella from a stand by the door and rushed out of the house before the shocked expressions on the officers' faces could get any worse.

It had been raining for maybe half an hour, but to Amara, it seemed as though it had been raining all day. The moment she stepped outside, the steel-gray sky cracked open with thunder. She opened the umbrella and sprinted toward the mall.

Four blocks later, Amara was shaking off the excess water as she entered the entrance of Von Maur. She refused to believe that Nettie had been abducted. She hoped that she hadn't and prayed with all her heart that she had somehow wandered off and gotten lost in the crowd.

As she raced through the mall, eyes darting to every small face, in every cranny, thoughts of her ordeal replayed through her mind.

The store manager immediately closed the exits to the store as soon as Amara reported Nettie's disappearance. Then the message, repeated more times than Amara could count, had come through store loudspeaker. "Trinette Hayward, please go to any courtesy counter. Your family is lost and looking for you."

After nearly an hour of detaining customers and checking every person leaving to make sure there wasn't a little lost black girl tagging along beside them, they reopened the store and extended the search. Meanwhile security guards were alerted and all video cameras were checked. Either Trinity had disappeared into thin air, or she'd somehow been missed among the throng of people shopping.

"Help me," Amara remembered saying over and over, voice breaking with fright. "Please help me."

Unfortunately there was no sign of her. But Amara was undaunted. Fate could not have brought the girls into her life just to take one of them away. She'd already suffered a serious loss, she would not survive—or allow—another.

Large drops of rain struck her face. It was hard for her to see. Still she searched on as the bad thoughts that she'd worked so desperately to keep out of her mind pushed their way in.

What if she hadn't just wandered off? What if a stranger has her? What if she's hurt? What if an evil person is giving her something to eat that will make her sick? What if she's being molested? What if—

Amara's methodical search turned into a brisk run as one dizzying wave of terror after another hit her full force. She'd made quick work of one end of the park and headed for the other. The bad end. Where the homeless had created residences out of benches, boulders, and overhangs. She'd always told the girls to stay away from that end of the park. Blood pounded in her throat at the thought of her little girl there, all alone, or worse, with someone.

After a while Amara realized she was running and shouting. The rain did a good job of muffling her yells of "Nettie! Trinette!" But nothing could stop her. The gray sky made it even more difficult to see. Evening looked more like dusk and a normal, even-tempered woman looked more like a panic-stricken banshee as she rushed into the area where people wearing tattered and disheveled clothing clumped like throwaways around barrels and bushes.

If Amara had been more observant, she would have noticed the rain letting up just a little and the clouds moving swiftly, allowing intermittent flashes of sun to shine through.

But she didn't. The only thing she noticed was her own despair. Growing and insurmountable. She drifted past the people as if she'd been washed out to sea. Her daughter was gone and amidst twenty or so individuals, Amara felt disconnected and alone.

Without thinking, she did what she'd always done as a kid when she felt this way.

She sang.

Something silly that couldn't possibly cheer her up but held a long-standing comfort nonetheless.

First you get the bowl, and it's time to begin
Butter, sugar, flour, the ingredients go in

Her voice was faint, strained with tension. She walked slowly now, the umbrella no longer protecting her from the elements, but retracted—a plaything for idle hands.

She didn't realize she was singing the cookie song until she heard the echo of a voice singing it with her, between raindrops.

She stopped in her tracks.

There was nothing. She was hallucinating with her ears. Sound mirages, she'd heard them called once. "Dear God," she said, putting in an emergency request to talk to her Lord and savior, "please let me find her, please let me—"

"Cookie-face cookies—"

Amara sprinted in the direction of the sound. "Nettie!" she called, hope racing through her veins.

The voice she heard was faint and sob-choked. But it was a voice.

It was *Trinette's* voice.

Amara sang louder, hoping her daughter would join in.

"Round on the pan with lots of lovin'."

All the while thinking, *Tell me where you are, Trinette. Sing with me.*

She heard the voice again. It came from a group of women huddled together near a Dumpster.

"Cookie-face cookies." A little girl's voice trembled out the words.

Running toward the women, Amara saw a small person between two of them. She was holding on to a woman's hand.

If my daughter is hurt, I'm going to jail for murder, Amara thought, eyes narrowing at the old woman. Then a flicker of recognition registered in her vision. It was the panhandler from outside the mall.

"I *knew* you would come," the old woman said, walking toward Amara.

Amara halted in front of them—anguished, elated, and out of breath.

"Nettie," she said, grabbing Trinette and hoisting her into her arms.

Trinette looked as if she'd been playing in the mud, but aside from that everything looked fine.

The old woman rambled on. "I knew you would find us. I didn't want nothin' ta happen to this little missus here. I took care of her!"

"God bless you!" Amara said, tears mixing with the rain on her face.

"Mama," Trinette said, and hugged Amara so tight, she wondered how such a little girl could have so much strength.

"Let's go home, baby," Amara said, thanking God, and took her daughter home.

Chapter 19

The office of Atlanta Family Health was supposed to be pristine and relaxing. White walls, tepid prints of flat green leaves, and kaleidoscope flowers as a border, he supposed, to liven the mood.

It didn't. But at least the flowers were real instead of fake. Ross hated fake flowers—even the silk kind. All his life, he'd been a proponent of the real thing. Real flowers and plants, real butter, real sugar, not that saccharine crap, real hair and nails on a woman.

Real love.

What had led him to this point in his life, where he and his daughter were waiting to be called back into a psychologist's office for treatment? He couldn't believe where life had brought him and the lengths to which his life had been changed, and all in the span of a few months.

Amara sat with them. Well, not exactly *with* them. More like across from them. She sat there herself of her own accord. She knew better than to try and act like part of the family. She'd forfeited that right when she carelessly lost Trinette in the mall. And now, they were all paying for it.

A thin man emerged from a back room. He was tall and had an all-natural quality to him as if he spent many a day doing Pilates, meditating, and eating macrobiotic food. His expression was peaceful, serene.

Those kinds of people got on Ross's nerves.

"Mr. Hayward," the man said, his salt-and-pepper hair a bit wild and very shiny on his head. Ross thought he sounded like Mr. Roberts.

The man extended his hand. "I'm Jeremy."

Just like I thought, Ross mused. *He doesn't want to be called Dr. Park like it says on the door of the office.*

Beatnik, Ross said to himself and extended his hand anyway. If this man wasn't as good as his cousin Suzette said, Ross might never speak to her again.

"This must be your wife," Jeremy said, smiling.

Not for much longer, Ross thought while Amara and the psychologist shook hands. Then the tall man squatted until he was Trinette's height. "I'll bet your name is Trinette."

Trinette just stared and blinked a few times and clung on to her dad tightly.

Jeremy stood. "Come on back," he said.

As they walked into what Ross imagined was Jeremy's office, Ross smelled the faint aroma of what seemed to be peaches, baby powder, and rainwater. He didn't know if it was the psychologist's cologne or something the office piped in through the vents to relax the patients. Aromatherapy, he thought. Well, it wouldn't work on him. He was determined to keep his wits about him where his daughter was concerned. He slid a glance over to where Amara walked quietly in front of him. He had to have his wits about him when it came to her, too. Sadly he'd let his guard down, let her into his life, his soul. And now he was paying the price. Thank God he'd gotten Trinette back. Thank God nothing had happened to her.

The inside of Jeremy's office was more of the same. Plain, bland, neutral paint, plants, and accents. It was probably supposed to calm, but all it did to Ross was annoy him.

"I just want my little girl back," Ross said, not waiting for Jeremy to start.

"Well, that's a great beginning," the psychologist said. "Let's deal with that. You said you want your little girl back. Back from where?"

"From wherever she's gone." Ross said, glancing in his daughter's direction. From the neck down, she was the same little girl, give or take a few pounds. She wore the same pink frilly clothes, had the same tiny hands, the same scampering feet. But her face was a plain of sadness. It hurt Ross to see it. The pain cut him so deeply, he wondered if he would survive it.

"It's like only part of her is here. The lively part, the part that asks a million questions, the part that plays with her sisters, the part that spills things, and laughs . . . the part that loves and loves life—is gone. And I've tried everything." Although no tears fell, they were raining down inside. He could barely think or breathe. The truth of his daughter's pain came down on him like an avalanche. The feelings consumed him, stole his breath.

"I want Nettie back, from wherever she's hiding. I want her back."

Jeremy nodded. "Why do you think she's . . . gone?"

Trinette stared at her hands. They moved nervously in her lap as if she were trying to keep something important within her grasp and it kept slipping away.

"Death. Her mother died six months ago and she hasn't been the same since."

"Amara, you've been pretty quiet. How do you feel about what Ross is saying?"

"He's right."

Jeremy waited a beat and then asked, "Care to add anything or elaborate?"

"No," Amara said.

"Trinette?" Jeremy asked. "Is there anything you would like to say?"

The little girl with the large sad eyes scooted closer to her father and shook her head no.

Jeremy looked from one person to the other, wrote a few notes in his book, and then looked up. "So what would you like to accomplish during our time together?"

Ross's blood began to boil. He hated shrinks. They always asked stupid questions and got paid big bucks for doing it. You paid them over a hundred bucks an hour and all they would do was encourage you to solve your own problems. Well, it seemed to Ross that if people could solve their own problems, they wouldn't need shrinks.

"I want you to fix my daughter."

"He can't fix Nettie," Amara interrupted. "She's not a car that needs an oil change or a roof with missing shingles. She's a flesh-and-blood child who's grieving for her mother in the worst way!"

"Not to mention recently returned from the land of lost children!" Ross said, standing. He'd had enough of Amara and her goody-two-shoes, caped-crusader rescue missions. "If anyone is the fixer, it's you! You charged into this marriage on your white horse as if the girls and I were a broken family. Well, sorry to burst your ever optimistic bubble, but we're not. We never were! We don't need you to fix us . . . got it!"

Ross's heart slammed against his chest. His breaths came out in short, hot bursts, and he felt as though he could smash his fist into a wall and not feel a thing.

"You are the most ungrateful man I've ever met," Amara said, rising. "Do you know how hard it is becoming instant mother to three young triplets and instant wife to an ogre like you!"

The veins in Amara's neck bulged angrily. In another lifetime, Ross would have kissed that neck, would have sucked away all the tension, massaged away the frustration with his tongue. But not now. Now he just wanted to ring—

"Listen," Jeremy said, rising himself. "Why don't you two take a break outside? I'd like some time to speak with Trinette alone and you two need time to cool down. Now can I trust you to go out into the waiting area and not break anything, including each other?"

Ross and Amara glared at each other and said nothing.

"I'm going to take that as a yes."

Ross knelt down in front of where Trinette sat as still as a frightened mouse.

"Nettie, sweetheart. Remember when Daddy told you about the friend he wanted you to meet and talk to. Well, this is the friend. Do you think you can draw a nice picture for him while he asks you some questions?"

Ross threw a scalding frown at Amara, daring her to do or say anything. His tactic didn't work. She knelt beside him and took Nettie's hands into hers.

"Please, Nettie. Jeremy's here to make you feel better . . . to make us all feel better." She took the crayons and coloring book out of her shoulder bag. "Please . . ."

Surprisingly, Nettie responded. She nodded her head slowly, almost imperceptibly. If you weren't watching for it, you wouldn't have been able to see it.

Reluctantly, Ross left with his soon-to-be ex-wife trailing behind him.

"Daddy will be right outside," he added for good measure.

The first few moments in the waiting area were composed of blissful silence. Ross needed the silence, needed the not-talking to order his thoughts, to steel his anger and frustration. But he realized he was asking for too much of a good thing. It wasn't long before Amara lit into him with the same force and vengeance as in the doctor's office.

"You know, if you had brought her in for counseling months ago when I first asked you to, Trinette might not be in the shape she's in right now."

"Yeah, and if you hadn't lost her in a shopping mall, she'd be a lot better off."

"No, she wouldn't, Ross," Amara said, lowering her voice. "She'd still be lost. She'd just be lost within the confines of our home."

Ross gritted his teeth. He hated it when Amara was right. And she seemed to be right quite often.

"Amara—"

"Look," she said, interrupting. "All I'm saying is give me some credit for knowing that Trinette needed help. Give me some credit for finding her when she ran away. Heck, give me some credit for taking on a challenge that no woman in her right mind would take on and that's marrying a man who didn't love me—a man with a ready-made family at that. Give me some credit for trying to make this relationship work and trying to make the girls happy."

Her eyes grew serious. "Give me some credit for loving you."

Ross's anger prevented most of Amara's words from

getting to him, but some of them got through. Especially those about caring for his daughters. He did have to give her credit for that. And if he peeled back the layer of fear that had turned to anger when Nettie was missing, he'd see that as much as she cared about the girls, she couldn't have been negligent at the mall. Nettie's disappearance was one of those fluke incidents that happened. He'd like to think that it couldn't have happened to him. But if it could happen to someone who loved his children as much as Amara, then who knows? Maybe it could have happened to him, too.

"Amara—" he said, leaning in her direction.

"Mr. and Mrs. Hayward?" Jeremy said. "You can come back now."

The longest walk in Ross's life was the one he took back into that doctor's office. He knew he was about to hear the kind of news that people dread, like, "I'm sorry, it's a tumor. Mr. and Mrs. Hayward, your daughter needs serious therapy. The business resumption plan failed miserably, your ex-in-laws will be staying another week."

Dread filled his body like lead. He sat down heavily next to Amara, no longer caring about the self-imposed distance between them. The only thing he cared about was his daughter and what needed to happen to get her well.

He would do anything.

"You don't waste any time, Doctor," he said, wanting to get right to the matter. "We were barely gone half an hour."

A receptionist from the outer area came in behind them.

"Nettie, will you go with Felicia while I talk to your father and Amara?"

As his daughter took the hand of a stranger and walked out of the office, Ross noticed a sour taste in his mouth, as if he'd eaten something flat and metal.

"Doctor . . ." he said, impatience welling up inside him like a geyser.

Dr. Park removed a folder from the top of his desk and sat down in a chair across from Ross and Amara. It was the file they'd brought with them. For the past two weeks, they'd been keeping track of Nettie's moods, drawings, and play habits. His daughter's moods had mirrored his and Amara's. Distant. Solemn. Withdrawn. Only more pronounced than ever before. She no longer played with her sisters. Only sat away from them and watched or sometimes waited in another room while Trinity and Trina laughed and carried on with dolls, Chutes and Ladders, or cartoons. Her drawings were always of her standing alone. If she chose to include anything else in the picture, it always towered over her as if she was just an insignificant speck on the page.

And there was something else. He and Amara had treated each other as if they were insignificant. He wondered now if that behavior had somehow hurt Nettie.

Jeremy glanced up after examining the contents of the folder for what seemed like an eternity. "Some of what I'm going to tell you, you are probably already aware of. Some of what I'm about to tell you will come as a surprise, but I'm asking you to listen first. Process what I'm saying to you, and react afterward. It might be hard, but—"

"Doctor!" Amara's exasperated shout told Ross that she was as impatient as he was.

"Yes," he said, stretching his long neck like a giraffe.

"Trinette is in transition. She's grieving her mother's passing."

Ross and Amara looked at each other as if to say, Duh!

"And she's frightened," Jeremy continued. "Frightened that she's going to lose her other parent. But the only way she can deal with that is to take herself out of the equation so that if something does happen to you, Mr. Hayward, maybe, just maybe she won't feel as bad as she does now with her mother being gone."

Ross nodded. It made sense. "That's why she ran away," he said.

"She didn't run away," Jeremy said. "She told me she saw her mother and went to go be with her."

"A hallucination?" Amara asked, eyes sick with worry.

"I don't think so. I believe she may have seen someone who looked like her mother and simply followed her out of the mall."

"So what do we do now?" Amara asked.

"Yeah," Ross chimed in. "Do we schedule her for regular therapy sessions?"

"Absolutely," Jeremy said. "I also want to spend time with her sisters."

Ross's jaw set determinedly. "Anything, Doctor, if you think it will help Nettie."

"Not only will it help Nettie, but it will help them as well. They are probably going through their own grieving process."

Ross stroked his chin thoughtfully. "You're right."

"You two have talked quite a bit about Trinity and what seems to be bothering her. Is there anything you'd like to say about yourselves?"

"No," Ross answered quickly.

Amara found the question disarming and shifted in her seat. "What do you mean?"

"I practice a holistic approach to therapy and healing, Mrs. Hayward. In order for Trinette and her sisters to truly come to terms with their mother's death, they are going to need help. And the only way you can help them is if you've come to terms with not only their mother's death, but the result of that death, which is your marriage."

Amara tried to focus on the words Jeremy said with difficulty. But the fact was, being called Mrs. Hayward bothered her. She didn't feel like a wife right now.

Suddenly she noticed how cold it was in the room. And how the hum of the air conditioner droned on softly in the background. She was aware of her own skin, and how uncomfortable she was in it. And she was aware of Ross and the power she'd given him over her heart. She thought that she'd healed him and the girls. But if that were true, they probably wouldn't be in a psychologist's office trying to get in touch with their feelings.

Ross sighed deeply. "We've come to terms with it," he said.

"I'm going to ask you to speak only for yourselves. Can we agree to that?"

They nodded.

"I've come to terms with it," Ross said, then slid a glance over to Amara that threatened her against saying anything different.

"Can you give me an example of how you've come to terms with the loss of your previous wife?"

Ross drew himself up as if preparing for battle. "Well, the fact that you've just said previous wife ought to tell you something. I mean, I *am* remarried."

Jeremy nodded and wrote a few notes on his pad. "And how do you feel about that?"

"About being remarried?"

"Yes."

Amara straightened in her chair. In the six months they'd been married, they never talked about how they felt about the situation. They just went along with it as if it was something to be endured. And then when things changed, when things got good between them, they acted as if their relationship had been ordained. But now, they treated each other like unwelcome guests in each other's lives.

"I felt . . ." Ross crossed his arms. "I felt imposed upon."

Jeremy took a few more notes. Amara had to clench her teeth not to butt in and scream, *What about me! I'm the one who was imposed upon!* But instead she took slow full breaths and listened.

"So what did you do?" Jeremy continued his probing with flat, measured questioning.

Ross was thoughtful, almost as if he didn't want to say what was really on his mind.

"I, um . . . I wasn't the most easy person to live with."

"I see. And how'd that work for you?"

"It made me dread coming home," he answered.

Amara flinched as if he'd physically swung at her. She was ready to provide her side of the story, but waited to make sure Ross was finished.

"You said you felt imposed upon. Is that still how you feel?"

"No," he said without hesitation.

"No?" Amara asked, surprised at her interruption and the startling way Ross's response felt inside her.

"I'm sorry for interrupting," she said. Ross stared at her for a few moments. His eyes not so hard. Not so accusatory.

"The timing is actually good, Amara." Jeremy flipped to a clean page in his pad.

Amara looked away from the two faces in the room as if that would absolve her from answering the questions she knew were coming. Then as she considered it. She derived more from the truth—a truth she was tired of hiding, ignoring, and trying to push away.

She loved Ross Hayward. She'd loved him for years. And what brought her the most pain was the fact that she knew he loved her. But a pain greater than love would keep them apart.

"So, Amara, have you come to terms with Brenda's death?"

She gathered her resolve and stared into Jeremy's eyes. "No."

"How do you feel about that?"

"Sometimes I feel like I'll never come to terms with it. How can you get over losing your best friend?"

She didn't want to cry in front of Ross. No telling how he would react. But she knew her tears were part of the truth she needed to tell. "Brenda Hayward was more of a mother to me than my own mother and I . . ." Amara took a few collective breaths to steady herself. "I owe her for that."

"So what did you do about this debt you owe?"

"I married Ross," she said, sneaking a glance at her husband. His eyes had grown softer. Were these the eyes she remembered holding her, kissing her, loving her? She wanted to touch him so badly.

But she didn't.

"I tried to—"

"Make everything right," Ross said, finishing her sentence.

Jeremy frowned. "Ross—"

"It's okay," Amara said, relief washing over her like a cool wave of air. "He's right."

There was no sarcasm in Ross's voice. Only honest understanding.

"How'd that work for you, Amara?"

"At first it—"

"Was frustrating as hell."

A smile cracked through the pain and tears. She turned to Ross. "Yes. It was. But then things changed, and I discovered that—"

"The man you married wasn't such a monster after all." Ross allowed a slight smile to pierce his stoic features.

Jeremy continued to take notes, but it was almost as if he'd left the room.

"And how'd that work for you, Mrs. Hayward?"

"Everything was working fine until . . ." She paused, wondering if Ross would go with her all the way. Could he empathize into his pain?

"Until I allowed Nettie's grief, and my own, to come between us."

Jeremy looked up, bright concern shining from his eyes. "I'd also like to schedule sessions with you two."

"Us!" the couple shouted together.

Ross sat up straight on the couch. "We don't need any counseling."

Jeremy smirked like a cat with a sweet secret. "That's not what Nettie had to say."

"Ross is right. We don't need any counseling," Amara said, emphatically.

"Denial," Jeremy retorted. "That's one of the first stages of transition. There are others. You can move through them without my help and potentially set back any progress I make with Nettie or you can go through them with my help and perhaps gain the tools you'll need to help all of your daughters through the transition of leaving one family behind and moving on with another."

Ross glanced at Amara. She was already looking at him, disdain prominent in her features.

"What if Amara and I are no longer a couple? Would we need counseling then?"

The thin therapist looked like a balloon that had just been popped. "That depends."

"On what?" Amara asked, folding her arms.

"On whether you want to send Nettie into deeper, extended, more complex treatment. If you two split up, imagine what that would do to a child who has already lost one parent. Now if you don't love each other, and you know in your heart that it would be best for the girls if you split up, then by all means, don't make them suffer another moment. But if you two love each other, and recent events have thrown a monkey wrench into your romance, then hang on. Like MLK said, you can overcome this."

Ross and Amara looked away from each other and fell silent.

Jeremy rose and walked behind his desk. "These are big questions, I know. It would be best if you answered them before we proceed with treatment. I'm willing to move forward for a while, but not for long. Not only do I need an answer, but your daughters deserve one."

Now Ross was the one who was deflated. And if he gave an honest opinion of Amara, it seemed that she was, too.

Did they love each other?

Despite his anger, frustration, and fear behind his daughter being missing, he did love Amara. Loved her in a way he thought he'd never love again. But did he love her beyond the desire he had for getting his daughter, his daughters, well?

"Why don't you schedule another appointment with Felicia for next week? Maybe by then you two will have decided what you really want."

As they walked out, Ross couldn't remember Amara ever being so quiet. Had she given up completely? If her recent actions were any indication, it would seem that she had. And that bothered him.

He'd known all along that he'd planned to get an annulment if the slightest thing went wrong in the marriage. Then, when he and Amara consummated their relationship and Nettie disappeared, Ross had been determined to get a divorce.

Now, faced with the cold hard reality of that possibility, Ross found himself backpedaling. Reexamining his position and realizing that despite everything, he wanted to stay married to Amara.

And it wasn't for the girls. It was for him. His peace of mind. His contentment. His inner peace. His love.

His life.

He'd married Amara for the wrong reasons, but now he wanted to stay married to her for the right ones.

Nettie took their hands and they stood at the receptionist cubicle.

Ross stared into Amara's tired beautiful eyes. "I'd like to make an appointment for us all next week."

"That's fine, Ross. But I won't be coming."

His heart plunged in his chest. "Why?"

"Because it's the same old thing again. We tried to stay together for the sake of the children. Or at least I did. It didn't work. I don't have to be slapped with the truth twice."

"What if we stay together for each other?" he asked, really wanting to know.

"Ross, don't. I know you. You would do anything for your girls. Anything, including staying married to me if you thought it would help them. Two wrongs don't make a right. I learned that a long time ago. It's time you learned it too."

The expression on Nettie's face reflected the feeling in Ross's heart. Amara had been reading his mind. But she'd missed all the important parts.

As they walked hand in hand to the car, Ross knew the only thing he had left to do was to prove to Amara that she was wrong.

Chapter 20

She hadn't moved out, but for all practical purposes, she might as well have. When she wasn't tending to the girls, she was scarcely around. And since Jeremy had encouraged Ross to spend as much time with the girls as possible, that meant that Amara could spend her time elsewhere if she so chose.

And she did.

She still completed some of her wifely functions, like cooking, cleaning, and that sort of thing. And she still poured her heart and soul into mothering the triplets. In that, Ross had no complaint. But in a perfect family scenario between a man and a woman, the time that they would normally spend together, Amara was nowhere to be found—conveniently running errands, visiting her parents, or spending time with her aunts. She was also spending an awful lot of time with Shasta. Anyone, it seemed, except him.

As therapy with the girls progressed, Ross and Amara did an excellent job at dodging the question about their love for each other. And Ross hadn't brought it up since they left the doctor's office that day. There didn't seem to be time. Between rearranging his work schedule, spending more time with the girls, following the doctor's instructions of maintaining a daily routine, and talking about feelings, and then visiting the doctor regularly, Ross could barely find a spare moment to breathe normally, let alone make amends with his estranged wife. But somehow, some way, he vowed to himself that he would do it. And do it soon before it was too late. It wasn't until he was tossing and turning in his sleep one night, desperately missing the company of Amara's mind, body, and soul beside him, that he came up with a plan.

"Where are the girls?" Amara asked, noticing that the house was especially quiet. It had become unusually quiet since she and Ross had all but stopped speaking. Or rather, she had stopped speaking to Ross. She just didn't have much to say to a man whom she'd given her heart to and who only wanted her around for the sake of convenience.

She stayed away as much as possible. To give Ross the time he needed to spend with the girls, but mostly to distance herself from the feelings she had for both him and the triplets. If she could put some space between them, maybe the blow wouldn't be so painful when he broached the subject about divorce.

She knew it was coming. What else made sense? He'd trusted her, and in his mind she'd betrayed that trust. And she was tired of trying to convince him otherwise. If her love for him and the girls wasn't enough, then she'd rather not be there. Rather not be in a relationship based on a lie and not love.

"Tinis has the girls," he said, standing very still in the living room.

Amara held her position near the doorway—wanted an out to retreat by if need be. She wasn't about to stand here and be verbally lashed by him. She would leave him mumbling where he stood if it came to that.

"Tinis? I thought she was in—"

"Detroit. I know. She came to pick up the girls for the week. I asked her to."

Here it comes, she thought, bracing herself. The *I think it would be better for everyone involved if we ended this marriage.* She steadied her nerves. She would not show emotion. Instead, she imagined that she was a steel pole. A steel pole facing down an oncoming hurricane. Well, damn it! She would not be moved. He would not make her cry or plead for them to stay together. She would accept his decision with the dignity of a tree—sturdy, majestic, strong.

There will be no breaking down, she told herself.

"We need to talk, Amara. And I think you should sit down for this."

Amara knew if she sat down, she'd never be able to get up after hearing the news of the end of her marriage. "I'll stand, thank you."

"As you wish." Ross took a long breath, then exhaled through flared nostrils. "I've been doing a lot of thinking. A lot of internal examination. A lot of reflecting about the last six months."

Oh, God . . . Amara thought. Emotions churned in her mind as if they were moving through thick goo. She tried to concentrate on the words he was saying, knowing all along that she didn't want to hear them.

Ross thrust his hands into his pockets. "I've been thinking . . . about us."

"Maybe I will sit down," she said, feeling a weakness in her knees.

Ross sat down across from her. "That question that Jeremy asked us, it really . . . well, it definitely helped me to see some things more clearly." He slid to the edge of the chair, his jean-clad legs gapped as if poised for action. "We need to talk about the answer to that question, or rather, I need to make it clear what my answer to that question is."

Amara sat forward, determined not to back away. "What's your answer, Ross?" she asked, knowing full well what he would say next and dreading every word of it.

"My answer . . ." he said, sounding unsure for the first time since she'd known him. "On second thought, I'd rather *show* you my answer." He stood. "Will you come?"

Amara stood and followed him upstairs. Since she'd been gone all morning, she wondered if he'd packed all of her belongings and had them stored in a room on the upper level.

When she saw where he was headed, her heart turned over in her chest.

His bedroom.

The room that had been the source of intense pleasure and remorse since she'd arrived those many months ago. Dread and anxiety twisted together inside her, constricting her words, jumbling her thoughts. She slowed her progress down the corridor.

"Please," he said, noticing her hesitancy.

Her breathing came more heavily now, but she did as he asked. When they rounded the corner into the bedroom, her breathing stopped altogether. For several moments, she forgot to breathe. It wasn't until he said, "Well?" that she let out a breath and quickly took another.

In the time it had taken her to have breakfast with her parents, Ross had gotten rid of all the old furniture in the bedroom. In its place was a pristine oak bedroom set complete with dressers, nightstands, lamps, an armoire, and a brand-new queen-size bed.

Every coherent thought Amara owned flew right out of her mind. If someone had asked her what her name was, she wouldn't have been able to answer. As her senses slowly returned, she realized that Ross was not demanding an end to their marriage. This gesture was quite the opposite.

Happiness welled up inside her like a fountain of love, and a wellspring of tears flowed from her eyes.

"I love you, Amara. I told you that a long time ago. I meant it then and I mean it now."

Tentatively he touched her hand. His palm was warm and strong and reassuring.

"The girls need you. I can't deny that. I'd be lying if I said your relationship with them doesn't touch me— doesn't add to my love for you. But just as important, and maybe even more so, is the truth that I love you, Amara. I need you, Amara. I want you, Amara. And the answer to Jeremy's question is I want to stay married to you. You're not a convenience.

"You're my family."

He pulled her close, brought her into his heat. "I can't lose you, Amara. I can't." He stroked her shoulders, her back, her arms. "I won't lose you."

She swept a glance at the bed. His eyes followed hers. "No more ghosts. Just us," he whispered. "Just us."

A dizzying cyclone of relief, confusion, elation, frustration, and awe nearly toppled Amara where she stood. Ross was finally saying to her what she had waited weeks, months, years for him to say, that he loved her. *Truly* loved her.

He loved her not as a mentor or the husband of a mentor or disgruntled spouse.

Amara blinked in surprise. She knew her heart was beating, but it felt more like the wings of butterflies fluttering in the middle of her chest. She took a long, deep breath. The scent of fresh oak filled her nostrils. The aroma was new, heavy, and spicy. As if the wood was freshly cut, newly put together. She stood there staring as if she'd been shot and was just waiting to fall from the impact.

But she didn't fall.

Neither did she back away. She stood her ground and turned her astonishment to Ross.

His eyes regarded her with a fond openness. Something she hadn't seen or felt from him for a mighty long time. There was also something else in his eyes. Hope. And hesitancy.

That surprised her. Ross Hayward was a man who was hesitant about nothing. He went after whatever he wanted with force and determination.

But now, he was waiting.

"If you don't like it, we can get something else. I just remembered a comment you made when we were in Savannah about liking oak furniture."

Amara was still too stunned to speak. Although her heart was already reaching out to him.

"If that doesn't work," he said, taking a step toward her, "we could build a new master suit onto the house."

She closed her eyes, barely believing what she was hearing. His words and conviction melted the distance to her heart.

He took a step closer, reached out, stroked the side of her face. "We could demolish the house and rebuild."

Ross took her hands and knelt on one knee. "We could move into another house, but whatever we do, we have to do it together. Amara. Please," he asked, kissing the backs of her hands, then pressing them against his face. "Be my wife. Be the mother of my children . . . our children. Let me be your husband."

He took a deep breath and squared his jaw. "Will you marry me again?"

At Ross's proposal, the world fell silent. There were no friends telling her Ross was a good catch. No family members asking her if she knew what she was doing. No nagging inner voice telling her this was her only chance. And this time, there was no voice from the grave haunting her, beseeching her to fulfill a promise.

No, this time Amara only heard the voice of her heart telling her that without a doubt she loved Ross Hayward and he loved her. The voice said that they had three wonderful daughters to love and raise and a lifetime of love and happiness to look forward to.

Without hesitation her heart voice became her speaking voice and she answered, "Yes!"

Relief washed over Ross's face in heavy waves. He stood and cupped her face in his hands. "Then I have one more lesson to teach you."

"What?" she asked, too happy to think.

"How good it feels to make up!" he said, and carried her reverently to their new bed.

Chapter 21

Over the course of the next few weeks, the Hayward family learned a lot about the grieving process. With Dr. Park's help, they each began to face and move through their grief in their own way.

Trinette expressed her feelings through drawing and coloring and clay figures. Slowly Jeremy along with Ross and Amara got her to talk about her art. Soon Trinette's conversations moved away from her drawings and back into the family when they sat down to dinner or took family outings.

Ross and Amara healed their wounds too. They both came to realize that they had not allowed themselves to fully grieve after Brenda's death and instead had jumped right into a situation that would not allow them to for a long time. When they finally did take time to release their feelings, it was a lot easier for them to help Trinity and Trina do the same.

In an exercise in Jeremy's office, Jeremy asked the couple to speak at random about some of the things they would have done differently in their relationship.

Jeremy had looked as if he'd just been presented the psychologist of the year award by Freud himself. *We must be making progress,* Ross thought.

"Now, Ross. Think about this carefully. Is there

anything you'd like to say to Amara? Something that's been bothering you?"

Ross looked away. There were lots of things he wanted to say to Amara, to tell her, ask her. Even at this stage in their relationship, he knew they still had a lot of healing to do.

He also knew that it would never occur unless they were totally honest with each other and had thoroughly committed themselves to the process of healing.

"Yes," he said, his voice heavy with honesty. He turned to her. Her expression was familiar, determined. The face of a woman who had weathered too many storms in her young years. The face he loved.

"You can't fix everything," he said, and a wave of relief moved through him.

"I never—"

"This is Ross's turn to speak," Jeremy said. "Your job now is to listen."

In a motion Ross could have predicted with certainty, Amara's slender fingers swept across the hair hanging in straight black lines against the side of her face and tucked it behind her ears. Her lips pursed, she exhaled.

"Ross, do you have anything more to say?"

He realized that the crux of what he had to say was just laid out before them. "You came charging into our lives, my life, like Ms. Fix-it. Not everything can be repaired," he said, thinking about his relationship with his ex-sisters-in-law. "Not everything should be repaired. And for those things that can, you shouldn't bear the responsibility of repairing them on your own. At least, not anymore. We can work on whatever it is . . . together."

Jeremy nodded, not so much proud of himself but of his client. "Amara, now you. Not so much focusing on a response to what Ross just said, but what is it that you would like him to know? What have you wanted to say to him?"

She leaned back on the couch, closed her eyes for a moment. Ross felt the muscles in his jaw tighten with concern.

"What I have to say is a response to your comment, Ross," Amara said, opening her eyes.

"What do you do for a living?"

"You know what I do." Seeing the displeasure on Jeremy's face, Ross understood that he'd answered inappropriately. "I'm a Disaster Recovery Specialist."

"More specifically?" Amara asked.

"I help businesses plan for and recover from disasters."

She crossed her arms. "What hurt me the most is that that's your chosen career, yet you couldn't seem to do it for your own family. For us."

A stone of regret fell in the pit of Ross's stomach. He nodded in acknowledgement.

Jeremy sat back in his thick leather chair, crossed one lanky leg over the other. "Any reaction to what you just heard? From either of you?"

"You're right," they said in unison.

During that session, when Ross heard Amara's description of the wedding she wished she could have had, he wasted no time making that dream come true.

Less than a month after her disclosure in the doctor's office, Amara and Ross Hayward renewed their wedding vows in a fairytale wedding of Amara's design with flowers and decorations provided by another of Shasta's sweepstakes winnings. Their family and friends were in attendance and the triplets shared the responsibility of being flower girls.

This time, they wrote their own vows. Not separate

vows, but words they both created and said to each other in unison.

My darling,
I give myself to you this day, this moment
and promise
with all that is my soul
to love you completely
and to
respect, support, uphold, cherish, embrace,
  protect, revere, and follow that love
every day that I live and breathe—
I will forever be
the companion of you
the reflection of you
the completion of you
to rear, raise, adore, mold, and shape our
  children together
and allow the almighty God to be the bond that
  unites us in love

That night, as man and wife in mind, body, and heart, Mr. and Mrs. Ross Hayward read a bedtime story to their three daughters, then made love in the master suite of their bedroom until the sun came up and the only energy they had left was to hold each other until they fell asleep.

Epilogue

From the hill upon which they stood, Ross and Amara Hayward could see for miles. Under a cloudless sky, the husband and wife held hands and gazed upon the final resting place of a woman who had meant so much to them that words could not explain the depth and breadth of that meaning.

They stood for a time thinking, reminiscing, praying. Both of them in silent recollection and quiet appreciation for life and the time they'd been given.

After a while, Amara knelt and placed the bouquet of flowers she'd held so tightly to her chest on top of the headstone that read BRENDA HAYWARD . . . BELOVED WIFE, MOTHER, AND FRIEND . . . WE WILL NEVER FORGET.

Amara stood and Ross took her hand, tucked it inside his own. She chewed on her bottom lip and then turned to her husband. "Do you think she knew?"

Amara didn't have to say any more than that. He understood what she was asking. Did Brenda know they would fall in love? Did she know she was making the right choice for her daughters when she made Amara and Ross promise to marry? Did she know they would be so perfect for each other that they could work through anything—even the tragedy of her death?

Ross stared into the crisp blue sky, as if he could see

Brenda there watching—eyes happy, a sweet twist on her lips, winking knowingly.

A warm ripple of understanding moved through Amara when Ross turned to her. His entire being lit up like the bright sun above them, and he smiled at her with his soul. The ripple ebbed and pulsed inside her, and she knew his answer was yes.

Then she smiled too, because the connection between them was strong now. So strong, she believed she could strum it like a chord between them and make the most beautiful sound in the world. A sound that said they belonged together. They would make a good family—a good mom and dad—for the girls. Good friends for each other.

Good lovers.

They turned and headed home to the place where they knew their daughters would rush from the babysitter and jump into their arms. The place where they would start a new life and build a great love the way heaven ordained.

Together.

Dear Reader,

Thank you for reading Amara and Ross's story. There were several wounded souls in this novel who found healing through their love of each other.

I was recently reminded that no matter what happens, you don't have to go through it alone as long as you have someone who cares about you. In their own way, both Amara and Ross had to learn this lesson.

Good friends and beloved family are priceless blessings. I live by the motto of giving those I love "flowers" while they are alive. Too many people that I care about have been touched by cancer. Some of them have been taken away. This story is for you, the readers. This book is for them.

As always, I love to hear from readers. Please contact me by mail or Internet at P.O. Box 31554, Omaha, NE 68131, http://www.kimlouise.com, or MsKimLouise@aol.com

Until next time, peace and blessings!

Kim

P.S. Remember your breast exam every month.

ABOUT THE AUTHOR

Kim Louise resides in Omaha, Nebraska. She's been writing since grade school and has always dreamed of penning "the Great American Novel." She has an undergraduate degree in journalism and a graduate degree in adult learning. She has one son, Steve, and one grandson, Zayvier. In her spare time she enjoys reading and songwriting, and has recently become addicted to scrapbooking.

Kim is a two-time finalist for Romance Slam Jam's Emma Awards and was selected as a Rising Star by *Romance in Color*. Her poetry has appeared in *Fine Lines Literary Journal, Cathartic,* and *Role Call* published by Third World Press.

COMING IN MARCH 2004 FROM
ARABESQUE ROMANCES

SIMPLY WILD
by Shelby Lewis   1-58314-326-2 $6.99US/$9.99CAN
Holly Hunter thought she liked her quiet life . . . until Jake Fishbone walked
in. Clouded in mystery, he quickly captures her curiosity—and her heart.
Their budding romance runs off course when she discovers he's the prime
suspect in a murder investigation, but Jake's passionate love will gently reel
her back in. As he hunts down his friend's killer to exact his own revenge,
Holly joins in the dangerous search, anxious to clear his name and show him
that justice *can* see love . . .

REFLECTIONS OF YOU
by Celeste O. Norfleet   1-58314-404-8 $6.99US/$9.99CAN
Architectural designer Angela Lord didn't know quite what to expect when
she decided to fly to Puerto Rico to learn the truth about her family background. She was stunned to discover that not only was she the exact double
of club owner Marco Santos' dead wife, but that someone would go to any
lengths to keep Angela from uncovering the past. And the closer Angela gets
to Marco, the more they must reveal each other's deepest truths if they are to
survive to love forever . . .

THE BEST OF EVERYTHING
by Francine Craft   1-58314-447-1 $5.99US/$7.99CAN
Sherrie Pinson was devastated when her husband, Michael, was killed. Now,
as she struggles to make a new life for herself and her young daughter Tressa,
Byron Tate intrudes on her sorrow. Her husband's best friend is the last man
she wants to see; Byron let him down when Michael needed him most. But
when Byron asks to spend time with Tressa, Sherrie finds it hard to refuse.
Even harder to resist is her attraction to this caring man who has awakened
powerful feelings of yearning and desire.

LET IT BE ME
by Melanie Schuster   1-58314-424-2 $5.99US/$7.99CAN
Vera is a woman on top of her game. Just turned forty, she feels fabulous,
loves her job as editor in chief of a magazine, and has her own television
show about to go into syndication. She's had disappointments—her marriage
wasn't nearly as wonderful as everyone believed—but life seems plenty sat-
isfying without a man . . . until Marcus Deveraux declares his feelings. Just
as Vera realizes she's fallen hard, a secret from Marcus's past resurfaces. Is
her new love a foolish gamble, or the one thing she's been missing?

Available Wherever Books Are Sold!

Visit our website at www.BET.com.